CRITICAL RAVES FOR
DANIELLE STEEL

"STEEL IS ONE OF THE BEST." —*Los Angeles Times*

"THE PLOTS OF DANIELLE STEEL'S NOVELS TWIST AND WEAVE AS INCREDIBLE STORIES UNFOLD TO THE THRILL AND DELIGHT OF HER ENORMOUS READING PUBLIC."
—United Press International

"A LITERARY PHENOMENON . . . ambitious . . . prolific . . . and not to be pigeonholed as one who produces a predictable kind of book."
—*The Detroit News*

"There is a smooth reading style to her writings which makes it easy to forget the time and to keep flipping the pages." —*The Pittsburgh Press*

"Ms. Steel excels at pacing her narrative, which races forward, mirroring the frenetic lives chronicled here; men and women swept up in bewildering change, seeking solutions to problems never before faced."
—*Nashville Banner*

By Danielle Steel

DANIELLE STEEL

THE
PROMISE

A NOVEL

BASED ON A SCREENPLAY BY
GARRY MICHAEL WHITE

DELL
NEW YORK

To Nicholas
with all my love

The Promise is a work of fiction. Names, characters, places,
and incidents either are the product of the author's
imagination or are used fictitiously. Any resemblance to actual
persons, living or dead, events, or locales is entirely
coincidental.

2011 Dell Mass Market Edition

ISBN: 978-0-345-52708-0

Cover design: Andrew M. Newman
Cover illustration: Mark Gerber

Printed in the United States of America

www.bantamdell.com

9 8 7 6 5 4 3 2 1

Dell mass market edition: May 2011

Chapter 1

The early morning sun streamed across their backs as they unhooked their bicycles in front of Eliot House on the Harvard campus. They stopped for a moment to smile at each other. It was May and they were very young. Her short hair shone in the sunshine, and her eyes found his as she began to laugh.

"Well, Doctor of Architecture, how do you feel?"

"Ask me that in two weeks after I get my doctorate." He smiled back at her, shaking a lock of blond hair off his forehead.

"To hell with your diploma, I meant after last night." She grinned at him again, and he rapidly swatted her behind.

"Smartass. How do *you* feel, Miss McAllister? Can you still walk?" They were hitching their legs over the bicycles now and she looked back at him teasingly in answer.

"Can you?" And with that, she was off, pulling ahead of him on the pretty little bike he had bought her for her birthday only a few months before. He was in love with her. He had always been in love with her. He had dreamed of her all his life. And he had known her for two years.

It had been a lonely time at Harvard before that, and well into his second year of graduate school he was resigned to more of the same. He didn't want what the others wanted. He didn't want Radcliffe or Vassar or Wellesley in bed with him. He had known too many of those girls during his undergraduate days, and for Michael there was always something missing. He wanted something more. Texture, substance, soul. He had solved the problem for himself very nicely the summer before, with an affair with one of his mother's friends. Not that his mother had known. But it had been fun. She was a damned attractive woman in her late thirties, years younger than his mother, of course, and she was an editor at *Vogue*. But that had been merely sport. For both of them. Nancy was different.

He had known from the first moment he had seen her in the Boston gallery that showed her paintings. There was a haunting loneliness about her country-sides, a solitary tenderness about her people that filled him with compassion and made him want to reach out to them and to the artist who painted them. She had been sitting there that day in a red beret and an old raccoon coat, her delicate skin still glowing from her walk to the Charles Street gallery, her eyes shining, her face alive. He had never wanted any woman as he wanted her. He had bought two of her paintings, and taken her to dinner at Lockober's. But the rest had taken longer. Nancy McAllister wasn't quick to give her body or her heart. She had been too lonely for too long to give herself easily. At nineteen she was already wise and well versed in pain. The pain of being alone. The pain of being left. It had plagued her since she had been put in the orphanage as a child. She could no longer remember the day her mother had left her there shortly before she died. But she remembered the chill of the halls. The smells of the strange people. The sounds in the morning as she lay in her bed fighting back tears. She would remember those things for the rest of her life. For a long time she had thought nothing could fill the emptiness inside her. But now she had Michael.

Theirs wasn't always an easy relationship, but it was a strong one, built on love and respect; they had meshed her world and his, and come up with something beautiful and rare. And Michael was no fool either. He knew the dangers of falling in love with someone "different," as his mother put it—when she got the chance. But there was nothing "different" about Nancy. The only thing different was that she was an artist, not just a student. She wasn't still searching, she already *was* what she wanted to be. And unlike the other women he knew, she wasn't auditioning candidates, she had chosen the man she loved. In two years he had never let her down. She was certain he never would: they knew each other too well. What could there possibly be that she hadn't already learned? She knew it all. The funny stuff, the silly secrets, the childhood dreams, the desperate fears. And through him she had come to respect his family. Even his mother.

Michael had been born into a tradition, groomed

since childhood to inherit a throne. It wasn't something he took lightly, or even joked about. Sometimes it actually frightened him. Would he live up to the legend? But Nancy knew he would. His grandfather, Richard Cotter, had been an architect, and his father as well. It was Michael's grandfather who had founded an empire. But it was the merging of the Cotter business with the Hillyard fortune, through the marriage of Michael's parents, that had created the Cotter-Hillyard of today. Richard Cotter had known how to make money, but it was the Hillyard money—old money—that had brought with it the rites and traditions of power. It was, at times, a heavy mantle to wear, but not one Michael disliked. And Nancy respected it too. She knew that one day Michael would be at the helm of Cotter-Hillyard. In the beginning they had talked about it incessantly, and then again later, when they realized how serious their affair really was. But Michael knew that he had found a woman who could handle it, the family responsibilities as well as the business duties. The orphanage had done nothing to prepare Nancy for the role Michael knew she would fill, but the groundwork seemed to be laid in her very soul.

He watched her now with almost unbearable pride as she sped ahead of him, so sure of herself, so strong, the lithe legs pedaling deftly, her chin tucked over her shoulder now and then to look at him and laugh. He wanted to speed ahead and take her off the bike . . . there . . . on the grass . . . the way they had the night before . . . the way . . . He swept the thought from his mind and raced after her.

"Hey, wait for me, you little twerp!" He was abreast of her in a few moments, and as they rode along, more quietly now, he held out a hand across the narrow gap between them. "You look beautiful today, Nancy." His voice was a caress in the spring air, and around them the world was fresh and green. "Do you know how much I love you?"

"Oh, maybe half as much as I love you, Mr. Hillyard?"

"That shows what you know, Miss Nancy Fancypants." She laughed, as always, at the nickname. Michael always made her happy. He did wonderful things. She had thought so from the first moment he walked into the gallery and threatened to take off all his clothes if she didn't sell him all her paintings. "I happen to love you at least seven times as much as you love me."

"Nope." She grinned at him again, put her nose in the air, and sped ahead again. "I love you more, Michael."

"How do you know?" He was pressing to catch up.

"Santa Claus told me." And with that she sped ahead again, and this time he let her move out on the narrow path. They were in a festive mood and he liked watching her. The slim shape of her hips in jeans, the narrow waist, the trim shoulders with the red sweater loosely tied about them, and that wonderful swing of dark hair. He could watch her for years. In fact, he was planning to do just that. Which reminded him . . . he had been meaning to talk to her about that all morning. He narrowed the gap between them again, and tapped her gently on the shoulder.

"Excuse me, Mrs. Hillyard." She jumped a little at the words, and then smiled shyly at him as the sun shone across her face. He could see tiny freckles there, almost like gold dust left by elves on the creamy surface of her skin. "I said . . . Mrs. Hillyard . . ." He mouthed the words with infinite pleasure. He had waited for two years.

"Aren't you rushing things a little, Michael?" She sounded hesitant, almost afraid. He hadn't spoken to Marion yet. No matter what he and Nancy had agreed to between themselves.

"I don't think I'm rushing anything. And I was thinking about doing it two weeks from now. Right after graduation." They had long since agreed on a small, intimate wedding. Nancy had no family, and Michael wanted to share the moment with Nancy, not a cast of thousands or an army of society photographers. "In fact, I was planning to go down to New York to talk to Marion about it tonight."

"Tonight?" There was an echo of fear in the word, and she let the bicycle come to a slow stop. He nodded in answer, and she grew pensive as she looked out at the lush hills around them. "What do you think she'll say?" She was afraid to look at him. Afraid to hear.

"Yes, of course. Are you really worried about it?" But it was a stupid question and they both knew it. They had plenty to worry about. Marion was no flower girl. She was Michael's mother, and she had all the tenderness of the *Titanic*. She was a woman of power, of determination, of concrete and steel. She had car-

ried on the family business after her father died and
again with renewed determination after her husband's
death. Nothing stopped Marion Hillyard. Nothing.
Certainly not a chit of a girl, or her only son. If she
didn't want them to get married, nothing would make
her grant that "yes" Michael pretended to be so sure
of. And Nancy knew exactly what Marion Hillyard
thought of her.

Marion had never made any secret of her feelings,
or at least, not from the moment she decided that
Michael's "fling" with "that artist" might be for real.
She had called Michael down to New York and cooed,
soothed, and charmed, after which she had stormed,
threatened, and baited. And then she had resigned
herself or seemed to. Michael had taken it as an en-
couraging sign, but Nancy wasn't so sure. She had a
feeling that Marion knew what she was doing; for the
present she had clearly decided to ignore "the situation." Invitations were not extended, accusations were
not made, apologies for things said to Michael in the
past were never forthcoming, but no fresh problems
had sprung up either. For her, Nancy simply did not
exist. And oddly, Nancy was always surprised to find
just how much that hurt. Having no family of her
own, she had always had odd dreams about Marion.
That they might be friends, that Marion would like
her, that she and Marion would go shopping for
Michael . . . that Marion would be . . . the mother
she had never had or known. But Marion was not
easily cast in that role. In two years, Nancy had had
ample opportunity to understand that. Only Michael

obstinately held to the position that his mother would come around, that once she had accepted the inevitable, they would be great friends. But Nancy was never that sure. She had even forced Michael to discuss the possibility of Marion's never accepting her, never agreeing to the marriage. Then what? . . . "Then we hop in the car and head for the nearest justice of the peace. We're both of age now, you know." Nancy had smiled at the simplicity of his solution. She knew it would never be as easy as that. But what did it matter? After two years together, they felt married anyway.

They stood in silence for a long moment, looking at the view, and then Michael took Nancy's hand. "I love you, babe."

"I love you too." She looked at him worriedly and he silenced her eyes with a kiss. But nothing could still the questions that either of them had. Nothing except the interview with Marion. Nancy let her bike fall, and with a sigh, slipped slowly into Michael's arms. "I wish it were easier, Michael."

"It will be. You'll see. Now come on. Are we going to ride, or just stand here all day?" He swatted her behind again and she smiled as he picked up her bike for her. And in a moment they were off again, laughing and playing and singing, pretending that Marion didn't exist. But she did. She always would. Marion was more an institution than a woman. Marion was forever. In Michael's life anyway. And now in Nancy's.

The sun rose higher in the sky as they pedaled through the countryside, alternately riding ahead of each other or side by side, at one moment raucously teasing, at the next growing silent and thoughtful. It was almost noon when they reached Revere Beach and saw the familiar face riding toward them. It was Ben Avery, with a new girl at his side. Another leggy blonde. They all looked like homecoming queens, and most of them were.

"Hi, you two. Going to the fair?" Ben grinned at them, and then with a vague wave of his hand introduced Jeannette. They all exchanged a round of hellos, and Nancy shielded her eyes to glance ahead at the fair. It was still several blocks away.

"Is it worth stopping for?"

"Hell, yes. We won a pink dog"—he pointed at the ugly little creature in Jeannette's basket—"a green turtle, which somehow got lost, and two cans of beer. Besides, they have corn on the cob and it's terrific."

"You just sold me." Michael looked over at Nancy and smiled. "Shall we?"

"Sure. You guys going back already?" But she could see that they were. Ben had a recognizable gleam in his eyes, and Jeannette seemed to be in agreement. Nancy smiled to herself as she watched them.

"Yeah, we've been out since about six this morning. I'm beat. What are you two doing for dinner tonight, by the way? Want to stop in for a pizza?" Ben's room was only a few doors down from Mike's.

"What are we doing for dinner, señor?" Nancy looked at Michael with a broad smile, but he was shaking his head.

"I have some business to attend to tonight. Maybe another time." It was a rapid reminder of the meeting with Marion.

"Okay. See ya." Ben and Jeannette waved and were off, as Nancy stared at Michael.

"You're really going down to see her tonight?"

"Yes. And stop worrying about it. Everything is going to be just fine. By the way, Mother says he's got the job."

"Ben?" Nancy looked up questioningly as they started pedaling toward the fair.

"Yes. We start at the same time. Different areas, but we start the same day." Mike looked pleased. He had known Ben since prep school, and they were like brothers.

"Does Ben know yet?"

Michael shook his head with a secretive smile. "I thought I'd let him get the thrill of hearing the news officially. I didn't want to spoil it for him."

Nancy smiled back at him. "You're a nice guy and I love you, Hillyard."

"Thank you, Mrs. H."

"Stop that, Michael." She wanted the name too much to hear it bandied about, even by Michael.

"I won't stop it. And you'd better get used to it." He suddenly looked serious.

"I will. When the time is right. But until then, Miss McAllister will do just fine."

"For about two more weeks, to be exact. Come on, I'll race ya."

They sped ahead, side by side, panting and laughing, and Michael reached the entrance to the fair a full thirty seconds before she did. But they both looked tanned and healthy and carefree.

"Well, sir, what's first?" But she had already guessed, and she was right.

"Corn, of course. Need you ask?"

"Not really." They parked their bikes next to a tree, knowing that in that sleepy countryside no one would steal them, and they walked off arm in arm. Ten minutes later they stood happily dripping butter as they ate their corn, and then they gobbled hot dogs and sipped ice-cold beer. Nancy followed it all up with a huge stick of cotton candy.

"How can you eat that stuff?"

"Easy. It's delicious." The words were garbled through the sticky pink stuff, but she wore the delighted face of a five-year-old.

"Have I told you lately how beautiful you are?" She grinned at him, wearing a faceful of pink candy, and he took out a handkerchief and wiped her chin. "If you'd clean up a little we could have our picture taken."

"Yeah? Where?" As she gobbled another pink cloud, her nose disappeared again.

"You're impossible. Over there." He pointed to a booth where they could stick their heads through round holes and have their photographs taken over outlandish outfits. They wandered over and chose Rhett Butler and Scarlett O'Hara. And strangely enough, they didn't even look foolish in the picture. Nancy looked beautiful over the elaborately painted costume. The delicate beauty of her face and the precision of its features were perfect with the immensely feminine costume of the Southern belle. And Michael looked like a young rake. The photographer handed them their photograph and collected his dollar.

"I ought to keep that, you two look so good."

"Thank you." Nancy was touched by the compliment, but Mike only smiled. He was always so damned proud of her. Just another two weeks and . . . but Nancy's frantic tugging on his sleeve distracted him from his daydreams. "Look, over there! A ring toss!" She had always wanted to play that at the fair when she was a little girl, but the nuns from the orphanage always said it was too expensive. "Can we?"

"But of course, my dear." He swept her a low bow, offered her his arm, and attempted to stroll toward the ring toss, but Nancy was far too excited to stroll. She was almost leaping like a child, and her excitement delighted him.

"Can we do it now?"

"Sure, sweetheart." He put down a dollar and the man at the counter handed her four times the usual allotment of rings. Most customers only paid a quarter. But she was inexperienced at the game, and all her tries fell wide. Michael was watching her with amusement. "Just exactly which prize are you trying for?"

"The beads." Her eyes shone like a child's and her words were barely more than a whisper. "I've never had a gaudy necklace before." It was the one thing she had always wanted as a child. Something bright and shiny and frivolous.

"You're certainly easy to please, my love. You sure you wouldn't rather have the pink doggie?" It was just like the one Jeannette had had in her basket, but Nancy shook her head determinedly.

"The beads."

"Your wish is my command." And he landed all three tosses perfectly on target. With a smile, the man behind the counter handed him the beads, and Michael quickly put them around Nancy's neck. "Voilà, mademoiselle. All yours. Do you suppose we should insure them?"

"Will you stop making fun of my beads? I think they're gorgeous." She touched them softly, enchanted to know they were sparkling at her neck.

"I think *you're* gorgeous. Anything else your heart desires?"

She grinned at him. "More cotton candy."

He bought her another stick of cotton candy, and they slowly wended their way back to the bikes. "Tired?"

"Not really."

"Want to go on a little further? There's a lovely spot up ahead. We could sit for a while and watch the surf."

"It sounds perfect."

They rode off again, but this time more quietly. The carnival atmosphere was gone, and they were both lost in their own thoughts, mostly of each other. Michael was beginning to wish they were back in bed, and Nancy wouldn't have disagreed. They were nearing Nahant when she saw the spot he had chosen at the tip of a land spit, under a lovely old tree, and she was glad they had come this last leg of the trip.

"Oh Michael, it's beautiful."

"It is, isn't it?" They sat down on a soft patch of grass, just before the narrow lip of sand began, and in the distance they watched long smooth waves break over a reef that lay just beneath the surface of the water. "I've always wanted to bring you here."

"I'm glad you did." They sat silently, holding hands, and then Nancy suddenly stood up.

"What's up?"

"I want to do something."

"Over there, behind the bushes."

"No, you creep. Not that." She was already running toward a spot on the beach, and slowly he followed her, wondering what she had in mind. She stopped at a large rock and tried earnestly to move it, with no success.

"Here, silly, let me help you with that. What do you want to do with it?" He was puzzled.

"I just want to move it for a second . . . there." It had given way under Michael's firm prodding, and it rolled back to show a damp indentation in the sand. Quickly, she took off the bright blue beads, held them for a moment, her eyes closed, and dropped them into the sand beneath the rock. "Okay, put it back."

"On top of the beads?"

She nodded, her eyes never leaving the sparkle of blue glass. "These beads will be our bond, a physical bond, buried fast for as long as this rock, and this beach, and these trees stand here. All right?"

"All right." He smiled softly. "We're being very romantic."

"Why not? If you're lucky enough to have love, celebrate it! Give it a home!"

"You're right. You're absolutely right. Okay, here's its home."

"Now let's make a promise. I promise never to forget what is here, or to forget what they stand for. Now you." She touched his hand, and he smiled down at her again. He had never loved her more.

"And I promise . . . I promise never to say goodbye to you . . ." And then, for no reason in particular, they laughed. Because it felt good to be young, to be romantic, even to be corny. The whole day had felt good. "Shall we go back now?" She nodded assent, and hand in hand they wandered back to where they had left the bikes. And two hours later, they were back at Nancy's tiny apartment on Spark Street, near the campus. Mike looked around as he let himself fall sleepily onto the couch and realized once again how much he enjoyed her apartment, how much like home it was to him. The only real home he had ever known. His mother's mammoth apartment had never really felt like home, but this place did. It had all Nancy's wonderful warm touches in it. The paintings she had done over the years, the warm earth colors she had chosen for the place, a soft brown velvet couch, and a fur rug she had bought from a friend. There were always flowers everywhere, and the plants she took such good care of. The spotless little white marble table where they ate, and the brass bed which creaked with pleasure when they made love.

"Do you know how much I love this place, Nancy?"

"Yeah, I know." She looked around nostalgically. "Me, too. What are we going to do when we get married?"

"Take all these beautiful things of yours to New York and find a cozy little home for them there." And then something caught his eye. "What's that? Something new?" He was looking at her easel, which held a painting still in its early stages but already with a haunting quality to it. It was a landscape of trees and fields, but as he walked toward it, he saw a small boy, hiding in a tree, dangling his legs. "Will he still show once you put the leaves on the tree?"

"Probably. But we'll know he's there in any case. Do you like it?" Her eyes shone as she watched his approval. He had always understood her work perfectly.

"I love it."

"Then it'll be your wedding present—when it's finished."

"You've got a deal. And speaking of wedding presents—" He looked at his watch. It was already five o'clock, and he wanted to be at the airport by six. "I should get going."

"Do you really have to go tonight?"

"Yes. It's important. I'll come back in a few hours. I should be at Marion's place by seven thirty or eight, depending on the traffic in New York. I can catch the last shuttle back, at eleven, and be home by midnight. Okay, little worrywart?"

"Okay." But she was hesitant. She was bothered by his going. She didn't want him to, and yet she didn't know why. "I hope it goes all right."

"I know it will." But they both knew that Marion did only what she wanted to do, listened only to what she wanted to hear, and understood only what suited her. Somehow he knew they'd win her over though.

They had to. He had to have Nancy. No matter what. He took her in his arms one last time before slipping a tie around the collar of the sport shirt he was wearing and grabbing a lightweight jacket on the back of a chair. He had left it there that morning. He knew it would be hot in New York, but he knew, too, that he had to appear at Marion's apartment in coat and tie. That was essential. Marion had no tolerance for "hippies," or for nobodies . . . like Nancy. They both knew what he was facing when they kissed good-bye at the door.

"Good luck."

"I love you."

For a long time Nancy sat in the silent apartment looking at the photograph of them at the fair. Rhett and Scarlet, immortal lovers, in their silly wooden costumes, poking their faces through the holes. But they didn't look silly. They looked happy. She wondered if Marion would understand that, if she knew the difference between happy and silly, between real and imaginary. She wondered if Marion would understand at all.

Chapter 2

The dining room table shone like the surface of a lake. Its sparkling perfection was disturbed only on the edge of the shore, where a single place setting of creamy Irish linen lay, adorned by delicate blue and gold china. There was a silver coffee service next to the plate, and an ornate little silver bell. Marion Hillyard sat back in her chair with a small sigh as she exhaled the smoke from the cigarette she had just lit. She was tired today. Sundays always tired her. Sometimes she thought she did more work at home than she did at the office. She always spent Sundays answering her personal correspondence, looking over the books kept by the cook and the housekeeper, making lists of what she had noticed needed to be repaired around the apartment and of items needed to complete her wardrobe, and planning the menus for the week. It was tedious work, but she had done it for years, even before she'd begun to run the business. And once she'd taken over for her husband, she still spent her Sundays attending to the household and taking care of Michael on the nurse's day off. The memory made her smile, and for a moment she closed her eyes. Those Sundays had been precious, a few hours with him without anyone interfering, anyone taking him away. Her Sundays weren't like that anymore; they hadn't been in too many years. A tiny bright tear crept into her lashes as she sat very still in her chair, seeing him as he had been eighteen years before, a little boy of six, and all hers. How she loved that child. She would have done anything for him. And she had. She had maintained an empire for him, carried the legacy from one generation to the next. It was her most valuable gift for Michael. Cotter-Hillyard. And she had come to love the business almost as much as she loved her son.

"You're looking beautiful, Mother." Her eyes flew open in surprise as she saw him standing there in the arched doorway of the richly paneled dining room. The sight of him now almost made her cry. She wanted to hug him as she had all those years ago, and instead she smiled slowly at her son.

"I didn't hear you come in." There was no invitation to approach, no sign of what she'd been feeling. No one ever knew, with Marion, what went on inside.

"I used my key. May I come in?"

"Of course. Would you like some dessert?"

Michael walked slowly into the room, a small nervous smile playing over his mouth, and then like a small boy he peered at her plate. "Hm . . . what was it? Looks like it must have been chocolate, huh?"

She chuckled and shook her head. He would never

23

grow up. In some ways anyway. "Profiteroles. Care for some? Mattie is still out there in the pantry."

"Probably eating what's left." They both laughed at what they knew was most likely true, but Marion reached for the bell.

Mattie appeared in an instant, black-uniformed and lace-trimmed, pale-faced and large-beamed. She had spent a lifetime running and fetching and doing for others, with only a brief Sunday here and there to call her own, and nothing to do with it once she had the much coveted "day." "Yes, madam?"

"Some coffee for Mr. Hillyard, Mattie. And . . . darling, dessert?" He shook his head. "Just coffee then."

"Yes, ma'am."

For a moment Michael wondered, as he often had, why his mother never said thank you to the servants. As though they had been born to do her bidding. But he knew that was what his mother thought. She had always lived surrounded by servants and secretaries and every possible kind of help. She had had a lonely upbringing but a comfortable one. Her mother had died when she was three, in an accident with Marion's only brother, the heir to the Cotter architectural throne. The accident had left only Marion to become a substitute son. She had done so very effectively.

"And how is school?"

"Almost over, thank God. Two more weeks."

"I know. I'm very proud of you, you know. A doctorate is a wonderful thing to have, particularly in architecture." For some reason the words made him want to say, "Oh, Mother!" as he had when he was nine. "We'll be contacting young Avery this week, about his job. You haven't said anything to him, have you?" She looked more curious than stern; she didn't really care. She had thought it a little childish that Michael thought it so important to surprise Ben.

"No, I haven't. He'll be very pleased."

"As well he should be. It's an excellent job."

"He deserves it."

"I hope so." She never gave an inch. "And you? Ready for work? Your office will be finished next week." Her eyes shone at the thought. It was a beautiful office, wood-paneled the way his father's had been, with etchings that had belonged to her own father, an impressive leather couch and chairs, and a roomful of Georgian furniture. She had bought it all in London over the holidays. "It really looks splendid, darling."

"Good." He smiled at his mother for a moment. "I have some things I want to get framed, but I'll wait till I take a look at the decor."

"You won't even need to do that. I have everything you'll need for the walls."

So did he. Nancy's drawings. There was sudden fire in his eyes now, and an air of watchfulness in hers. She had seen something in his face.

"Mother—" He sat down next to her with a small sigh and stretched his legs as Mattie arrived with the coffee. "Thank you, Mattie."

"You're welcome, Mr. Hillyard." She smiled at him as warmly as she always did. He was always so pleasant to her, as though he hated to bother her, not like . . . "Will there be anything else, madam?"

"No. As a matter of fact . . . Michael, do you want to take that into the library?"

"All right." Maybe it would be easier to talk in there. His mother's dining room had always reminded him of ballrooms he had seen in ancestral homes. It was not conducive to intimate conversation, and certainly not to gentle persuasion. He stood up and followed his mother out of the room, down three thickly carpeted steps, and into the library immediately to their left. There was a splendid view of Fifth Avenue and a comfortable chunk of Central Park, but there was also a warm fireplace and two walls lined with books. The fourth wall was dominated by a portrait of Michael's father, but it was one he liked, one in which his father looked warm—like someone you'd want to know. As a small boy he had come to look at that portrait at times, and to "talk" aloud to his father. His mother had found him that way once, and told him it was an absurd thing to do. But later he had seen her crying in that room, and staring at the portrait as he had.

His mother ensconced herself in her usual place, in a Louis XV chair covered in beige damask and facing the fireplace. Tonight her dress was almost the same color, and for a moment, as the firelight glowed, Michael thought her almost beautiful. She had been once, and not so long ago. Now she was fifty-seven. Michael had been born when she was thirty-three. She hadn't had time for children before that. And she had been very beautiful then. She had had the same rich honey-blonde hair that Michael had, but now it was graying, and the life in her face had faded. It had been replaced by other things. Mostly the business. And the once cornflower-blue eyes looked almost gray now. As though winter had finally come.

"I have the feeling that you came down here tonight to speak to me about something important, Michael. Is anything the matter?" Had he gotten someone pregnant? Smashed up his car? Hurt someone? Nothing was irreparable, of course, as long as he told her. She was glad he had come down.

"No, nothing's the matter. But there is something I want to discuss with you." Wrong. He cringed almost visibly at his own words. "Discuss." He should have said there was something he wanted to *tell* her, not *discuss* with her. Damn. "I thought it was about time we were honest with each other."

"You make it sound as though we usually aren't."

"About some things we aren't." His whole body was tense now, and he was leaning forward in his chair, conscious of his father looking over his shoulder. "We aren't honest about Nancy, Mother."

"Nancy?" She sounded blank, and suddenly he wanted to jump up and slap her. He hated the way she said her name. Like one of the servants.

"Nancy McAllister. My friend."

"Oh, yes." There was an interminable pause as she shifted the tiny vermeil and enamel spoon on the saucer of her demitasse cup. "And in what way are we not honest about Nancy?" Her eyes were veiled by a sheet of gray ice.

"You try to pretend that she doesn't exist. And I

try not to get you upset about it. But the fact is, Mother . . . I'm going to marry her." He took another breath and sat back in his chair. "In two weeks."

"I see." Marion Hillyard was perfectly still. Her eyes did not move, nor her hands, nor her face. Nothing. "And may I ask why? Is she pregnant?"

"Of course not."

"How fortunate. Then why, may I ask, are you marrying her? And why in two weeks?"

"Because I graduate then, because I'm moving to New York then, because I start work then. Because it makes sense."

"To whom?" The ice was hardening, and one leg crossed carefully over the other with the slippery sound of silk. Michael felt uncomfortable under the constancy of her gaze. She hadn't shifted her eyes once. As in business, she was ruthless. She could make any man squirm, and eventually break.

"It makes sense to us, Mother."

"Well, not to me. We've been asked to build a medical center in San Francisco, by the same group who were behind the Hartford Center. You won't have time for a wife. I'm going to be counting on you very heavily for the next year or two. Frankly, darling, I wish you'd wait." It was the first softening he'd seen, and it almost made him wonder if there was hope.

"Nancy will be an asset to both of us, Mother. Not a distraction to me, or a nuisance to you. She's a wonderful girl."

"Maybe so, but as for being an asset . . . have you thought of the scandal?" There was victory in her eyes now. She was going in for the kill, and suddenly Michael held his breath, a helpless prey, not knowing where she would strike, or how.

"What scandal?"

"She's told you who she is, of course?"

Oh, Jesus. Now what? "What do you mean, *who* she is?"

"Precisely that. I'll be quite specific." And in one smooth, feline gesture, she set down the demitasse and glided to her desk. From a bottom drawer she removed a file, and silently handed it to Michael. He held it for an instant, afraid to look inside.

"What *is* this?"

"A report. I had a private investigator look into your artistic little friend. I was not very pleased." An understatement. She had been livid. "Please sit down and read it." He did not sit down, but unwillingly he opened the folder and began to read. It told him in the first twelve lines that Nancy's father had been killed in prison when she was still a baby, and her mother had died an alcoholic two years later. It explained as well that her father had been serving a seven-year sentence for armed robbery. "Charming people, weren't they, darling?" Her voice was lightly contemptuous, and suddenly Michael threw the folder on the desk, from which its contents slid rapidly to the floor.

"I won't read that garbage."

"No, but you'll marry it."

"What difference does it make who her parents were? Is that her Goddamn fault?"

"No. Her misfortune. And yours, if you marry her.

Michael, be sensible. You're going into a business where millions of dollars are involved in every deal. You can no longer afford the risk of scandal. You'll ruin us. Your grandfather founded this business over fifty years ago, and you're going to destroy it now for a love affair? Don't be insane. It's time you grew up, my boy. High time. Your salad days are over. In exactly two weeks." She burned as she looked at him now. She was not going to lose this battle, no matter what she had to do. "I won't discuss this with you, Michael. You have no choice." She had always told him that. Goddammit, she had always . . .

"The hell I don't!" It was a sudden roar as he paced across the room. "I'm not going to bow and scrape before you and your rules for the rest of my life, Mother! I won't! What exactly do you think, that you're going to pull me into the business, groom me until you retire, and then run me as a puppet from a chaise longue in your room? Well, to hell with that. I'm coming to work for you. But that's all. You don't own my life, now or ever, and I have a right to marry anybody I bloody well please!"

"Michael!"

They were interrupted by the sudden peal of the doorbell, and they stood eying each other like two jaguars in a cage. The old cat and the young one, each slightly afraid of the other, each hungry for victory, each fighting for his survival. They were still standing at opposite ends of the room, trembling with rage, when George Calloway walked in, and instantly sensed that he had stepped into a scene of great passion. He was a gentle, elegant man in his late fifties who had been Marion's right hand man for years. More than that, he was much of the power behind Cotter-Hillyard. But unlike Marion, he was seldom in the forefront; he preferred to wield his strength from the shadows. He had long since learned the merits of quiet strength. It had won him Marion's trust and admiration years ago, when she first took her husband's place in the business. She had been only a figurehead then, and it had been George who actually ran Cotter-Hillyard for the first year, while he determinedly and conscientiously taught her the ropes. And he had done his job well. Marion had learned all he had taught, and more. She was a power in her own right now, but she still relied on George on every major deal. That meant everything to him. Knowing that she still needed him after all these years. Knowing that she always would. He understood that now. They were a team, silent, inseparable, each one stronger because of the other. He sometimes wondered if Michael knew just how close they were. He doubted it. Michael had always been the hub of his mother's life. Why would he ever have noticed just how much George cared? In some ways, even Marion didn't understand that. But George accepted that. He lavished his warmth and energies on the business. And perhaps, one day . . . George looked at Marion now with instant concern. He had learned to recognize the tightness around the mouth and the strange pallor beneath the carefully applied powder and rouge.

"Marion, are you all right?" He knew more about

her health than anyone did. She had confided in him years before. Someone had to know, for the business. She had appallingly high blood pressure, and a serious problem with her heart.

For a moment there was no answer, and then she pulled her eyes away from her son to look at her longtime associate and friend. "Yes . . . yes, I'm fine. I'm sorry. Good evening, George. Come in."

"I think I've come at a bad time."

"Not at all, George, I was just leaving." Michael turned to look at him and couldn't even pretend to smile. Then he looked at his mother again, but made no move to approach her. "Good night, Mother."

"I'll call you tomorrow, Michael. We can discuss this over the phone."

He wanted to say something hateful to her, to frighten her, but he couldn't, he didn't know how. And what was the point?

"Michael . . ."

He didn't answer her; he merely shook hands solemnly with George and walked out of the library without looking back. He never saw the look in his mother's eyes, or the concern in George's as she sank slowly back into her chair and brought her trembling hands to her face. There were tears in her eyes which she hid even from George.

"What on earth happened?"

"He's going to do something insane."

"Maybe not. We all threaten mad things now and then."

"At our age we threaten, at his age they do." All her

efforts for nothing. The investigators' reports, the phone calls, the . . . She sighed and slowly sat back against the delicate chair.

"Have you taken your medicine today?" She shook her head almost imperceptibly. "Where is it?"

"In my bag. Behind the desk." He walked to the desk, saying nothing of the pages of the report scattered there and on the floor, and found the black alligator handbag with the eighteen-karat-gold clasp. He knew it well; he had given it to her three Christmases before. He found the medicine and returned to her side, holding the two white pills in his hand. She heard the rattle of the demitasse cup and opened her eyes. This time she smiled at him. "What would I do without you, George?"

"What would I do without you?" He couldn't even bear the thought. "Shall I leave now? You should get some rest."

"I'd just get upset thinking about Michael."

"Is he still coming to work for the firm?"

"Yes, it was something else."

The girl then. George knew about that too, but he didn't want to press Marion now. She was distressed enough, but at least the color was coming back to her face, and after swallowing the pills she took a cigarette out of her case. He lit it for her as he watched her face. She was a beautiful woman. He had always thought so. Even now, as she grew tired and increasingly ill. He wondered if Michael knew how ill. He couldn't possibly or he wouldn't upset her like this.

What George did not know was that Michael was

equally distressed at that moment. Hot tears burned his eyes as he sat in the back of a cab on his way to the airport.

He called Nancy as soon as he got to the terminal. His flight would leave in twenty minutes.

"How did it go?" She couldn't tell much from his voice when he said hello.

"Fine. Now I want you to get busy. I want you to pack a bag, get dressed, and be ready in an hour and a half when I get there."

"Ready for what?" She was puzzled as she sat curled up on the couch, holding the phone.

He paused for a moment and then smiled. It was his first smile in two hours. "An adventure, my love. You'll see."

"You're crazy." She was laughing her wonderful soft laugh.

"Yeah, crazy about you." He felt like himself again. Once more it was all beginning to make sense: he was back with Nancy. No one could ever take that away from him, not his mother, not a report, no one and nothing. He had vowed that day, on the beach where they had buried the beads, never to say good-bye to her, and he had meant it. "Okay, Nancy Fancy-pants, get moving. Oh, and wear something old, something new . . ." He wasn't just smiling now, he was grinning.

"You mean . . ." Her voice trailed off in astonishment.

"I mean we're getting married tonight. Okay with you?"

"Yes, but—"

"But nothing, lady. Get your ass in gear and make like a bride."

"But why tonight?"

"Instinct. Trust me. Besides, it's a full moon."

"It must be." She was smiling now, too. She was going to be married. She and Michael were going to be married!

"I'll see you in an hour, babe. And . . . Nancy?"

"Yes?"

"I love you." He hung up the phone and ran toward the gate. He was the last passenger to board the plane to Boston. Nothing could stop him now.

Chapter 3

He had been pounding on the door for almost ten minutes, but he wasn't going to give up. He knew Ben was in there.

"Ben! Come on, you ... *Ben!* ! ... For Chrissake, man ..." Another rash of pounding and then at last the sound of footsteps and a sudden crash. The door opened to reveal a sleepy Ben, standing confusedly in his underwear and rubbing his shin. "Christ, it's only eleven o'clock. What are you doing asleep at this hour?" But the grin on Ben's face told him with a second glance. "Jesus. You're smashed."

"To the very tips of my toes." Ben looked down at his feet with an elfin smile and an unsteady wobbling of the legs.

"Well, you're going to sober up real quick, podner. I need you."

"The hell you do. Six Beefeaters and tonic and you think I'm gonna waste it? Bullsh—"

"Never mind that. Get dressed."

"I *am* dressed." He squinted unhappily as Mike turned on the lights. "Hey, what the hell are you doing?" But Mike only smiled as he headed toward the tiny, disheveled kitchen.

"What'd you do in here? Detonate a hand grenade?"

"Yeah. And I'm gonna shove one up your—"

"Now, now, this is a special occasion." Mike turned to smile at him from the kitchen doorway, and for a moment there was hope in Ben's eyes.

"Can we drink to it?"

"All you want. But later."

"Crap." He let himself fall into a chair, and let his head loll back against the soft cushions.

"Don't you want to know what the occasion is?"

"Not if I can't drink to it. I'm graduating from graduate school. That I can drink to."

"And I'm getting married."

"That's nice." And then he sat up straight, and the eyes came open. "You're what?"

"You heard me. Nancy and I are getting married." Mike said it with the quiet pride of a man who knows his mind.

"This is an engagement party?" Ben sat up with a look of delight. Hell, that was worth at least another six Beefeaters. Maybe even seven or eight.

"Not an engagement party, Avery. I told you. It's a wedding."

"Now?" Confusion again. Hillyard was a real pain in the ass. "Why now?"

"Because we want to. Besides, you're too loaded to understand anyway. Can you get it together enough to be our best man?"

"Sure. Son of a bitch, you're actually going to—"

He leapt out of his chair, lurched horribly and stubbed his toe on the coffee table. "Goddamn—"

"Go put some clothes on without killing yourself. I'll make you some coffee."

"Yeah . . ." He was still muttering to himself when he disappeared into the bedroom, but he looked slightly more composed when he returned. He was even wearing a tie, with a blue and red striped T-shirt. Mike looked at him and shook his head with a grin.

"You could've at least picked a tie that went with the shirt." The tie was a dark maroon with a beige and black design.

"Do I need a tie?" He suddenly looked worried. "I couldn't find one that matched."

"Just zip up your fly and we're all set. You might want to find the other shoe, too." Ben looked down to see only one loafer, and then he started to laugh.

"Okay, so I'm gassed. But did I know you'd need me tonight? You could've at least told me this morning."

"I didn't know this morning."

That brought a look of sudden seriousness to Ben's eyes. "You didn't?"

"Nope."

"Are you sure about this?"

"Very much so. And look, don't make me speeches. I've had enough of those tonight. Just get yourself decent so we can pick up Nancy." He handed his friend a mug of steaming coffee, and Ben took a long hard swallow, then grimaced.

"What a waste of good gin."

"We'll buy you another round after the wedding."

"Where are you doing this, by the way?"

"You'll see. It's a beautiful little town I've been in love with for years. I spent a summer there once as a kid. It's only about an hour from here. It's the perfect place."

"You've got a license?"

"Don't need one. It's one of those crazy towns where you do it all in one shot. You ready?"

Ben downed the last of the coffee and nodded. "I think so. Jesus, I'm getting nervous. Aren't you scared?" He looked at Mike more soberly now, but Mike looked strangely calm.

"Not a bit."

"Maybe you know what you're doing. I don't know . . . it's just that . . . marriage . . ." He shook his head again and stared at his feet. It reminded him that he had another loafer to find. "Nancy's a hell of a nice girl though."

"Better than that." Mike spotted the other loafer under the couch and handed it to him. "She's everything I've always wanted."

"Then I hope the marriage brings you both everything you want, Mike. Always." There was a bright glaze of tenderness in his eyes, and for a moment Mike held him by both arms.

"Thanks." And then they both looked away, anxious to get going, to laugh again, to taste the moment with glee instead of solemnity.

"Do I look all right?" Ben checked his pants for his wallet, then searched for his keys.

"You look gorgeous."

"Oh shove it . . . damn . . . where're my keys?" He looked around helplessly as Mike laughed at him. The keys were attached to one of the belt loops on his trousers.

"Come on, Avery. Let's get you out of here." The two left, arm in arm and singing the beer hall songs of summers before. The entire building could hear them but no one really cared; the whole place was populated by students living off campus, and two weeks before the end of school everyone was raising hell.

They pulled up outside Nancy's place on Spark Street ten minutes later, and she waved nervously from the window as Mike honked. She felt as though she'd been ready for hours. A moment later she was standing beside the car, and for a few seconds both young men fell silent. It was Mike who spoke first.

"My God, Nance . . . you look beautiful. Where did you get that?"

"I had it." They exchanged a long smile, and none of them moved. She suddenly felt every bit a bride, despite the late hour and the unorthodox circumstances. She was wearing a long white eyelet dress and there was a little blue satin cap on her shiny black hair. She had worn the dress as a bridesmaid at a friend's wedding three years before, but Mike had never seen it. She was wearing white sandals and carrying a very old, very beautiful lace handkerchief. "See, something old, something new . . . the handkerchief was my grandmother's." And the cap was blue. She looked so beautiful that for a moment Mike didn't know what to say. Even Ben seemed totally sobered as he looked at her.

"You look like a princess, Nancy."

"Thanks, Ben."

"Hey, listen, you got something borrowed?"

"What do you mean?"

"You know . . . something old, something new . . . something borrowed . . ." She laughed and shook her head. "Okay, here." He bent his head forward and began to fumble with something at his neck. A moment later he held out a narrow, handsome gold chain. "Now, this is just a loan. My sister gave it to me for graduation, but I opened it early. You can borrow it for the wedding." He leaned out of the car to fasten it around her throat and it fell just above the delicate neckline of the dress.

"It's perfect."

"So are you." Mike said it as he got out of the car and held the door for her. He had been so stunned by the way she looked that he hadn't been able to move. "Get in the back, Avery. Darling, you sit in front."

"Can't she sit on my lap?" Ben made a feeble protest as he scrambled toward the back, and Mike gave him the finger. "Okay, man, okay, don't get excited. I just thought maybe since I was the best man, and—"

"You'll be the dead man if you don't watch it." But the mood was strictly a teasing one as Nancy settled herself on the front seat and beamed at the man she was about to marry. She felt a moment's queasiness about Marion, but she pushed it from her mind. This was the time to think only of herself, and Michael.

41

"What a crazy night . . . but I love it."

They alternately joked and fell silent on the road to the tiny town Mike had in mind, and at last none of them spoke. They had a lot on their minds. Michael was thinking back to his interview with his mother, and Nancy was thinking of all that this day meant to her.

"Is it much farther, love?" Nancy was getting fidgety and her grandmother's handkerchief was beginning to look crumpled as it passed through her hands.

"Only about five more miles, guys. We're almost there." Michael reached briefly for Nancy's hand. "Just a few more minutes, babe, and we'll be married."

"Then speed it up, mister, before I get cold feet," Ben sang out from the back, and all three of them laughed. Mike put his foot on the gas and swerved around the next curve, but the laughter rapidly shrank to a gasp as Michael veered helplessly to avoid a diesel truck occupying both lanes as it plowed mercilessly toward them, going too fast, and almost out of control. The driver must have been half-asleep, and the only sounds Nancy remembered hearing were Ben's anguished "Oh no!" and her own voice screaming in her ears. Then there was endless shattering of glass . . . shattering . . . breaking . . . metal grinding, crunching, roaring, engines meeting and locking and arms flying and leather tearing and plastic cracking as everything was covered with a blanket of glass. And then at last everything stopped, and the world was black.

It seemed years later when Ben woke up, lying with his head jammed into the dashboard and a horrible pounding in his ears. Everything was dark around him and there seemed to be a handful of sand in his mouth. It felt like hours before he could open his eyes, and the effort it took made him feel sick. At first he couldn't understand what he saw. Nothing seemed to make sense, and then he realized that he was looking into Michael's right eye. He was in the front seat with him, but all he could see was Michael, and there was a thin river of blood trickling slowly down the side of Mike's face, onto his neck. It was strange to watch it, but for a while that was all Ben did . . . watch . . . Mike . . . bleeding . . . Jesus. It dawned on him what was happening. Accident . . . there had been an accident . . . he and Mike had been driving and . . . he lifted his head from where it had lain and tried to look up but a blow as if from iron forced him back down. It was minutes before he caught his breath and could open his eyes again. Mike was still lying there, bleeding, but now Ben could see that he was breathing, and this time when he stirred nothing happened. He could lift his head, and what he saw just beyond Mike was the truck that had hit them, lying flipped over the side of the road. What he did not see was the driver, lying dead beneath the cab of the truck. It would be a long time before anyone saw that. And then Ben realized something more, that he was seeing it all through open windows. There was no more glass left anywhere in the car, they were wearing it all, crushed into tiny particles all around them. And on Mike's side there was also no door. And then he remembered something more. Somebody else had been in the car . . . Nancy was . . . and where were they going? It was all so hard to hold onto, and his head hurt so badly, and as he moved a horrible pain shot though his leg, into his side. He moved to get away from the pain, and then he saw her. Nancy . . . Jesus . . . it was Nancy in some kind of red and white dress, lying face down on the hood . . . Nancy . . . she had to be dead . . . he didn't even care about the pain in his leg now, he dragged himself over the dashboard and to her side. He had to . . . turn her over . . . get to her . . . help her . . . Nancy . . . And then he saw the fine powder that dusted Nancy's hair. She was wearing the windshield all over her dress, all over the back of her head, all over . . . My God. With the last of his strength he rolled her slowly to her side and then pitifully, like a terrified little boy, he began to whimper.

"Oh, my God . . ." There was no face left beneath the blood-soaked blue satin cap. He couldn't tell if she were dead or alive, but for one horrible instant, he hoped she was dead, because there was simply no more Nancy. There was no one there at all, not even a remnant of the once beautiful face. And then mercifully, in her blood and his tears, he passed out.

Chapter 4

He looked so painfully pale as his mother sat there watching him. Marion Hillyard sat in a corner of the room with a bleak expression on her face. She had been there before, in that room, on that day, watching that face . . . not really that face, or that room, but she felt as though nothing had changed. It was just like when Frederick had the massive coronary that had killed him within hours. She had sat there, just as still, just as frightened, just as alone. And he had . . . Frederick . . . she felt a sob catch in her throat again and she took a deep, sharp breath. She couldn't cry. She couldn't let herself think those thoughts. Her husband was gone. Michael wasn't. Nothing was going to happen to Michael. She wouldn't let anything happen. She was holding on to him now with every ounce of strength she could give.

For a moment she turned her gaze to the nurse's face. The woman was watching Michael intently, but with no sign of alarm. He had been in a coma all that day, since the accident the night before. Marion had gotten there at five in the morning. She had called a twenty-four-hour limousine service and been driven up from New York. But she would have walked if she'd had to. Nothing would have kept her from Michael's side; she had to be there to keep him alive. He was all she had now. Michael, and the business . . . and the business was for him. She had done it all for him . . . well, not all for him, but for the most part. It was the greatest gift she could give him. The gift of power, of success. He couldn't throw that away on that little bitch . . . he couldn't throw it away by *dying*. Jesus. It was all her fault, that damned girl. She had probably talked him into this. She had . . .

The nurse got up quickly and pulled at Michael's eyelids, as Marion went tense and forgot what she had been thinking. She stood up silently and quickly and walked to the nurse's side. Whatever there was to see, she wanted to see it. But there was nothing. No change. The expressionless woman in white held his wrist for a moment and then mouthed the same words again. "No change." She motioned toward the corridor then and Marion followed her outside. This time the woman's concern was not for Michael, but for his mother.

"Dr. Wickfield told me to ask you to leave by five o'clock, Mrs. Hillyard. And I'm afraid . . ." She looked menacingly at her watch, and then smiled apologetically. It was five fifteen. Marion had been at Michael's side for exactly twelve hours. She had sat there uninterrupted all day, with only two cups of coffee to keep her going. But she wasn't tired, she wasn't hungry, she wasn't anything. And she wasn't leaving.

"Thank you for the thought. I'll just walk down the hall for a moment and come back." She wasn't leaving him. Not ever. She had left Frederick. Only for an hour, to have dinner. They had insisted that she eat something, and it had happened then. He had died while she was gone. That wasn't going to happen this time. She knew that as long as she sat there, Michael wouldn't die. The damage was mostly internal, but even Wickfield felt he'd come out of the coma soon. Still, she wasn't taking any chances. They had thought Frederick would make it, too. There were tears in her eyes now as she stood staring blankly at the pale blue wall behind the nurse.

"Mrs. Hillyard? The woman gently touched her arm, and Marion started. "You ought to get some rest. Dr. Wickfield set aside a room for you on the third floor."

"There's no need." She smiled blankly at the nurse and walked away toward the far end of the hall. The sun was still bright in the window there, and she sat carefully on the ledge, to smoke her first cigarette in hours and watch the sun set over a white church in the pretty New England town. Thank God the town only looked remote, and was actually less than an hour from Boston. They had had no trouble bringing in the best doctors to consult, and as soon as he could stand it, Michael would be moved to a hospital in New York. But at least she knew that in the meantime he was in good hands. Medically, Michael had taken the worst of it. The Avery boy was pretty badly broken up, but he was awake and alive, and his father had had him taken to Boston by ambulance that afternoon.

He had broken an arm, a thigh, a foot, and a collarbone, but he'd be all right. And the girl . . . well, it was her fault, there was no reason why she should . . . Marion stubbed out the cigarette with a quick crushing motion of her foot. The girl would be all right too. She'd live anyway. The only thing she had lost was her face. And maybe that was just as well. For a fraction of a second Marion wanted to fight the anger, wanted to make herself sorry for the girl—just in case all that crap about Christian charity was true, just in case her feelings made some difference for Michael . . . just in case there was a God who would punish her by taking him. But she couldn't do it. She hated the girl with every ounce of her being.

"I thought I left orders for you to get some rest." Marion turned toward the voice with a start, and then smiled tiredly when she saw her own Dr. Wickfield. Wicky. "Don't you ever listen to anyone, Marion?"

"Not if I can help it. How's Michael?" Her brow furrowed and she reached for another cigarette.

"I just looked in on him. He's stable. I told you, he'll come out of it. Give him time. His entire system received one hell of a shock."

"So did mine when I got the news." He nodded sympathetically. "You're sure there won't be permanent damage from this?" She paused for a moment and then said the dread words. "Brain damage?"

Wickfield patted her arm and sat next to her on the window ledge. Behind them the little town made a scene pretty enough for a postcard. "I told you, Marion. As best we can tell, he'll be fine. A lot depends of course on how long he stays under. But I'm not frightened yet."

"I am." They were two tiny words in the mouth of a very strong woman, and they surprised her doctor, as he looked at her closely. There were sides to Marion Hillyard that no one even guessed at. "What about the girl?" she went on. Now she was the Marion he knew again, eyes narrowed behind the smoke from her cigarette, face hardened, fear gone.

"Not much is going to change for her. Not for the time being anyway. She's been in stable condition all day, but there's not a damn thing we can do for her. For one thing, it's much too soon, and for another, there are only one or two men in the country who can cope with that kind of total reconstruction. There is simply nothing left of her face, not a single bone intact, not a nerve, not a muscle. The only thing not totally wiped out are her eyes."

"The better to see herself with." Dr. Wickfield jumped at the tone of Marion's voice.

"Michael was driving, Marion. She wasn't." But Marion only nodded in answer. There was no point in going over it with him. She knew whose fault it was. It was the girl's.

"What happens to someone like that if there's no repair work done? Will she live?"

"Unfortunately, yes. But she'll lead a tragic life. You can't take a twenty-two-year-old girl and turn her into a horror like that and expect her to adjust. No one could. Was she . . . was she pretty before?"

"I suppose so. I don't know. We'd never met." Her tone was rock hard, and her eyes equally so.

"I see. In any case, she's in for some tough realities. They'll do what they can here at the hospital when she's a little more recovered, but it won't be much. Does she have money?"

"None." Marion spoke the word like a death sentence. It was the worst thing she could say of anyone.

"Then she won't have many alternatives. I'm afraid the men who do this kind of thing don't do it for charity."

"Do you have anyone particular in mind?"

"Well, I know some of the names. Two, actually. The best one is out in San Francisco." A little fire kindled in Dr. Wickfield's heart. With all her money, Marion Hillyard could . . . if only . . . "His name is Peter Gregson. We met several years ago. He's really an amazing guy."

"Could he do this?"

Wickfield felt a rush of admiration for the woman. He almost wanted to hug her, but he didn't dare. "He may well be the only man who could. Shall I . . . do you want me to call him?" He hesitated to say the words, and then she looked at him with those cold, calculating eyes and he wondered what she had in mind. The wave of admiration almost turned to fear.

"I'll let you know."

"Fine." He looked at his watch then, and stood up. "I'd like you to go downstairs and rest now. I really mean that."

"I know." She favored him with a wintry smile. "But I'm not going to. You know that too. I have to be with Michael."

"Even if you kill yourself doing it?"

"I won't. I'm too mean to die, Wicky. Besides, I still have a lot of work to do."

"Is it worth it?" He looked at her curiously for a moment. If he had had one tenth of her ambition, he would have been a great surgeon, but he didn't and he wasn't. And he wasn't even sure that he envied her. "Is it worth it?" He said it more softly the second time, and she nodded.

"Absolutely. Don't ever doubt it for a second. It's given me everything I want out of life." Unless I lose Michael. She closed her eyes and pushed away the thought.

"Well, I'll give you another hour with him, and then I'm coming back up here. And I don't care if I have to shoot you with Nembutal and drag you away myself, you're going. Is that clear?"

"Very." She stood up, dropped another cigarette to the floor where she crushed it, and patted his cheek. "And Wicky—" She looked up at him from under long chestnut lashes, and for a moment she was all softness and elegant beauty. "—thank you." He gently kissed her cheek, squeezed her arm, and stood back for a moment.

"He'll be all right, Marion, you'll see." He didn't dare mention the girl again. They could talk about that later. He only smiled and walked away, as she stood there looking vulnerable and alone. He was glad he had called George Calloway a few hours before. Marion needed someone with her. He thought about her all the way down the corridor, as she stood watching him go. She hadn't moved from the spot where he had left her, and then slowly, she began the lonely walk up the hall, back towards Michael's room, past open doors and closed ones, heartbreaks to come and hopes never to be known again. And a few who would make it. This was a floor set aside for the critically ill, and there was no sound from any of the rooms as she walked slowly by, until she was halfway down the hall, where she heard little jerking sobs come from an open door. The sounds were so soft that at first she wasn't sure what she was hearing. And then she saw the room number, and she knew. She stopped as though she had come to a wall, staring at the door, and the darkness beyond.

She could see the bed dimly outlined in the corner, but the room was dark; all the blinds and curtains had been drawn, as though the patient could not be touched by light. Marion stood there for a long moment, afraid to go in, but knowing that she had to; and then slowly, one foot after the other, softly, gliding, she walked a few feet into the room and stopped again. The sobs were a little louder now, and coming at quicker intervals, with little panicky gasps.

"Is someone there?" The girl's entire head was covered with bandages, and the voice was muffled and strange. "Is someone . . ." She cried harder now. "I can't see."

"Your eyes are just covered with bandages. There's nothing wrong with your eyes." But the words were met by fresh sobs. "Why are you awake?" Marion spoke to her in a monotone. They were not words of reassurance, they were devoid of all feeling, and Marion herself felt as though she were standing in a dream. But she knew that she had to be there. Had to. For Michael's sake. "Didn't they give you something to make you sleep?"

"It doesn't work. I keep waking up."

"Is the pain very bad?"

"No, everything is numb. Who . . . who are you?"

She was afraid to tell her. Instead, she moved toward the bed and sat down in the narrow blue vinyl chair the nurse must have pulled up next to it. The girl's hands were wrapped in bandages, too, and lay useless at her sides. Marion remembered Wicky telling her that the girl had naturally used her hands to try to shield her face. The damage to them was almost as great as to her face, which would be devastating to her as an artist. In essence, her whole life was over. Her youth, her beauty, her work. And her romance. But now Marion knew what she had to say.

"Nancy—" It was the first time she had said the name, but now it didn't matter. She had no choice. "Did they . . ." Her voice was smooth and silky as she sat next to the broken girl. "Did they tell you about your face?" There was total silence in the room for an endless amount of time, and then a small broken sob freed itself from the bandages. "Did they tell you how bad it was?" Her stomach turned over as she said the words, but she could not stop now. She had to free Michael. If she freed him, he would live. She felt that in her guts. "Did they tell you how impossible it would be to put you back together?"

The sobs were angry now. "They lied to me. They said . . ."

"There's only one man who can do it, Nancy, and it would cost hundreds of thousands of dollars. You can't afford it. And neither can Michael."

"I'd never let him do that." She was angry at the voice now, as well as at fate. "I'd never let him . . ."

"Then what will you do?"

"I don't know." And the sobs began again.

"Could you face him like that?" It took minutes for the stifled "no" to emerge. "Do you think he would love you like that? Even if he tried, because he felt some bond of loyalty, some obligation, how long could it last? How long could you bear knowing what you looked like and what you were doing to him?" The sounds Nancy made now were frightening. She sounded as though she were going to be sick, and Marion wondered if she herself would be as well. "Nancy, there's nothing left of you. Nothing. There's nothing left of the life you had before today." They sat in interminable silence, and Marion thought she would hear those sobs forever. But it had to be painful or it would never work. "You've already lost him. You couldn't do this to him. And he . . . he deserves better than that. If you love him, you know that. And . . . and so do you. But you could have a new life, Nancy." The girl didn't even bother to answer as her sobs went on. "You *could* have a new life. A whole new world." She waited until the sobs grew angrier again and then stopped. "A whole new face."

"How?"

"There's a man in San Francisco who could make you beautiful again. Who could make you able to paint again. It would take a long time, and a lot of money, but it would be worth it, Nancy . . . wouldn't it?" There was the tiniest of smiles at the corners of Marion's mouth. Now she was on familiar ground. It was just like making a multimillion-dollar deal. A hundred-million-dollar deal. They were all the same.

A small jagged sigh emerged from the faceless bandages. "We can't afford it." Marion almost shuddered at the "we." They were not a "we" anymore. They never had been. She and Michael were the "we." Not this . . . this . . . She took a deep breath and composed herself. She had work to do. That was the only way she could think of it. She couldn't think of the girl. Only of Michael.

"You can't, Nancy. But I can. You do know who I am, don't you?"

"Yes."

"You do understand that you've already lost Michael? That he could never survive the pressure and tragedy of what has happened to you, if he survives at all. You understand that, don't you?"

"Yes."

"And you know that it would be a vicious thing to do, to try to put him through it, to make him prove his loyalty to you?" She wouldn't say the word "love." The girl wasn't worthy of it. Marion had to believe that. "Do you understand that, Nancy?" There was a silent pause. "Do you?"

This time it was a very tired little word. She was sounding spent. "Yes."

"Then you've already lost everything you can lose, haven't you?"

"Yes." The word had no tone, no life to it. It was as though life itself were seeping away from the girl.

"Nancy, I'd like to propose a little deal to you." It was Marion Hillyard at her best. If her son had heard her, he would have wanted to kill her. "I'd like you to think about that new face. About a new life, a new Nancy. Think about it. About what it would mean. You'd be beautiful again, you could have friends again, you could go places—to restaurants, to movies, to stores—you could wear pretty clothes and go out with men. The other way . . . people would shriek when you walked near them. You couldn't go anywhere, do anything, be anyone. Children would cry if they saw you. Can you imagine what that would be like? But you have a choice." She let the words sink in.

"No, I don't."

"Yes, you do. I want to give you that choice. I will give you that new life. A new face, a new world. An apartment in another city while the work is being done—anything you need, anything you want to do. There'll be no struggle, Nancy, and in a year or so, the nightmare will be over."

"And then?"

"You're free. The new life is yours." There was an endless pause as Marion prepared to lower the boom Nancy was waiting for. "As long as you never contact Michael again. The new face is yours only if you give up Michael. But if you don't accept my . . . my gift, you know that you've already lost him, anyway. So

why live the rest of your life as a freak if you don't
have to?"

"What if Michael doesn't honor the agreement?
What if I stay away from him, but he doesn't stay
away from me?"

"All I want from you is the promise that you'll stay
away from him. What Michael does is up to him."

"And you'll honor that? If he wants me . . . anyway
. . . if he comes after me, then it's up to him?"

"I'll honor that."

Nancy felt victorious as she lay there. She knew
Michael infinitely better than his mother did. Michael
would never give up on her. He'd find her, and want
to help her through the ordeal, but by then she'd already be on her way to becoming herself again. His
mother couldn't win this one, no matter how hard she
tried. Accepting the deal would make Nancy a cheat,
because she knew what the outcome would be. But
she had to do it. She had to. There was no other way.

"Will you do it?" Marion almost held her breath as
she waited for the one word she prayed for, the word
that would free Michael, and at last it came.

But it would be a word of victory, not of defeat. It
would be filled with all Nancy's faith in Michael. She
remembered the words he had said to her at the rock
where they'd hidden the beads the morning before.
"I promise never to say good-bye to you." She knew
he never would.

"Your answer, Nancy?" Marion couldn't wait any
longer. Her heart wouldn't bear it.

"Yes."

Chapter 5

Marion Hillyard stood in the doorway of the hospital in a black wool dress and black Cardin coat watching them load the girl into an ambulance. It was six o'clock in the morning, and she had never spoken to her again. They had made their agreement the night before, and Marion had immediately asked Wicky to call the man he knew in San Francisco. Wickfield had been overjoyed. He had kissed Marion on the cheek and gotten hold of Peter Gregson at his home. Gregson would do it. He wanted Nancy out west immediately, and Marion had arranged for a special compartment and two nurses in first class on a jet heading for San Francisco at eight o'clock that morning. She was sparing no expense. "She's a lucky girl, Marion." Wickfield looked at her in admiration as she crushed out another cigarette.

"I think so. And I don't want Michael to know, Wicky. Is that clear?" It was, and so was the "or else" in her voice. "If someone does tell him, I cancel her treatment."

"But why? He has a right to know what you've done for the girl."

"It's between the two of us. The four of us, including you and Gregson. Michael doesn't need to know anything. When he comes out of the coma, you're not to mention the girl to him at all. It will only agitate him."

If he ever came out of the coma. Marion had dozed in the chair at his side all night long despite Wicky's protests. But she had felt strangely revived after her talk with the girl. She had freed Michael at last. Now he could live. In a way, she had given them both life. She knew she had been right to do what she'd done. "You won't say anything then, will you, Robert?" She never called him that, except to remind him what the Hillyard money had done for his hospital.

"Of course not, if that's what you want."

"It is."

There was the dull clank of the ambulance door closing, and the last of the blue blankets swathing the girl disappeared with the two nurses' backs. The nurses would be with her for the first six or eight months in San Francisco. After that, Gregson had said, she wouldn't need them. But for those six or eight months, she would spend much of her time with her eyes bandaged, as he worked on her lids and her nose, her brow and her cheekbones. He had a whole face to reconstruct. There would be other expenses involved, too. Nancy would need almost constant care by a psychiatrist as she underwent the emotional shock of becoming a new person. There was no way Gregson could give her back the self she had been. He had to create a whole new woman. And Marion liked that idea just fine: the girl would be that much more removed from

Michael. It took away the possibility of an accident, a chance meeting in an airport five years later. Marion didn't want that to happen. Her mind ran over the list of arrangements she had made with Gregson on the phone at four o'clock that morning, one o'clock San Francisco time. He had sounded bright and alive and dynamic, a man in his forties with an extraordinary international reputation in his field. She was a damn lucky girl. He said he'd have his secretary work it all out. The apartment, the clothes. They had quickly run over the cost of eighteen months of surgery, and the additional expense of psychiatric help, constant nurses for a while, and even general support. They had settled on four hundred thousand dollars as a reasonable figure. Marion would call the bank at nine and have it transferred to Gregson's account on the coast. It would be there when his own bank opened at nine. Not that he was worried. He knew who Marion Hillyard was. Who didn't?

"Why don't you come inside and have some breakfast, Marion?" Wickfield was losing hope of having any influence on her at all, and Calloway had said that he couldn't leave New York until that morning. Wickfield didn't know that Marion had told him not to. She had wanted to be alone to work out her "business" arrangements. And everything had worked out just perfectly. "Marion?"

"Hm?"

"Breakfast?"

"Later, Wicky. Later. I want to see Michael."

"I'll go up and take a look at him now."

Marion stopped in the ladies' room for a moment, while Wickfield went ahead to see Michael. But he didn't expect any immediate change; he had checked him only an hour before.

But there was a strange stillness when Marion came into the room five minutes later. Wicky was standing back from the bed with a look of solemnity, and the nurse had left the room. The New England sun was streaming across the bed, and from somewhere there was the steady sound of water dripping into a sink. Everything was much too still, and suddenly her heart flew to her mouth. It was like when Frederick ... oh God ... her hand went unwillingly to her heart and she stood frozen in the doorway looking from Wicky to the bed. And then she saw him, and her eyes filled with tears. He was smiling at her . . . her boy. It wasn't like Frederick at all. A sob caught in her throat and she walked to the bed with trembling legs, and then she bent down and touched his face with her hands.

"Hi, Mom." They were the most beautiful words she had ever heard, and the tears poured down her face as she smiled.

"I love you, Michael."

"I love you, too." Even Wickfield had tears in his eyes as he watched them. The boy, so young and handsome and alive again, and the woman who had given so much in the past two days. He slipped quietly from the room, and they never heard him go.

She held her son gently in her arms for a long moment as he ran a hand over her hair. "Take it easy,

Mom. Everything's okay. Christ, I'm hungry." Marion laughed. He sounded so good. He was alive again. And all hers.

"We will get you the biggest, bestest, superest breakfast you've ever seen, if Wicky says it's all right."

"To hell with Wicky. I'm starving."

"Michael!" She couldn't be angry at him, though. She could only love him. But then as she looked at him, she saw his face cloud over as though he were suddenly remembering why he was there. Before that, he had acted as if he had just awakened from having his tonsils out. All he wanted was ice cream and his mom. But now there was a great deal more in his face, and he tried to sit up. He didn't know how to say the words, but he had to ask. He searched her face, and she kept her eyes on his and his hand tightly held in hers. "Take it easy, darling."

"Mom . . . the others . . . the other night . . . I remember . . ."

"Ben has already gone back to Boston with his father. He's pretty badly banged up but he's all right. A lot more all right than you were." She said it with a sigh and tightened her grip on his hand. She knew what was coming next. But she was prepared for it.

"And . . . Nancy?" His face was ivory white as he said her name. "Nancy, Mom?" The tears already stood out in his eyes. He could see the answer in his mother's face as she sat down carefully in the chair next to him and ran a gentle hand along the outline of his face.

"She didn't make it, darling. They did all they could. But the damage was just too great." She paused for only the slightest of seconds and then went on. "She died early this morning."

"Did you see her?" He was still searching her face for something more.

"I sat with her for a while last night."

"Oh, God . . . and I wasn't there. Oh, Nancy . . ." He turned his head into the pillow and cried like a child as Marion held his shoulders. He said her name over and over and over again, until at last he could cry no more. And when he turned to look at his mother again, she saw something in his face that she had never seen there before. It was as though he had lost something of himself in those moments when he said Nancy's name. As though part of him had bled away and died.

Chapter 6

Nancy heard the landing gear grind out of the plane's belly, and for the hundredth time since the flight began she felt the touch of the hand that had touched her arm before. It was strangely comforting to feel the nurse's hand, and it pleased her that she could already tell the difference between them. One woman had thin, delicate hands with long narrow fingers; her hands were always cold but there was great strength in the way she held on to Nancy. It made Nancy feel brave again just to touch her. The other nurse had warm, chubby soft hands that made one feel safe and loved. She patted Nancy's arm a lot, and it was she who had given Nancy the two shots for the pain. She had a soft soothing voice. The first woman had a slight accent. Nancy had already come to like them both.

"It won't be much longer now, dear. We can see the bay now. We'll be there in no time at all."

Actually, it would be another twenty minutes. And Peter Gregson was counting on that as he raced along the freeway in the black Porsche. The ambulance was meeting him there. He could have one of the girls from his office pick his car up later that morning. He wanted to ride into the city with the girl. He was intrigued by her. She had to be Someone for Marion Hillyard to be so concerned about her. Four hundred thousand dollars was quite a sum, and only three of that was going to him. The other hundred was to keep the girl comfortable in the next year and a half. And she would be. He had promised Marion Hillyard that. But he would have seen to that anyway. It was part of what he did. He would get to know the girl's very soul. They would become more than friends; he would mean everything to her and she to him. It had to be that way, because by the time that new face was born, she would be the person she looked like. Peter Gregson was going to give birth to Nancy McAllister, after a pregnancy of eighteen long months. She was going to have to be a very brave girl. But she would be. He would see to that. They would face it together. The very idea excited him. He loved what he did, and in an odd way he already loved Nancy. What he would make of her. What she would be. He would give her all that he had to give.

He looked at his watch and stepped on the gas. The car was one of his favorite releases. He also flew his own plane, went scuba diving whenever he had time, skied, and had climbed several mountains in Europe. He was a man who liked to scale heights, in every possible way. To defy the impossible and win. It was why he loved his work. People accused him of playing God. But it wasn't really that. It was the thrill of insuperable odds that stimulated him. And he had never yet been defeated. Not by women or mountains or sky, not even by a patient. At forty-seven he had won at everything he touched, and he was going to win now. He and Nancy were going to win together. His dark hair blew softly in the breeze and his eyes almost crackled with life. He still had a tan from his recent week in Tahiti, and he was wearing gray slacks and a soft blue cashmere sweater that was just the color of his eyes. He was always impeccably dressed, perfectly put together. He was an exceptionally good-looking man, but there was more to him than that. It was his vitality, his electricity, that caught one's attention even more than his looks did.

He pulled up to the curb at the airport precisely at the moment Nancy's plane was touching down. He showed a special pass to a policeman, who nodded and promised to keep an eye on the car. Even the policeman smiled at Gregson. Peter was a man no one could ignore. He had an almost irresistible charm, and a strength that showed through everything he did. It made people want to be near him.

He wove his way expertly into the airport lobby and spoke rapidly to a ground supervisor. The man picked up a phone, and within moments Peter was ushered through a door, down a flight of stairs, and into a tiny airport vehicle, then rushed out to the runway, where he saw the ambulance standing by, the attendants waiting for the patient to be taken off the plane. He thanked his driver and hurried to the ambulance, where he quickly checked inside to see that his orders had been carried out. They had been, to the letter. Everything was there that he needed. It was hard to tell what kind of shape she might be in after the flight, but he had wanted her in San Francisco immediately, so he could keep a close eye on things. He had a lot of planning to do, and work would begin in just a few days.

The other passengers were held back a few more minutes while Nancy was carried out through the forward hatch. The stewardesses hung back, looking grave, averting their gazes from the bottles and transfusions that hung over the bandaged girl, but the nurses seemed to be speaking to her as she was carried out. He liked the look of the nurses, young but competent, and they seemed to work well as a team. That was what he wanted. They were all going to be part of a team for the next year and a half, and everyone was important. There was no room for reluctance or incompetence. Everyone had to be the very best they could be, including Nancy. But he would see to that. She was going to be the star of this show. He watched her being carried toward him and waited until the stretcher had been gently set down inside the ambulance. He smiled at the nurses but said nothing, and held up a hand gesturing them to wait as he eased in beside Nancy and sat down on a seat next to her. He reached for her hand and held it.

"Hello, Nancy. I'm Peter. How was the trip?" As though she were for real. As though she were still someone, not just a faceless blob. She could feel relief wash over her at the sound of his voice.

"It was okay. You're Dr. Gregson?" She sounded tired but interested.

"Yes. But Peter sounds a little less formal between two people who're going to be working together." She liked the way he said it, and if she could have, she would have smiled.

"You came out to meet me?"

"Wouldn't you have come out to meet me?"

"Yes." She wanted to nod, but she couldn't. "Thank you."

"I'm glad I did. Have you ever been to San Francisco before, Nancy?"

"No."

"You're going to love it. And we're going to find you an apartment you like so much you'll never want to leave here. Most people don't, you know. Once they dig in their heels, they want to stay here forever. I came out here from Chicago about fifteen years ago, and you couldn't get me back there on a bet." She laughed at the way he said it, and he smiled down at her. "Are you from Boston?" He was treating her as though they had been introduced by friends. But he wanted her to relax after the long flight. And a few minutes without movement would do her good. The nurses were also glad of the opportunity to stretch as they chatted with the two ambulance attendants. Now and then they glanced in to see Dr. Gregson still talking to Nancy, and they liked him already. He exuded warmth.

"No, I was from New Hampshire. That's where I grew up anyway. In an orphanage. I moved to Boston when I was eighteen."

"It sounds very romantic. Or was the orphanage straight out of Dickens?" He gave everything a light touch, a happy note. Nancy laughed at the question about Dickens.

"Hardly. The nuns were wonderful. So much so that I wanted to be one."

"Oh, God. Now listen, you—" And she laughed at the tone of his voice. "When we're through with our project, young lady, you're going to be ready for Hollywood. If you go hide in a convent somewhere I'll . . . I'll . . . why, I'll head off the bridge, damn it. You'd better promise me you won't go off and become a nun somewhere." That was easy. She had Michael to get ready for. Her dreams of being Sister Agnes Marie had faded years ago, but she wanted to tease Gregson a little. She already liked him.

"Oh, all right." She said it begrudgingly but with laughter in her voice.

"Is that a promise? Come on, say it . . . I promise."

"I promise."

"What do you promise?" They were both laughing now.

"I promise not to be a nun."

"Whew. That's better." He signaled to the two nurses to join them, and the attendants moved toward the front. She was ready to go now, and he didn't want to tire her with too much patter. "Why don't you introduce me to your friends."

"Well, let's see, the cold hands are Lily, and the warm ones are Gretchen." All four of them laughed.

"Thanks a lot, Nancy." Lily laughed benevolently as Nancy smiled to herself. She felt safe with her new-found friends, and all she could think of now was what she would look like for Michael after it was all over. She liked Peter Gregson, and suddenly she knew that he was going to make her someone very special, because he cared.

"Welcome to San Francisco, little one." Lily's cool hands were replaced by his strong, graceful ones, and he kept a light hand on her shoulder all the way into the city. In an odd way, he made her feel as though she had come home.

Chapter 7

The ambulance doors swung open and they carried the stretcher expertly into the hotel. The manager was waiting to greet them, and the entire penthouse suite had been reserved for their use. They were only planning to stay for a day or two, but the hotel would provide a breather between hospital and home. Marion had business meetings in Boston, and besides, for some reason Michael had insisted on a few days in a hotel before going home. And his mother was ready to indulge his every whim.

The ambulance attendants set him down carefully on the bed, and he made a face. "For Chrissake, there's nothing wrong with me, Mother. They all said I was fine."

"But there's no need to push."

"Push?" He looked around the suite and groaned as she tipped the ambulance attendants, who promptly vanished. The room was filled with flowers, and there was a huge basket of fruit on the table near the bed. His mother owned the hotel. She had bought it years before as an investment.

"Now relax, darling. Don't get overexcited. Do you want anything to eat?" She had wanted to keep the nurse, but even the doctor had said that was unnecessary, and it would have driven Michael crazy. All he had to do now was take it easy for another couple of weeks, and then he could go to work. But he had something else to do first. "How about some lunch?" Marion asked.

"Sure. Escargots. Oysters Rockefeller. Champagne. Turtles' eggs and caviar." He sat up in bed like a mischievous child.

"What a revolting combination, my love." But she wasn't really listening to him. She was looking at her watch. "But do order yourself something. George should be here any minute. Our meeting downtown is at one." She walked out of the room distractedly, to look for her briefcase, and Mike heard the doorbell at the front of the suite. A moment later, George Calloway walked into his room.

"Well, Michael, how are you feeling?"

"After two weeks in the hospital, doing absolutely nothing, I feel mostly embarrassed." He tried to make light of his situation, but there was still a broken look around his eyes. His mother saw it too, but put it down to fatigue. She had closed any alternative explanation from her mind, and she and Michael never discussed it. They talked about the business, and the plans for the medical center in San Francisco. Never the accident.

"I stopped in at your office this morning. It looks very handsome indeed." George smiled and sat down at the foot of the bed.

"I'm sure it does." Michael watched his mother as she came into the room. She was wearing a light gray Chanel suit with a soft blue silk blouse, pearl earrings, and three strands of pearls around her neck. "Mother has excellent taste."

"Yes, she does." George smiled at her warmly, but she waved nervously at them both.

"Stop throwing roses; we're going to be late. George, do you have the papers we need?"

"Of course."

"Then let's go." She walked quickly toward Michael's bed and bent down to kiss the top of his head. "Rest, darling. And don't forget to order lunch."

"Yes, ma'am. Good luck at the meeting."

She raised her head and smiled with pure anticipation. "Luck has nothing to do with it." The two men laughed, and Michael watched them go. And then he sat up.

He sat patiently and quietly, waiting and thinking. He knew exactly what he was going to do. He had planned it for two weeks. He had lived for this moment. It had been all he could think of. It was why he had suggested the hotel, insisted on it in fact, and urged her to attend the meetings herself for the new Boston library building. He needed the afternoon to himself. He just didn't want to spoil anything by having them catch him. He wanted to be sure they were gone. So he sat exactly where he was for exactly half an hour. And then he was sure. He had rehearsed it a hundred times in his head. He went quickly to the suitcase on the rack at the foot of his bed and took out what he needed. Gray slacks, blue shirt, loafers, socks, underwear. It seemed a thousand years since he had worn clothes, and he was surprised at how wobbly he felt as he got dressed. He had to sit down three or four times to catch his breath. It was ridiculous to feel that weak, and he wouldn't give in to it. He wasn't going to wait another day. He was going there now. It took him nearly half an hour to dress and comb his hair, and then he called the desk and asked for a cab. He was pale on his way down in the elevator, but the excitement of his plan made him feel better. Just the thought of it gave him life again, as nothing had done in two weeks. The cab was waiting for him at the curb.

He gave the driver the address, and sat back with a feeling of great exhilaration. It was as though they had a date, as though she were expecting him, as though she knew. He smiled to himself all the way over, and gave the driver a large tip. He didn't ask the man to wait. He didn't want anyone waiting for him. He would stay there alone, for as long as he wanted. He had even toyed with the idea of continuing to pay rent on the place, so that he could come there whenever he liked. It was only an hour's flight from New York, and that way he would always have their apartment. Their apartment. He looked up at the building with a familiar glow of warmth, and almost in spite of himself, he heard himself say the words he'd been thinking. "Hi, Nancy Fancypants, I'm home." He had said the words a thousand times before, as he walked in the door and found her sitting at her easel, with paint splattered all over hands and arms and occasionally her face. If she was terribly involved in the work, she sometimes didn't hear him come in.

He walked slowly up the stairs, tired but buoyed by the feeling of homecoming. He just wanted to go upstairs and sit down, near her, with her . . . with her things. . . . All the same familiar smells pervaded the building, and there was the sound of running water, of a child, a cat meowing in a hallway below, and outside a horn honking. He could hear an Italian song on the radio, and for a strange moment he wondered if the radio was on in her studio. He had his key in his hand when he reached the landing, and he stopped for a long, long moment. For the first time all day, he felt tears burn his eyes. He still knew the truth. She wouldn't be there. She was gone forever. She was dead.

He still tried the word out loud from time to time, just to make himself say it, to make himself know. He didn't want to be one of those crazy people who never faced the truth, who played games of pretend. She would have been scornful of that. But now and then he let the knowledge go, only to have it return with a slap. As it did now. He turned the key in the lock and waited, as though maybe someone would come to the door after all. But there was no one there. He opened the door slowly, and then he gasped.

"Oh, my God! Where is . . . where . . ." It was gone. All of it. Every table, every chair, the plants, the paintings, her easel, her paints. Her clothes, her . . . Jesus Christ, Nancy!" And then he heard himself crying as hot angry tears stung his face and he pulled open doors. Nothing. Even the refrigerator was gone. He stood there dumbly for a moment and then flew down the stairs two at a time until he reached the manager's apartment in the basement. He pounded on the door until the little old man opened it just the width of the protective chain and stared out with a look of fear in his eyes. But he recognized Michael and opened the door as he started to smile, until Michael grabbed him by the collar and began to shake him.

"Where is her stuff, Kowalski? Where the hell is it? What did you do with it? Did you take it? Who took it? Where are her things?"

"What things? Who . . . oh, my God . . . no, no, I didn't take anything. They came two weeks ago. They told me—" He was trembling with terror, and Michael with rage.

"Who the hell is 'they'?"

"I don't know. Someone called me and said that the apartment would be vacant. That Miss McAllister was . . . had . . ." He saw the tears still wet on Michael's face and was afraid to go on. "You know. Well, they told me, and they said the apartment would be empty by the end of the week. Two nurses came and took a few things, and then the Goodwill truck came the next morning."

"Nurses? What nurses?" Michael's mind was a blank. And Goodwill? Who had called them?

"I don't know who they were. They looked like nurses though—they were wearing white. They didn't take much. Just that little bag, and her paintings. Goodwill got the rest. I didn't take nothing. Honest. I wouldn't do that. Not to a nice girl like . . ." But Michael wasn't listening to him. He was already wandering up the stairs to the street, dazed, as the old man watched him, shaking his head. Poor guy. He had probably just heard. "Hey . . . hey." Michael turned around, and the old man lowered his voice. "I'm sorry." Michael only nodded and went out to the street. How did the nurses know? How could they have done it? They'd probably taken the little jewelry she had, a few trinkets, and the paintings. Maybe someone had said something to them at the hospital. Vultures, picking over what was left. God, if he'd seen them, he'd . . . His hands clenched at his sides, and then his arm shot out to hail a cab. At least . . . maybe . . . it was worth a try. He slid into the cab, ignoring the ache that was beginning to pound at the back of his head. "Where's the nearest Goodwill?"

"Goodwill what?" The driver was chewing a soggy cigar and was not particularly interested in Goodwill of any kind.

"Goodwill store. You know, used clothes, old furniture."

"Oh yeah. Okay." The kid didn't look like one of their customers, but a fare was a fare. It was a five-minute drive from Nancy's apartment, and the fresh air on his face helped revive Michael from the shock of the emptiness he had found. It was like looking for your pulse and finding that your heart had stopped beating. "Okay, this is it."

Michael thanked him, absentmindedly paid twice the fare, and got out. He wasn't even sure he wanted to go inside. He had wanted to see her things in her apartment, where they belonged. Not in some stinking, musty old store, with price tags on them. And what would he do? Buy it all? And then what? He walked into the store feeling lonely and tired and confused. No one offered to help him, and he began to wander aimlessly up one aisle and down another, finding nothing he knew, seeing nothing familiar, and suddenly aching, not for the "things" that had seemed so important to him that morning, but for the girl who had owned them. She was gone, and nothing he found or didn't find would ever make any difference. The tears began to stream down his face as he walked slowly back out to the street.

This time he didn't hail a cab. He just walked. Blindly and alone, in a direction his feet seemed to know, but his head didn't. His head didn't know anything anymore. It felt like mush. His whole body felt like mush, but his heart was a stone. Suddenly, in that stinking old store, his life had come to an end. He understood now what it all meant, and as he stood at a red light, waiting for it to change, not giving a damn if it did, he passed out.

He woke up a few moments later, with a crowd around him as he lay on a small patch of grass where someone had carried him. There was a policeman standing over him, looking sharply into his eyes.

"You okay, son?" He was certain the kid was neither drunk nor stoned, but he looked a terrible gray color. More likely he was sick. Or maybe just hungry or something. Looked like he had money though, couldn't have been a case of starvation.

"Yeah. I'm okay. I got out of the hospital this morning, and I guess I overdid it." He smiled ruefully, but the faces around him did cartwheels when he tried to get up. The cop saw what was happening and urged the crowd to disperse. Then he looked back at Michael.

"I'll get a patrol car to give you a lift home."

"No, really, I'm okay."

"Never mind that. Would you rather go back to the hospital?"

"Hell, no!"

"All right, then we'll take you home." He spoke into a small walkie-talkie and then squatted down near Michael. "They'll be here in a minute. Been sick for a long time?"

Michael shook his head silently, and then looked down at his hands. "Two weeks." There was still a narrow scar near his temple, but too small for the policeman to notice.

"Well, you take it easy." The patrol car slid up alongside them, and the policeman gave Michael a hand up. He was all right now. Pale, but steadier than he had been at first.

Michael looked over his shoulder and tried to smile at the cop. "Thanks." But the attempted smile only made the cop wonder what was wrong. There was a kind of despair in the kid's eyes.

He gave the men in the patrol car an address a block from the hotel, and thanked them when he got out. And then he walked the last block. The suite was still empty when he got there, and for a moment he

79

thought about taking off his clothes and going back to bed, but there was no point in playing that game anymore. He had done what he'd wanted to do. It had gotten him nowhere, but at least he'd gone through with it. What he'd been looking for was Nancy. He should have known that he wouldn't find her there, or anywhere else. He would only find her in the one place she still lived, in his heart.

The door to the suite opened as he stood looking out the window, and for a moment he didn't turn around. He didn't really want to see them, or hear about the meeting, or have to pretend that he was all right. He wasn't all right. And maybe he never would be again.

"What are you doing up, Michael?" His mother made it sound as though he were going to be seven in a few days, instead of twenty-five. He turned around slowly and said nothing at first, and then tiredly he smiled at George.

"It's time for me to get up, Mother. I can't stay in bed forever. In fact, I'm going to New York tonight."

"You're what?"

"Going to New York."

"But why? You wanted to stay here." She looked totally confused.

"You had your meeting." And I had mine. "We have no reason to hang around here anymore. And I want to be in the office tomorrow. Right, George?"

George looked at him nervously, frightened by the pain and grief he saw in the boy's eyes. Maybe it would do him good to get busy. He didn't look terribly strong yet, but lying about had to be difficult for him. It gave him too much time to think. "You might be right, Michael. And you can always work half days at first."

"I think you're both crazy. He just got out of the hospital this morning."

"And you, of course, are famous for taking such good care of yourself. Right, Mother?" He cocked his head at her, and she sank down slowly on the couch.

"All right, all right," she said with a slow smile.

"How was the meeting?" Michael sat down across from her and tried to look as though he cared. He was going to have to do a lot of that, because that afternoon he had made a decision. From now on he was going to live for one thing and one thing only. His work. There was nothing else left.

Chapter 8

"Ready?"

"I guess so." She couldn't feel anything above her shoulders; it was as though her head had been cut off. And the bright lights of the operating room made Nancy want to squint, but she couldn't even do that. All she could see clearly was Peter's face as he bent over her, his neatly trimmed beard covered by a blue surgical mask, and his eyes dancing. He had spent almost three weeks studying the X-rays, measuring, sketching, drawing, planning, preparing, and talking to her. The only photograph of Nancy he had was the one taken the day of the accident, at the fair. But her face had been partially obscured by the silly boardwalk facade she and Michael had stuck their heads through to have their picture taken. It gave him an idea though, a starting point, but he was going much farther than that. She was going to be a different girl when he was through, a person anyone would dream of being. He smiled down at her again as he saw her eyelids grow heavy.

"You're going to have to stay awake now, and keep

talking to me. You can get drowsy but you can't go to sleep." Otherwise she might choke on her own blood, but she didn't need to know that. Instead he kept her amused with stories and jokes, asked her questions, made her think of things, dig up answers, remember the names of all the nuns she knew when she was a child. "And you're sure you don't still want to be Sister Agnes Marie?"

"Uh uh. I promised." They teased back and forth during the whole three hours that the procedure took, and his hands never stopped moving. For Nancy it was like watching a ballet.

"And just think, in another couple of weeks we'll get you your own apartment, maybe something with a view, and then . . . Hey, sleepyhead, what do you think of the view? Do you want to see the bay from the bedroom?"

"Sure. Why not?"

"Just 'sure'? You know, I think you're getting spoiled by the view from your room here at the hospital, Nancy."

"That's not true. I love it."

"Okay, then we'll go out together and find you something even better. Deal?"

"Deal." Even with the sleepy voice, she sounded pleased. "Can't I go to sleep yet?"

"You know what, Princess, you just about can. Just a few more minutes and we'll whisk you back to your room and you can sleep all you want."

"Good."

"Have I been boring you then?" She giggled at his

mock hurt. "There, love . . . all . . . set." He looked
up at his assistant with a nod, stood back for a moment, and a nurse gave Nancy a quick shot in the
thigh. Then Peter stepped back to her side and smiled
down at the eyes he already knew so well. He didn't
even see the rest. Not yet. But he saw the eyes. And
knew them intimately. Just as she knew his. "Did you
know that today is a special day?"

"Yes."

"You did? How did you know?"

Because it was Michael's birthday, but she didn't
want to tell him that. He was going to be twenty-five
years old today. She wondered what he was doing.

"I just knew, that's all."

"Well, it's special to me because this is the beginning. Our first surgery together, our first step on a
wonderful road toward a new you. How about that?"
He smiled at her then, and she quietly closed her
eyes and fell asleep. The shot had taken effect.

"Happy birthday, boss."

"Don't call me that, you jerk. Christ, you look lousy,
Ben."

"Thanks a lot." Ben looked over at his friend as he
hobbled into the office with crutches and the assistance of a secretary. She eased him into a chair and
withdrew from Michael's overstuffed and much paneled office. "This is some place they fixed up for you.
Is mine gonna look like this?"

"If not, you can have this one. I hate it."

"That's nice. So what's new?" The talk between
them was still strained. They had seen each other

twice since Ben arrived from Boston, but the effort of staying off the subject of Nancy was almost too much for them. It was all either of them could think of. "The doctor says I can start work next week."

Michael laughed and shook his head. "You're stark staring crazy, Ben."

"And you're not?"

A cloud passed over Mike's eyes. "I didn't break anything." Nothing you could see anyway. "I told you, you've got a month. Two if you need it. Why don't you go to Europe with your sister?"

"And do what? Sit in a wheelchair and dream about bikinis? I want to come to work. How about two weeks?"

"We'll see." There was a long silence and then suddenly Mike looked at his friend with an expression of bitterness Ben had never seen before. "And then what?"

"What do you mean, Mike, 'and then what?'"

"Just that. We work our asses off for the next fifty years, screw as many people as we can, make as much money as we can, and so what? So Goddamn what?"

"You're in a wonderful mood. What happened? Slam your finger in your desk this morning?"

"Oh for Chrissake, be serious for a change, will you? I mean it. Don't you ever think of that? What the hell does it all mean?" Ben knew what he meant, and there was no avoiding the questions now.

"I don't know, Mike. The accident made me think of that, too. It made me ask myself what's important in my life, what I believe in."

"And what did you come up with?"

"I'm not sure. I think I'm just grateful to be here. Maybe it taught me how important life is, how good it is while you have it." There were tears in his eyes as he spoke. "I still don't understand why it happened the way it did. I wish . . . I wish . . ." His voice broke on the words. "I wish it had been me."

Mike closed his eyes on the tears in his own eyes and then came slowly around the desk to his friend. They stood there for a moment, the two of them, tears running slowly down their faces, holding tight to each other, and feeling the friendship of ten years comfort them as little else could. "Thanks, Ben."

"Hey, listen." Ben wiped the tears from his cheeks with the sleeve of his jacket. "You want to go out and get smashed? Hell, it's your birthday, why not?" For a minute Mike laughed, and then like a small boy drawn into a conspiracy, he nodded.

"Hell, it's almost five o'clock. I don't have any more meetings I'm supposed to be at. We'll go to the Oak Room and tie one on." He assisted Ben from the room, and then into a cab, and half an hour later they were well on their way to a major blow-out. Mike didn't get back to his mother's apartment until after midnight, and when he did he required a considerable amount of help from the doorman to get upstairs. The next morning when the maid came in, she found him asleep on the floor of his room. But at least he had gotten through the birthday.

He could hardly see when he got to the breakfast table the next morning. His mother was already there, in a black dress, reading *The New York Times*.

He wanted to throw up when he smelled the sweet rolls and coffee.

"You must have had an interesting time last night." Her tone was glacial.

"I was out with Ben."

"So your secretary told me. I hope you won't make a habit of this."

Oh, Jesus. Why not? "What? Getting smashed?"

"No. Leaving early. And actually, the other, too. You must have looked charming when you came home."

"I can't remember." He was trying desperately not to gag on his coffee.

"There's something else you didn't remember." She put the paper down on the table and glared at him. "We had a dinner date last night, at Twenty-one. I waited for you for two hours. With nine other people. Your birthday—remember?"

Christ. That would have been all he needed. "You never told me about nine people. You just asked me to dinner. I thought it would have been just the two of us." It was a moot point now, of course.

"And it was all right to stand up just me, is that it?"

"No, I just forgot, for Chrissake. This wasn't exactly my favorite birthday."

"I'm sorry." But she didn't sound as though she remembered why this birthday was different, or as though she really cared. She sounded miffed.

"And that brings up another point, Mother. I'm going to move out and get my own place."

She looked up, surprised. "Why?"

"Because I'm twenty-five years old. I work for you, Mother. I don't have to live with you, too."

"You don't 'have' to do anything." She was beginning to wonder about the Avery boy and just what kind of influence he was. This sounded like his idea.

"Mother, let's not get into this now. I have an incredible headache."

"Hangover." She looked at her watch and stood up. "I'll see you at the office in half an hour. Don't forget the meeting with the people from Houston. Are you up to it?"

"I will be. And Mom . . . I'm sorry about the apartment, but I think it's time."

She looked at him sternly for a moment and then let out a small sigh. "Maybe it is, Michael. Maybe it is. Happy birthday, by the way." She bent down to kiss him, and he even smiled despite the terrible ache in his head. "I left you a little present on your desk."

"You shouldn't have." There was no present that mattered anymore. Ben had understood that. He had given him nothing.

"Birthdays are birthdays after all, Michael. See you at the office."

After she left he sat for a long time in the dining room, looking at the view. He knew just the apartment he wanted. Only it was in Boston. But he was going to do his damnedest to find one just like it in New York. In some ways he still hadn't given up the dream. Even though he knew he was crazy to cling to it.

Chapter 9

"Hi, Sue. Is Mr. Hillyard in?" Ben had the look of five o'clock as he arrived at Mike's office door: not quite disheveled, but relieved that the day was almost over. He'd barely had time to sit down all day long, let alone relax.

"He is. Shall I let him know you're here?" She smiled at him, and he felt his eyes drawn to the carefully concealed figure. Marion Hillyard did not approve of sexy secretaries, even for her son . . . or was it especially for her son? Ben wondered as he shook his head.

"No, thanks. I'll announce myself." He strode past her desk, carrying the files that had been his excuse, and knocked on the heavy oak door. "Anybody home?" There was no answer so he knocked again. And still got no reply. He turned questioningly to the secretary. "You're sure he's in there?"

"Positive."

"Okay." Ben tried again and this time a hoarse croak from the other side urged him in. Ben cautiously opened the door and looked around. "You asleep or something?" Michael looked up and grinned at his friend.

"I wish. Look at this mess." He sat surrounded by folders, mock-ups, drawings, designs, reports. It was enough to keep ten men busy for a year. "Sit down, Ben."

"Thanks, boss." Ben couldn't resist teasing him.

"Oh, shut up. What's with the files you brought me?" He ran a hand through his hair and sat back in the heavy leather desk chair he had grown accustomed to. He had even gotten used to the impersonal prints on the walls. It didn't matter anymore. He didn't give a damn. He never looked at the walls, or his office, or his secretary . . . or his life. He looked at the work on his desk and very little else. It had been four months. "Please don't tell me you've brought me another set of problems with that damn shopping center in Kansas City. They're driving me nuts."

"And you love it. Tell me, Mike, what was the last movie you saw? *Bridge on the River Kwai*, or *Fantasia*? Don't you ever get the hell out of here?"

"When I get the chance." Michael looked at some papers as he answered. "So what's with the files?"

"They're a decoy. I just wanted to come and talk to you."

"And you can't do that without an excuse?" Michael grinned up at him. It was like being kids again, visiting each other's study halls with fake homework to consult on.

"I keep forgetting your mother isn't old Sanders up at St. Jude's."

"Thank God." Actually they both knew she was worse, but neither of them could afford to admit it. She detested seeing people "float around" the halls, as she put it, and she was usually quick to glance at whatever files they were carrying. "So what's up, Ben? How were the Hamptons this summer?"

Ben sat very still for a moment, watching him, before he answered. "Do you really care?"

"About you, or the Hamptons?" Michael's smile looked pasted on, and he had the ghostly pallor of December, not September. It was obvious he had gone nowhere all summer. "I care a lot about you, Ben."

"But not about yourself. Have you looked in the mirror lately? You'd scare Frankenstein's mother."

"Gee, thanks."

"Don't mention it. Anyway, that's why I'm here."

"On behalf of Frankenstein's mother?"

"No, mine. We want you to come up to the Cape this weekend. They do. I do. We all do. And listen, if you say no, I'll come across that desk and drag you out of here. You need to get out of here, damn it." Ben wasn't smiling anymore. He was dead serious, and Mike knew it. But he shook his head.

"I'd love to, Ben. But I can't. I've got Kansas City to worry about, and forty-seven thousand problems with it that we just can't seem to solve. You know. You were in that meeting yesterday."

"So were twenty-three other people. Let them handle it. For a weekend at least. Or is your ego such that you can't let anyone else touch your work?"

But they both knew it wasn't that. Work had become his drug. It numbed him to everything else. And he had been abusing the job since the day he walked into the office.

"Come on, Mike. Be good to yourself. Just this once."

"I just can't, Ben."

"Goddamn it, man, what do I have to say to you? Look at yourself. Don't you care? You're killing yourself, and for what?" His voice roared across the office and hit Michael with an almost physical force as he watched his friend's face convulse with emotion. "What the hell's the use, Mike? If you kill yourself, it won't bring her back. You're alive, damn it. Twenty-five years old and alive—and wasting your life, driving yourself like your Goddamn mother. Is that what you want? To be like her? To live, eat, sleep, drink, and die this Goddamn business? Is that it for you now? Is that who you are? Well, I don't believe it. I know someone else in that skin of yours, mister, and I love that other person. But you happen to be treating him like a dog, and I won't let you do it. You know what you should be doing? You should be out there, living. You should be out there making it with that good-looking secretary who sits outside your office, or ten other broads you meet at the best parties in town. Get off your ass and get out of your casket, Mike, before—"

But Mike cut him off before he could finish. He was leaning halfway across the desk at him, shaking, and even paler than he had been before. "Get the hell out

of my office, Ben, before I kill you. *Get out!!"* It was
the roar of an injured lion, and for a moment the two
men stood staring at each other, shaken and frightened by what they had felt and said. "I'm sorry."
Mike sat down again and dropped his head into his
hands. "Why don't we just let this go for today?" He
never looked up at Ben, who walked slowly across
the room, squeezed his shoulder, and walked out,
closing the door quietly behind him. There was
nothing left to say.

Michael's secretary looked at Ben questioningly as
he walked past, but said nothing. She had heard
Mike's roar at the very end. The whole floor could
have, if they'd been listening. Ben passed Marion in
the hall on the way back to his office, but she was
busy with something Calloway was showing her and
Ben wasn't in the mood for the usual pleasantries. He
was sick of her, and what she was letting Mike do to
himself. It served her purposes to have him work like
that; it was good for the business, for the empire, for
the dynasty . . . and it made Ben Avery sick.

He left the office at six thirty that night, and when
he looked up from the street, he could still see the
lights burning in Mike's office. He knew they would
still be lit at eleven or twelve that night. And why
not? What the hell did he have to go home to? The
empty apartment he had rented three months before?
He had found an attractive little apartment on Central Park South, and something about the layout had
reminded Ben of Nancy's place in Boston. He was
sure Mike had noticed that, too. Maybe that was

why he had taken it. But then something had happened. What little life had been left had gone out of him. He had begun this insane work thing, a marathon of madness. So he never bothered to do anything with the apartment. It just sat there, cold and empty and lonely. The only furniture he had put in it were two folding chairs, a bed, and an ugly old lamp which stayed on the floor. The whole place rang with empty echoes; it looked as though the tenant had been evicted that morning. Ben got depressed just thinking about coming home to such a place, and he could imagine what it did to Mike—if he even noticed his surroundings anymore, which Ben was beginning to doubt. He had given him three plants for the place in early July, and all of them had been dead by the end of the month. Like the ugly lamp, they just sat there, unloved and forgotten.

Ben didn't like what was happening, but there was nothing anyone could do. No one except Nancy, and she was dead. Thinking about her still gave Ben an almost physical pang, like the twinge he felt in his ankle and his hip when he got tired. But the breaks had repaired quickly; youth had served him well. He only hoped it did the same for Mike. But Mike's breaks were compound fractures of parts of him that didn't even show. Except in his eyes. Or his face at the end of a day . . . or the set of his mouth in an unguarded moment as he sat at his desk and looked into the distance, at the endless stretch of the view.

Chapter 10

"Well, young lady? Did I keep my promise? Do you
have the most spectacular view in town?" Peter Gregson sat on the terrace with Nancy, and they exchanged
a glowing look. Her face was still heavily bandaged,
but her eyes danced through the bandages and her
hands were free now. They looked different, but they
were lovely as she made a sweeping gesture around
her. From where they sat, they could see the entire
bay, with the Golden Gate Bridge at their left, Alca-
traz to their right, Marin County directly across from
them, and from the other side of the terrace, an equally spectacular city view toward the south and east.
The wraparound terrace also gave her an equal share
of sunrises and sunsets, and boundless pleasure as she
sat there all day. The weather had been glorious since
she'd gotten the apartment. Peter had found the place
for her, as promised.

"You know, I'm getting horribly spoiled."

"You deserve to be. Which reminds me, I brought
you something."

She clapped her hands like a little girl. He always

brought her something. A silly thought, a pile of magazines, a stack of books, a funny hat, a beautiful scarf to drape over the bandages, wonderful clattery bracelets to celebrate her new hands. It was a constant flow of gifts, but today's was the largest of all. With a mysterious look of pleasure, he left his seat on the terrace and went inside. The box he brought back was fairly large and looked as though it might be quite heavy. When he dropped it on her lap, she found her guess had been correct.

"What is it, Peter? It feels like a rock." She smiled through the bandages and he laughed.

"Yes, the largest emerald I could find in the dime store."

"Perfect!" But the gift was even more perfect than she suspected. The contents of the mysterious box proved to be a very expensive and highly elaborate camera. "Peter! My God, what a gift! I can't—"

"You most certainly can. And I expect to see some serious work done with it."

They both knew how disturbed she was that she didn't seem to want to paint anymore. And now she no longer had the excuse of bandaged hands. But she couldn't. Something in her stopped every time she even thought of it. The paintings the nurses had brought from her Boston apartment were still enclosed in the large black artist's portfolio shoved to the back of a storage closet. She didn't want to see them, let alone work on them. But a camera might be different. Peter saw the spark in her eyes and prayed that he had opened a new door. She needed new doors. None of the old ones were going to reveal what she wanted them to. It would be better for her to start fresh.

"There is a fabulously complicated instruction booklet, which ten years of medical school never prepared me for. Maybe you can figure it out."

"Hell, yes." She glanced into the thick booklet and sat lost in concentration for a few moments, holding the camera and forgetting her friend, and then waved the booklet absently. "It's fantastic, Peter. Look . . . this thing over here, if you flick that . . ."

She was gone, totally enthralled, and Peter sat back with a comfortable smile. It was half an hour later before she noticed him again. She looked up suddenly with delight in her eyes, and they told him how grateful she was. "It's the most beautiful gift I've ever had." Except for Michael's blue beads at the fair . . . but she forced them quickly from her mind. Peter was used to the sudden clouds which flitted across her eyes as old thoughts came to haunt her. He knew they would leave her in time. "Did you bring film?"

"Of course." He pulled another, smaller box out of the wrappings and plonked it in her lap. "Would I forget film?"

"No. You never forget anything." She was quick to load the camera and begin shooting photographs of him, and then of the view, and then a quick series of a bird as it flew past the terrace. "They'll probably be awful, but it's a start." He watched her silently for a long time, and then he put an arm around her shoulders and they went inside.

"You know, I have another gift for you today, Nancy."

"A Mercedes. See, I always guess."

"No. This one's serious." He looked down at her with a gentle, cautious smile. "I'm going to share a friend with you. A very special lady." For an insane moment, Nancy felt a ripple of jealousy course down her spine, but something in Peter's face told her that she didn't need to feel that way. He sensed her watching him closely, though, as he went on. "Her name is Faye Allison, and we went to medical school together. She is, without a doubt, one of the most competent psychiatrists in the West, maybe in the country, and she's a very good friend and a very special person. I think you're going to like her."

"And?" Nancy waited, tense but curious.

"And . . . I think it might be a good idea for you to see her for a while. You know that. We've talked about it before."

"You don't think I'm adjusting well?" She sounded hurt, and put the camera down to look at him more seriously.

"I think you're doing remarkably well, Nancy, but if nothing else, you need another person to talk to. You have Lily and Gretchen and me, and that's it. Don't you want someone else to talk to?"

Yes. Michael. He had been her best friend for so long. But for the moment, Peter was enough. "I'm not sure."

"I think you will be once you meet Faye. She is incredibly warm and kind. And she's been very sympathetic to your case from the beginning."

"She knows about me?"

"From the first." She had been there the night Marion Hillyard and Dr. Wickfield had called, but Nancy didn't need to know that. He and Faye had been lovers on and off for years, more as a matter of companionship and convenience than as a result of any great passion. They were friends most of all. "She's coming to join us for coffee this afternoon. All right with you?"

But she knew she had little choice. "I suppose so." She grew pensive as she settled herself in the living room. She wasn't at all sure she liked this addition to her scene, particularly a woman. She felt an instant sense of competition and distrust.

Until she met Faye Allison. Nothing Peter had said had prepared her for the warmth she felt from the other woman. She was tall, thin, blonde, and angular, but all the lines of her face were soft. Her eyes were warm and alert; there was an instant joke, an instant answer, an instant burst of laughter always ready in those eyes. Yet one sensed, too, that she was always ready to be serious and compassionate. Peter left them alone after the first hour, and Nancy was actually glad.

They talked about a thousand things, and none of them the accident. Boston, painting, San Francisco, children, people, medical school. Faye shared chunks of her life with Nancy, and Nancy gave her glimpses of herself that she hadn't given anyone for a long time, not since she had first gotten to know Michael. Views of the orphanage, real views, not the amusing ones she gave Peter. The loneliness of it, the questions about who she really was, why she had been left there, what it meant to be totally alone. And then for no reason she could think of, she told Faye about her arrangement with Marion Hillyard. There was no shock, no reproach, there was nothing but warmth and understanding in the way Faye Allison listened, and Nancy found herself sharing feelings which covered years, not just the past four months. But the relief of telling her about Marion Hillyard was enormous.

"I don't know, it sounds so strange to say it, but—" She hesitated, feeling foolish, and looking childlike as she glanced up at her new friend. "But I . . . I had never had any kind of family, growing up in the orphanage. The mother superior was the closest I had to a mother, and she was more like a maiden aunt. But despite what I knew about Marion, from Michael, from his friend Ben, just from what I sensed—despite all that, I always had these crazy dreams, fantasies, that she would like me, that we would be friends." Her eyes filled with unexpected tears and she looked away.

"Did you think that maybe she'd become your mother?"

Nancy nodded silently and then blinked away the tears with a terse laugh. "Isn't that insane?"

"Not at all. It was a normal assumption. You were in love with Michael. You have no family of your own. It's normal that you should want to adopt his. Is that why your deal with her hurt so much?" But she already knew the answer, as did Nancy.

"Yes. It was proof of just how much she hated me."

"I wouldn't go that far, Nancy. From the look of things, she's done an awful lot for you. She did send you out to Peter for a new face." Not to mention the extremely comfortable lifestyle she had provided during the process.

"As long as I gave up Michael. She was rejecting me, for him—and for herself. I knew then that I had never had a chance with her. It was a horrible moment." She sighed, and her voice became more gentle. "But I guess I've lost before and survived it."

"Do you remember losing your parents?"

"Not in any real way. I was too little to remember anything when my father died, and not much older when my mother left me at the home. I remember the day they told me she had died. I cried, but I'm not really even sure why I cried. I don't think I remembered her. Maybe I just felt abandoned."

"The way you do now?" It was a guess, but a good one.

"Maybe. That bottomless feeling of 'but who will take care of me now?' I think of that sometimes. Back then I knew the home would take care of me until I grew up. Now I know Peter will, and Marion's money will, until I'm all patched up. But then what?"

"What about Michael? Do you think he'll come back to you?"

"Sometimes I do. A lot of the time I do." There was a long pause.

"And the rest of the time?"

"I'm beginning to wonder. At first I thought that maybe he was afraid of the way I'd look, the way that would make him feel about me. But by now he knows about the surgery, and he must figure there's some improvement. So how come he's not here yet?" She turned to face Faye squarely. "That's what I wonder."

"Do you come up with any answers to that question?"

"Nothing very pretty. Sometimes I think she's gotten to him, and convinced him that a girl from my 'unsavory background' will harm him professionally. Marion Hillyard has helped build an empire, and she's counting on Michael to carry on in the best family traditions. That doesn't include marrying a nameless nobody out of an orphange, an artist yet. She wants him to marry some debutante heiress who can do him some good."

"Do you think that matters to him?"

"It didn't used to matter, but now . . . I don't know."

"What if you lose him?"

Nancy flinched but she didn't answer. Her eyes said everything though.

"What if he didn't feel able to cope with all that you're going through? That's possible, Nancy. Some men aren't as brave as we like to think they are."

"I don't know. Maybe he's waiting till it's all over."

"Wouldn't you resent him then? For not being here when you need him?"

Nancy let out a long sigh in answer. "Maybe. I don't really know. I think about it all a lot, but I don't have many answers."

"Only time has the answers. All you need to know is how you feel. That's all. How do you feel about you? The new you? Are you excited? Scared? Angry that you'll look different? Relieved?"

"All of the above." They both laughed at her honesty. "To tell you the truth, it terrifies me. Can you imagine looking in the mirror after twenty-two years and seeing someone else there? Christ, talk about freaking out!" She laughed but there was real fear in the laughter.

"Are you freaked out?"

"Sometimes. A lot of the time I don't think about it."

"What do you think about?"

"Honestly?"

"Sure."

"Michael. Peter sometimes. But mostly Michael."

"Are you falling in love with Peter?" There was no hesitation in the question. This was Dr. Allison speaking now, not Faye. She was thinking only of Nancy.

"No, I couldn't fall in love with Peter. He's a nice man, a good friend. He's sort of like the wonderful father I never had. He brings me presents all the time. But . . . I'm in love with Michael."

"Well, we'll just have to see what happens." Faye Allison looked at her watch and was amazed. The two of them had been talking for almost three hours. It was after seven o'clock. "Good Lord, do you know what time it is?" Nancy looked at her watch, too, and her eyes widened in surprise.

"Wow! How did we do that?" And then she smiled. "Will you come back and see me again sometime, Faye? Peter was right. You're a very special lady."

"Thank you. I'd love to. In fact . . . Peter was thinking that we might do it on a regular basis. What do you think?"

"I think it would be wonderful to have someone to talk to, like we did today."

"I can't always promise you three hours." They both laughed as Nancy walked her to the door. "How about three times a week for an hour, professionally? And we can get together separately, as friends. Sound okay to you?"

"Sounds wonderful."

They shook hands on it at the door, and Nancy was amazed to find herself already impatient for their first official session, only two days away.

Chapter 11

Nancy settled herself comfortably in the easy chair near the fire and sighed as she leaned her head back. She was five minutes early today, and anxious to talk to Faye. She heard the click-clack of her high heels coming across the hall to the study she used for seeing patients, and Nancy smiled and sat up straight in her chair. She wanted to give Faye the full benefit.

"Good morning, early bird. Don't you look pretty in red today." And then she stopped in the doorway and smiled. "Never mind the red. Let me see the new chin." Faye advanced on her slowly, looking at the lower part of Nancy's face, and at last, with a victorious smile, she found Nancy's eyes.

"Well, how do you like it?" But she could see the answer in Faye's face. Admiration for Peter's work, and pleasure for the girl.

"Nancy, you look beautiful. Just beautiful." Now one could see the lovely young neck, arching gracefully away from the slim shoulders, the delicate chin and gentle, sensuous mouth. What one could see was exquisite and perfectly suited the girl's personality.

Peter's endless sketches and sculptures had not been in vain. "My God, I want one like that too!"

Nancy chortled with glee, and sat back in the chair, hiding the rest of her face, which was still concealed by bandages, behind the dark brown felt hat she had bought a few weeks before at I. Magnin. It went well with the new brown wool coat and brown boots she was wearing with the red knit dress. Her figure had always been excellent, and with the striking new face she was going to be a very dazzling girl. She was even beginning to feel beautiful, now that she could see something of what was to come. Peter was keeping his promises.

"It's embarrassing, Faye. I feel so good I could squeak. And the weird thing is, it doesn't even look like me, but I love it."

"I'm glad. But what about it not looking like you? Does that bother you, Nancy?"

"Not as much as I thought it would. But maybe I still expect the rest to look like me. This is just one isolated part, and I never much liked my mouth before anyway. Maybe it'll seem stranger when the rest looks like someone else too. I don't know."

"You know something, Nancy? Maybe you ought to just sit back and enjoy it. Maybe you ought to play with this a little. Go with it."

"What do you mean?"

"Well, you're working on being Nancy, and we've been trying to adjust to giving up pieces of that Nancy as we go along. Maybe you ought to just stand back and look at the whole canvas. For instance, did you like your walk before?"

Nancy looked puzzled as she thought about it. This was a whole new idea, and something they had never discussed in the four months she'd been seeing Faye. "I don't know, Faye. I never thought about my walk."

"Well, let's think about it. What about your voice? Have you ever considered a voice coach? You have a marvelous voice, smooth and soft. Maybe with a little coaching you could make more of it. Why don't we play with what you've got and really make the most of it? Peter is. Why don't you?"

Nancy's face lit up at the idea, and she began to catch some of Faye's excitement. "I could develop all kinds of new sides to myself, couldn't I? Play the piano . . . a new walk . . . . I could even change my name."

"Well, let's not leap into any of this. You don't want to feel you've lost yourself. You want to feel you've added to yourself. But let's think about all this. I have a feeling it's going to take us in some very interesting directions."

"I want a new voice." Nancy sat back and giggled. "Like this." She lowered her voice by several octaves, and Faye laughed.

"If you do enough of that, Peter may have to give you a beard."

"Terrific." They were suddenly in a holiday mood, and Nancy got up and began to prance around the room. At times like that, Faye remembered how young she really was. Twenty-three now. Her birthday had come and gone, and she was growing up in ways many people never had to. But beneath the surface, she was still a very young girl.

"You know, I do want you to be aware of one thing though, Nancy." She sounded more serious now.

"And what's that?"

"I think you should understand why you're so willing to try out a new you. It's not unusual for orphans, as you were, to feel unsure of their identities. You're not certain what your parents were like, and as a result, you feel as though a piece of you is missing, a link to reality. So it's a lot easier for you to give up parts of the person you once were than it would be for someone who retained very clear images of her parents—and all the responsibilities that entails. In some ways it may make things simpler for you."

Nancy was silent, and Faye smiled at her as she sank back into the cozy chair near the fire. It was a wonderful room to see patients in: it set everyone instantly at ease. She had put her grandmother's Persian carpets to good use in the room, which also boasted splendid paneling and old brass sconces. The fireplace was also trimmed in brass, the curtains were old and lacy, there were walls of books, tiny paintings tucked away in unexpected corners, and everywhere was a profusion of leafy ferns. It looked like the home of an interesting woman, and that was exactly the effect Faye wanted. "Okay, it'll take you some time to think about that. For the moment, there's another serious subject we have to get into. What about the holidays?"

"What about them?" Nancy's eyes closed like two doors, and the laughter of moments before was now completely gone. Faye had known it would be this way, which was why the subject had to be broached.

"How do you feel about the holidays? Are you scared?"

"No." Nancy's face was immobile, as Faye watched.

"Sad?"

"No."

"Okay, no more guessing games, Nancy. Suppose you tell me. What do you feel?"

"You want to know what I feel?" Nancy suddenly looked straight back at her, dead in the eye. "You want to know?" She stood up and strode across the room and then back again. "I feel pissed."

"Pissed?"

"Very pissed. Superpissed. Royally pissed."

"At whom?"

Nancy sank into the chair again and looked into the fire. This time when she spoke her voice was soft and sad. "At Michael. I thought he'd have found me by now. It's been over seven months. I thought he'd have been here." She closed her eyes to keep back the tears.

"Who else are you mad at? Yourself?"

"Yes."

"Why?"

"For making the deal with Marion Hillyard in the first place. I hate her guts, but I hate mine worse. I sold out."

"Did you?"

"I think so. And all for a new chin." She spoke with contempt where moments before there had been pride. But they were delving deeper now.

"I don't agree with you, Nancy. You didn't do it for a new chin. You did it for a new life. Is that so wrong at your age? What would you think of someone else who did the same thing?"

"I don't know. Maybe I'd think they were stupid. Maybe I'd understand."

"You know, a few minutes ago we were talking about a new life. New voice, new walk, new face, new name. Everything is new, except one thing." Nancy waited, not wanting to hear her say it. "Michael. What about thinking of a new life without him? Do you ever think about that?"

"No." But her eyes filled with tears, and they both knew she was lying.

"Never?"

"I never think of other men. But sometimes I think about not having Michael."

"And how do you feel?"

"Like I wish I were dead." But she didn't really mean that, and they both knew it.

"But you don't have Michael now. And it's not so bad, is it?" Nancy only shrugged in answer, and then Faye spoke again, her voice infinitely soft. "Maybe you need to do some real thinking about all that, Nancy."

"You don't think he's coming back to me, do you?" She was angry again. This time at Faye, because there was no one else to be angry at.

"I don't know, Nancy. No one knows the answer to that except Michael."

"Yeah. The son of a bitch." She got up and paced

the room again, and then like a windup toy winding
down, the fury of her pacing slowed, until she finally
stood in front of the fire, with tears rolling down her
face and her hands clenched on the screen in front of
the fire. "Oh Faye, I'm so scared."

"Of what?" The voice was soft behind her.

"Of being alone. Of not being me anymore. Of . . .
I wonder if I've done a terrible thing that I'll be
punished for. I gave up love for my face."

"But you thought you'd already lost everything. You
can't blame yourself for the choice you made, and in
the end you may be glad."

"Yeah . . . maybe . . ." There were fresh sobs from
the fireplace, and Faye watched the slim shoulders
shake. "You know, I'm scared of the holidays too. It's
worse than being back at the orphanage. This time
there's no one. Lily and Gretchen left last month, and
you're going skiing. Peter's going to Europe for a
week, and . . ." She couldn't stop the tears. But these
were the realities of her life now. She had to face
them. Faye shouldn't be made to feel guilty for leaving, nor should Peter: they had their own lives, as
well as their time with her.

"Maybe it's time you got out and made some
friends."

"Like this?" She turned to face Faye again and
pulled off the soft brown hat, revealing a great deal
of bandaging. "How can I go out and meet anyone
like this? I'd scare them to death. Look guys, it's
Dracula!"

"It isn't frightening looking, Nancy, and in time it'll

be gone. It's not permanent. They're only bandages. People would understand."

"Maybe so." But she wasn't ready to believe that. "Anyway, I don't need friends. I keep busy with my camera." Peter's gift had been a godsend.

"I know. I saw your last batch of prints at Peter's the other day. He's so proud of them he shows them to everyone. It's beautiful work, Nancy."

"Thank you." Some of the anger drained out of her with the talk of her work. "Oh Faye . . ." She sat back in the chair again and stretched her legs. "What am I going to do with my life?"

"That's what we're working on figuring out, isn't it? And in the meantime, why don't you think about some of what we talked about today? The voice coach, music lessons—something to amuse you, and all part of the person you'll become."

"Yeah, I guess I will give it some thought. When are you coming back from skiing, by the way?"

"In two weeks. But I'll leave a number where you can reach me in an emergency." Faye was more worried about Nancy's getting through the holidays than she was willing to admit. Holidays were prime time for depression, even suicide, but Nancy seemed solid for the moment. She just didn't want her to become hysterical in her loneliness. It was rotten luck that she and Peter were going away at the same time, but on the other hand Nancy had to learn not to depend on them too much. "Why don't we make an appointment for two weeks from today. And I want to see a mountain of beautiful prints you made over the holidays."

"That reminds me." Nancy jumped up again and

vanished into the hallway, where she had left a flat package wrapped in brown paper. When she returned with it, she smilingly held it out to Faye. "Merry Christmas."

Faye opened it with a look of pleasure and then of awe. The gift was a photograph of herself that looked as though she had sat for it for hours, to allow the photographer to capture just the right look, the right mood. It had a dreamy, impressionistic quality; she had been standing on Nancy's terrace with the wind in her hair, wearing a pale pink silk shirt, and the sun had been setting in red and pink tones behind her. She remembered the day, but couldn't remember Nancy taking the picture. "When did you take it?" She looked stunned.

"When you weren't looking." Nancy looked pleased with herself, and she had every right to be. The photograph was magnificent. She had printed it herself and enlarged it, and then had it handsomely framed. It was as expressive as a painting.

"You're incredible, Nancy. What a beautiful, beautiful gift."

"I had a good subject."

The two women exchanged a hug, and Nancy regretfully shrugged back into her coat. "Have a wonderful ski trip."

"I will. I'll bring you some snow."

"Smartass." Nancy hugged her again and they wished each other a Merry Christmas as she left. There was a tug at Faye's heart after she was gone. Nancy was a beautiful girl. Inside. Where it mattered.

Chapter 12

"Mr. Calloway's on the line for you, Mr. Hillyard." The
snow had been falling for five or six hours on the
already slush-ridden streets of New York, but Michael
had noticed nothing. He had been at his desk since
six that morning, and it was after five o'clock now. He
grabbed for the phone while signing a stack of letters
for his secretary to mail. At least the job in Kansas
City was off his back. Now he had Houston to worry
about, and in the spring he'd be getting ulcers over
the medical center in San Francisco. His job was a
never-ending stream of headaches and demands, con-
tracts and problems and meetings. Thank God.

"George? Mike. What's up?"

"Your mother's in a meeting, but she asked me to
call and tell you that we'll be back from Boston tonight, if the snow lets up. Tomorrow if it doesn't."

"Is it snowing there?" Michael sounded surprised,
as though it were June and snow was preposterous.

"No." George sounded momentarily confused. "They
said there was a blizzard in New York . . . isn't there?"

Mike looked out his window and grinned. "Yeah,
there is. I just hadn't looked. Sorry."

114

The boy was killing himself, just as his mother always had. George wondered for a moment what it was about the breed that made them so hard on themselves, and on the people who loved them. "Anyway, now that we've gotten that settled." George chuckled for a moment. "She wanted me to call you and make sure you're home for Christmas dinner tomorrow night. She has a few friends coming and of course she wants you there."

Michael took a deep breath as he listened. A few friends. That meant twenty or thirty, all of them people he either disliked or didn't know, and the inevitable single girl, from a good family, for him. It sounded like a stinking way to spend Christmas. Or any other day. "I'm sorry, George. I'm afraid I owe Mother an apology. I've got a prior commitment."

"You do?" He sounded stunned.

"I meant to tell her last week and I totally forgot. I was so busy with the Houston center that I just never got to it. I'm sure she'll understand." He'd been working miracles with the Houston client so she'd damn well better understand. Michael knew he had her on that one.

"Well, she'll be disappointed of course, but she'll be pleased to know that you have plans. Something . . . uh . . . something exciting, I hope."

"Yeah, George. A real knockout."

"Anything serious?" Now George sounded worried. Christ, there was no satisfying them.

"No, nothing to worry about. Just some good clean fun."

"Excellent. Well, Merry Christmas and all that."

"Same to you, and give Mother my love. I'll call her tomorrow."

"I'll tell her." George was wreathed in smiles when he hung up, pleased that the boy was finally recovering. Michael had been leading a very strange life for a while there. Marion would be relieved, too, though undoubtedly she'd be mad as hell for a few minutes that he wouldn't be home for dinner with her friends. But he was young after all. He had a right to a little fun. George grinned to himself as he took a sip of his Scotch and remembered a Christmas in Vienna twenty-five years before. And then, as always, his thoughts wandered back to Michael's mother.

In Michael's office, the phone continued to ring. Ben wanted to be sure he had plans. Michael assured him that he would be at his mother's, boring but expected, and assorted clients called, alternately to complain, congratulate, and wish him a Merry Christmas. As he hung up after the last one he muttered to himself, "Ah go to hell," and then looked up in surprise when he heard unfamiliar laughter from the doorway. It was that new interior designer Ben had hired. A pretty girl, too, with rich auburn hair that fell in thick waves to her shoulders and set off creamy skin and blue eyes. Mike never noticed, of course. He never noticed anything anymore, unless it was lying on his desk and needed a signature.

"Do you always wish people Merry Christmas that way?"

"Only the people I truly enjoy hearing from." He smiled at her and wondered what she was doing there. He hadn't asked to see her, and she had no direct business with him, not that he knew of anyway. "Is there anything I can do for you, Miss . . ." Damn. He couldn't remember her name. What the hell was it?

"Wendy Townsend. I just came to wish you a Merry Christmas."

Ah. An apple polisher. Michael was amused and waved her to a chair. "Didn't they tell you I'm the original Scrooge?"

"I gathered that when you didn't show up at either the office party or the Christmas dinner last night. They also say you work too hard."

"It's good for my complexion."

"So are other things." She crossed one pretty leg over the other, and Michael checked it out. It did as little for him as anything else had since last May. "I also wanted to thank you for the raise I just got." She flashed a set of perfect teeth at him, and he returned the smile. He was beginning to wonder what she really wanted. A bonus? Another raise?

"You'll have to thank Ben Avery for that. I'm afraid I had nothing to do with it."

"I see." It was a pointless conversation, and she knew it. Regretfully, she stood up, and then glanced at the window. There were seven or eight inches of snow piled up on the window ledge. "Looks like it's going to be a white Christmas after all. It's also going to be practically impossible to get home tonight."

"I think you may be right. I probably won't even try." He pointed at the leather couch with a grin. "I

think that's why they put that there, to keep me
chained to my office." No, mister, you do that to yourself. But she only smiled and wished him a Merry
Christmas. Michael went back to signing letters, and
true to his word, he spent the night on the couch. And
the next night as well. It suited him perfectly. Christmas fell over a weekend this year, so no one knew
where he was. Even the janitor and the maids had
been given the holiday. Only the night watchman realized that Michael never left the office from Friday
until late Sunday night, and by then Christmas was
over. And when he got back to his empty apartment,
he had nothing more to fear. Christmas, with all its
memories and ghosts, was already a thing of the past.
There was a large, ostentatious poinsettia wilting outside his door, sent to him by his mother. He put it
near the trash can.

In San Francisco, Nancy had spent the holiday more
comfortably than Michael, but in equal solitude. She
had cooked a small capon, sung Christmas carols alone
on the terrace on Christmas Eve, after she came home
from church, and slept late on Christmas Day. She'd
hoped to keep the day from coming, but there was no
escaping it. It was relentless with its tinsel and trees,
its promises and lies. At least in San Francisco the
weather reminded her less of Christmases she had
known in the East. It was almost as though these
people were pretending it was Christmas, when she
knew it actually wasn't. The unfamiliarity made it a
trifle easier to bear. And she had two presents this

year, a beautiful Gucci handbag from Peter and a funny book from Faye. She curled up in a chair with it in the afternoon after she had eaten her capon and stuffing and cranberry sauce. It was all rather like celebrating Christmas at Schrafft's, with all the old ladies, and all your life's hopes stashed in a shopping bag. She had always wondered what they carried in those bags. Old letters maybe, or photographs, trinkets or trophies or dreams.

It was after six o'clock when she finally put down the book and stretched her legs. A walk would be nice; she needed to get some air. She slipped into her coat, reached for her hat and camera, and smiled at herself in the mirror. She still liked the new smile. It was a great smile. It made her wonder what the rest of her face would look like, when Peter was through. It was a little bit like becoming his dream woman. And once he had told her that he was making her his "ideal." It was an uncomfortable feeling, but still, she liked that smile. She slipped the camera over her shoulder and took the elevator downstairs.

It was a crisp breezy evening, with no fog—she knew it would be a good night for taking pictures—and she headed slowly down toward the wharf. The streets were mostly deserted. Everyone was recovering from Christmas dinner, recuperating in easy chairs and on couches, or snoring softly in front of the TV. The vision she created in her own head made Nancy smile, and then suddenly she tripped, making a little shrieking noise as she stumbled. Peter had warned her to be careful of falling. She couldn't indulge yet in any active sports because of that danger, and now she'd almost fallen on the street. Her arms had gone out to save her and she had regained her balance before hitting the pavement. And then she realized that she wasn't the only one who had shrieked. She had stumbled over a small shaggy dog, who looked greatly offended. Now he sat down, waved a paw at Nancy, and yipped. He was a tangled little fur ball of beige and brown. He stared at her and barked again.

"Okay, okay. I'm sorry. You scared me, too, you know." She bent to pat him and he wagged his tail and barked once more. He was a comical little dog, barely older than a puppy. She was sorry she had nothing to give him to eat. He looked hungry. She patted him again, smiled, and stood up, grateful that she hadn't dropped her camera. He barked at her again and she grinned. "Okay. Bye-bye." She started to walk away, but he immediately followed, trotting along at her side until she stopped and looked down at him again.

"Now listen you, go on home. Go on . . ." But each time she took a step, he did, too, and when she stopped he sat down, waiting happily for her to go on. She stood there and laughed at him. He was really a ridiculous little dog, but such a cute one. She stooped down to pat him again and felt his neck for a collar, but there was none. A totally naked dog. And then suddenly, in amusement, she decided to snap some pictures of him. He proved to be a natural, prancing, posing, waving, and having a marvelous time. Nancy had made a new friend, and at the end of half an hour he still showed no sign of deserting her. "All right, you, come on." So off they went, to the wharf, where she shot pictures of crab stalls and shrimp vendors, tourists and drunken Santa Clauses, boats and birds and a few more of the dog. She had a good time, and never succeeded in losing her friend. He remained at her side until at last she stopped for coffee. She had gotten quite good at going into coffee shops and fast food places, lowering her head so she concealed most of her face beneath her hat, and ordering whatever she wanted. Now she even had a smile to go with the thank you, and it wasn't as hard to pull off as she once had thought. This time she ordered black coffee for herself, and a hamburger for the dog. She put the red paper plate on the sidewalk next to him, and he gobbled it up and then barked his thanks.

"Does that mean thank you, or more?" He barked again and she laughed, and someone stopped to pat him and ask his name. "I don't know. He just adopted me."

"Did you report him?"

"I guess I should." The man told her how and she thanked him. She would call from her apartment if the dog stuck with her that far. And he did. He stopped at the door of her building as though he lived there, too. So she took him upstairs and called the ASPCA, but no one had reported losing a dog that looked like him, and they suggested she either resign herself to having a new dog, or drop him off at the shelter and have him put to sleep. She was outraged at the thought and put a protective arm around him as they sat side by side on the floor. "You look a mess, you know, kid. How about a bath?" He wagged tongue and tail simultaneously, and she scooped him up in her arms and deposited him in the bathtub. She had to be careful not to get splashed, so as not to get her face bandages wet, but he submitted to the bath with no resistance. And as they progressed, she discovered that he was not beige and brown, but brown and white. His brown was the color of milk chocolate, and his white was the color of snow. He was really an adorable dog, and Nancy hoped no one called to report him missing. She had never had a dog before, and she had already fallen in love with this one. It hadn't been possible to have a dog at the orphanage, and pets weren't allowed at her apartment building in Boston. But this building's management had no objection to pets. Nancy sat back on her heels and rubbed him again with the towel as he rolled over on his back, waving all four feet. And then she thought of a name. It was the name of a dog Michael had told her about, the first puppy he'd had as a child, and somehow it seemed the perfect name for this independent little dog. "How do you feel about Fred, little guy? Sound okay to you?" He barked twice, and Nancy took that to mean yes.

Chapter 13

Nancy peeked her head around the door to grin at Faye, already cozily settled near the fire.

"And what do you have up your sleeve today, young lady?" Faye smiled at her, relieved that she looked so well.

"I brought a friend."

"You did? I'm gone for two weeks and you already have a new friend? Well, how do you like that?" And with that, Fred bounced into the room, obviously proud of his new red collar and leash. No one had reported losing him, and as of that morning he officially belonged to Nancy. He had a license, a bed, a bowl, and about seventeen toys. Nancy was lavishing him with love.

"Faye, I'd like you to meet Fred." She smiled down at him with motherly pride, and Faye laughed.

"He's adorable, Nancy. Where'd you get him?"

"He adopted me on Christmas night. Actually, I should probably have called him Noel, but Fred seemed more appropriate." For once, she was embarrassed to tell Faye why. She was beginning to feel like a fool for clinging to Michael. "I also brought you a stack of my work to look at."

"My, haven't you been busy. Maybe I should go away more often."

"Do me a favor, don't." A glimpse into Nancy's eyes told Faye just how lonely she'd been. But at least she had made it through Christmas, and alone. That was no small accomplishment for anyone. "And . . ." She drew the word out with pride ". . . I've made arrangements for a voice coach. Peter says it's all part of the package. I start tomorrow at three. I can't do dance class yet, because my face isn't finished, but I can do that next summer."

"I'm proud of you, Nancy."

"So am I."

They had a good session that day, and for the first time in eight months, they didn't talk about Michael. Much to Faye's astonishment, it was spring again before Nancy mentioned his name. It was almost as though she were determined not to. All she talked about now was her plans. Her voice lessons. Her photography. The work she wanted to do with the photography when her techniques became more sophisticated. And in the spring she and Fred went for long walks in the park, through the rose gardens and along the remoter paths near the beach. She sometimes went on drives with Peter to out-of-the-way beaches where her bandages didn't matter. But little by little her face was emerging, and so was her personality. It was as though by remolding her cheekbones and her forehead and her nose, he was also revealing more of the soul that had been hidden by youth. She had matured a great deal in the year since the accident.

"Has it already been a year?" Faye was astonished as she looked at Nancy one afternoon. Peter was working on the area around her eyes just then, and she was wearing huge dark glasses which hid her cheekbones as well as her eyes.

"Yes. It happened last May. And I've been seeing you for eight months, Faye. Do you really think I'm making progress?" She sounded discouraged. But she was still tired from her last surgery three days before.

"Do you doubt your progress?"

"Sometimes. When I think of Michael too much." It was a heavy confession for her to make. She was still clinging to the last shreds of hope—that he would finally find her, and the deal with his mother would be off. "I don't know why I still do that to myself, but I do."

"Wait till you get out in the world a little more, Nancy. You have nothing to do now but look back at things you remember, or ahead at things you don't yet know. It's natural that you'd spend a fair amount of time looking back. You have no other people in your life just now, but you will. In time. Be patient."

Nancy sighed a long tired sigh. "I'm so sick of being patient, Faye, and I feel like this work on my face will go on forever. Sometimes I hate Peter for it, and I know it's not his fault. He's doing it as fast as he can."

"It'll be worth the time you invested in it. It already

is." She smiled, and Nancy smiled back. The delicate shape of the girl's face had already emerged, and each week there seemed to be changes. The voice coach had done her work well, too. Nancy's voice was pitched a little lower now, beautifully modulated, and she had far greater control over the smoothness of her voice than anyone without training could have. It gave Faye an idea. "Have you ever thought of acting when this is all over? The experience might give you an incredible amount of insight."

Nancy smiled at her and shook her head. "Making films maybe, acting in them, no. It's so plastic. I'd rather be at my end of the camera."

"Okay, it was just a thought. So what's on your agenda for this week?"

"I told Peter I'd take some pictures for him, we're flying down to Santa Barbara for the day on Sunday. He wants to see some people there, and he offered to take me along for the ride."

"I should lead such a life. Well, kiddo . . ." She looked at her watch. "See you on Wednesday."

"Yes ma'am." Nancy saluted with a smile, and Fred bounced out of the room with his leash in his mouth. He was used to the sessions in Faye's office. Nancy never left him behind.

When she left Faye's office, she decided to walk a few blocks toward a little park nearby, to see if there were any children to photograph in the playground. She hadn't taken any shots of kids in a while. When she got there, there was an ample supply of subjects, climbing and pushing and shoving and running. Nancy sat down on a bench for a while to watch them and get a feeling for who they were and what they were up to. It was a beautiful day, and she felt good about life.

"Do you come here often?"

Michael looked up in surprise from the bench where he sat. He had escaped to the park for an hour, just to get away from the office and see something green. There was always something magical about those first spring days, when New York turns from gray to lush green, bushes and trees and flowers exploding into life. But he had felt sure he would be alone in the secluded little spot where he had found an empty bench. The sudden voice surprised him. When he looked up he saw Wendy Townsend, the designer from his office.

"No . . . I . . . as a matter of fact, almost never. But I was having a rare case of spring fever today."

"So was I." She looked embarrassed as she held her dripping ice cream stick and then took a quick lick to keep from losing a big slice of chocolate.

"That looks delicious." He smiled at her in the warm spring air.

"Want some?" She held it out like a friendly third grader, but he shook his head.

"But thanks for the offer. Would you like to sit down?" He felt a little silly being caught in the park, but it was such a nice day he didn't mind sharing it, and she was a pleasant girl. Their paths had crossed a number of times since she'd walked into his office five months before, to wish him a Merry Christmas. She sat down next to him and ate the last of her ice cream. "What are you working on these days?" he asked.

"Houston and Kansas City. My work is always five or six months behind yours. It's kind of interesting to follow on your heels that way."

"I'm not quite sure how to take that." But he wasn't particularly worried about it.

"As a compliment." She smiled at him from under long auburn lashes.

"Thank you. Is Ben treating you decently or is he the slave driver I tell him to be?"

"He wouldn't know how."

"I know." Mike smiled at the thought. "We've known each other for half our lives. He's like my brother."

"He's a hell of a nice man."

Mike nodded silently, thinking how little he had seen of Ben in the past year. He never had time. He never made time. He didn't even know what was happening in Ben's life. It had been months since he'd taken the time to find out. It made him feel guilty as he sat next to the girl, lost in his own thoughts. But a lot had changed for him in the past year. He had changed.

"You're a long way away, Mr. Hillyard. Someplace pleasant, I hope."

He shrugged. "Spring does strange things to me. It kind of makes me stop from year to year and take stock. I think that's what I was doing today."

"That's a nice idea. For some reason, I always do

that in September. I think the idea of the 'school year' marked me forever. A lot of other people take stock in January. But spring makes the most sense. Everything is starting again, so why wouldn't we start our lives again each spring?" They exchanged a smile and Michael looked out over the little lake, still except for a few contented-looking ducks. There were no other people in sight. "What were you doing this time last year?" She went on. It was an innocent question, but it cut through him like a knife. A year ago on that day . . .

"Nothing very different from what I'm doing now." He furrowed his brow, looked at his watch, and stood up. "I'm afraid I have a meeting in ten minutes. I'd better be getting back. But it was nice chatting with you." He barely smiled at her before striding away, and she sat there wondering what she had said. She'd have to ask Ben sometime what was wrong with the guy. You couldn't get within a thousand miles of him.

Chapter 14

Much to Michael's surprise, Wendy was scheduled into the same meeting he was, ten minutes later. Ben had wanted her there. They were going to discuss the very early plans for the San Francisco Medical Center, and Interior Design would be a big factor. A lot of local art would be used to highlight the basic design. Ben was going to take care of finding that art himself, but Wendy would be doing a lot of the coordinating on the home front—more than usual, since Ben would be in San Francisco a lot of the time. The project was, of course, a long way away, but it was time to start working out the plans and the problems and the details.

It was a long, demanding, interesting meeting, run in great part by Marion, with George Calloway's assistance. But Michael took an almost equal part in the proceedings. This project was his; his mother had wanted it to be, from the first. Every major architectural firm in the country had been lusting after this job, and Marion intended to use it to establish Michael's name and reputation in the business.

It was almost six o'clock when the meeting ended,

and Wendy was drained. She had presented her ideas well, stood up to Marion when she had to, and made a great deal of sense to Mike. Ben was proud of her and patted her on the shoulder as they left.

"Nice job, kid. Damn nice job." He was called away by his secretary then, and Wendy continued down the corridor alone. She was surprised when Mike stopped her, too.

"I was very impressed with your work, Wendy. I think that together we're going to pull off a beautiful job out there."

"So do I." She virtually glowed with the praise, and from him of all people. "I . . . Michael, I . . . I'm really sorry if I said anything to offend you this afternoon. I really didn't mean to pry, and if it was an inappropriate question, I'm awfully . . ."

He felt a pang for her discomfiture and put up a hand to stop her as he smiled gently down at her. "I was rude and I apologize. I guess spring fever makes me crazy as well as dreamy. Can I make it up to you this evening with dinner?" He was as surprised as she was when the words tumbled out of his mouth. Dinner? He hadn't had dinner with a woman in a year. But she was a nice girl, she was doing a good job, and she meant well. And she was looking up at him, pink-cheeked and embarrassed.

"I . . . you don't have to . . ."

"I know, but I'd like to." And this time he meant it. "Are you free?"

"Yes. And I'd love to."

"Fine. Then I'll pick you up at your place in an hour." He jotted the address on the back of his notepad and smiled as he hurried back to his office. It was a crazy thing to do, but why the hell not?

He arrived punctually at her apartment an hour later, and he liked what he saw. It was a neat little brownstone with a shiny black door and a large brass knocker. The house was divided into four apartments, and Wendy had the smallest one, but hers boasted a perfectly kept little garden in the back. Her apartment was a wonderful mesh of old and new, antique shop, thrift shop, and good modern; it was all done in soft warm colors with soft lighting, plants, and candles. She seemed to have a great fondness for old silver, all of which she had polished to mirror perfection. He looked around him with pleasure, and sat down to enjoy the hors d'oeuvres she had made. They drank Bloody Marys and exchanged absurdities about the various projects they had worked on. An hour flew by in easy conversation, and Michael hated to break it up and move on to dinner, but he had made reservations at a French restaurant nearby, and they never held latecomers' tables for more than five minutes.

"I'm afraid we'll have to run if we want to make it. Or do we really care?" He was startled to hear her voice his own thoughts, and he wasn't quite sure what the mischief in her eyes meant. It had been so long since he'd been out with anyone that he was afraid to misinterpret and make the wrong move.

"Just exactly what are you thinking, Miss Townsend? Is the thought as outrageous as the look on your face?"

"Worse. I was thinking we could put together a

picnic and go watch the boats on the East River."
She looked like a little kid with a naughty idea. There
they both were, dressed for dinner, he in a dark suit
and she in a black silk dress, and she was proposing
a picnic on the East River.

"It sounds terrific. Do you have any peanut butter?"

"Certainly not." She looked offended. "But I make
my own pâté, Mr. Hillyard. And I have sourdough
bread." She looked very proud of herself, and Michael
was suitably impressed.

"My God. I was thinking more in the line of peanut
butter and jelly, or hot dogs."

"Never." With a grin, she disappeared into the kitch-
en, where in ten minutes she concocted the perfect picnic for two. Some leftover ratatouille, the promised pâté, a loaf of sourdough bread, a healthy hunk
of Brie, three very ripe pears, some grapes, and a
small bottle of wine. "Does that seem like enough?"
She looked worried, and he laughed.

"Are you serious? I haven't eaten that well since I
was twelve. I live mostly on leftover roast beef sand-
wiches and whatever my secretary feeds me when I'm
not looking. Probably dog food, I never notice."

"That's great. It's a wonder you don't die of starvation." He wasn't starving, but he was certainly very
thin. "Are we all set?" She looked around the living
room and picked up a delicate beige shawl while
Michael gathered up the picnic basket. Then they were
off. They walked the few blocks to the East River,
found a bench, and settled themselves happily to look
at the boats. It was a beautiful warm night with a
sky full of stars, and the river was well populated

with tugs, cabin cruisers, and even a few sailboats from time to time, out for an evening excursion. Mike and Wendy weren't the only ones with spring fever.

"Is this your first job, Wendy?" His mouth was half-full of pâté, and he looked younger than he had in a year.

She nodded happily. "Yes. First one I applied for, too. I was really glad I got it. As soon as I graduated from Parsons I came straight to you."

"That's nice. It's my first job, too." He was dying to ask her how she liked his mother, but he didn't dare. It wouldn't have been fair. Besides, if the girl had any sense at all, she must hate her. Marion Hillyard was a monster to work for; even Michael knew that.

"You should do well there, Michael." She was teasing him again, and he laughed.

"What are you going to do after this? Get married and have kids?"

"I don't know. Maybe. But if I do, it won't be for a long time yet. I want a career first. I can always have kids later, in my thirties."

"Boy, things sure have changed. Used to be everyone was hot to get married." He grinned at his new friend.

"Some girls still are hot to get married." She smiled at him and took a little piece of the Brie with a slice of pear. It had been an excellent dinner. "You want to get married?" She glanced at him curiously, and he shook his head as he looked out at the boats. "Never?" He turned to face her and shook his head again, and something in his eyes cried out to her. She wasn't sure if she should get off the question or not. She decided to ask him. "Should I ask why, or should I let it be?"

"Maybe it doesn't matter anymore. I've been running away from it for a whole year. I even ran away from you today at lunch. I can't run forever." He paused for a moment, looked down at his hands, then back up at her. "I was supposed to get married last year, and on the way to the wedding, Ben Avery, and . . . and . . . my fiancée and I . . . were in a car accident. The other driver was killed, and so was . . . She was, too." He didn't cry, but he felt as though his insides had been shredded. Wendy was looking at him with wide, horrified eyes.

"Oh God, Michael, how awful. It sounds like a nightmare."

"It was. I was in a coma for a couple of days, and when I came to, she was already gone. I . . . I . . ." He almost couldn't say the words, but now he had to. He had to tell someone. He had never even told Ben. "I went back to her apartment when I got out of the hospital two weeks later, but it was already empty. Someone had just called Goodwill, and her paintings had . . . had been stolen by a couple of nurses from the hospital. She was an artist." They sat in silence for a long time, and then he said the words again, as though to understand them better himself. "There was nothing left. Of me either, I guess." When he looked up he saw tears running down Wendy's face.

"I'm so sorry, Michael."

He nodded, and then for the first time in a year, he cried, too. The tears just slid slowly down his face as he took her into his arms.

Chapter 15

"Mike, what do you think of that woman running the Kansas City office of . . ." She looked over at him, sprawled out on a deck chair in her garden. He wasn't listening. "Mike." He was staring at the Sunday paper as they sat in their bathing suits, in the hot New York sun, but Wendy knew he wasn't paying attention to the paper either. "Mike."

"Hm? What?"

"I was asking you about that woman in the Kansas City office." But she had already lost him. She stared at him in irritation. "Do you want another Bloody Mary?"

"Huh? Yeah. I think I'll go to the office in a while." He gazed past her at an invisible spot just beyond her left shoulder.

"Wonderful."

"What's that supposed to mean?" He was watching her now, and he wasn't quite sure what he read in her face. If he'd tried a little harder, he would have understood instantly. But he never tried.

"Nothing."

"Look, the medical center in San Francisco is going to have me working my ass off for the next two years. It's one of the biggest jobs in the country."

"And if it weren't that it would be something else. You don't need an excuse. It's okay."

"Then don't make it sound like I'm punching a time clock around here." He shoved the paper away with his foot and glared at her as she started to steam.

"Time clock? You got here at twelve thirty last night. We were supposed to have dinner with the Thompsons, and you didn't even call me until nine forty-five, Michael. I should have gone out with them anyway."

"Then why didn't you? You don't have to sit around waiting for me."

"No, but I happen to be in love with you, so I do it anyway. But you don't even try to be considerate. What the hell is it with you? Are you afraid to be anywhere but at your desk, afraid someone will get their hooks into you? Are you afraid that maybe you'll fall in love with me, too? Would that be so awful?"

"Don't be ridiculous. You know what my work schedule is like. You should know better than anyone."

"I do. Which is why I also know that half the hours you work aren't justified. You use your work as a place to hide, a way of life. You use it to avoid me. And yourself." And Nancy. But she didn't say that.

"That's ridiculous." He got up and strode around the narrow, well-tended garden, the flagstone walk warm under his feet. It was September, but still hot in New York. After the first few happy weeks of their romance, he and Wendy had had an erratic summer. He had spent most of it working, but they managed one weekend away, on Long Island. "Besides, what the hell do you expect from me? I thought we cleared all that up in the beginning. I told you I didn't want to get—"

"You told me you didn't want to get too involved, that you were afraid to be hurt. You weren't sure you'd ever want to get married. You never told me you were afraid to be alive, for Chrissake, afraid to care at all, afraid to be a human being. Jesus, Michael, you spend more time with your dictaphone than you do with me. And you're probably nicer to it."

"So?"

She felt a little shiver run up her spine as she watched his face. He really didn't care. She was crazy to stay with him. But there was something about him, a beauty, a strength, a wildness to him, a sorrow, that drew her like a magnet. And more than that, she sensed how great his pain was, his need. She wanted to reach out to him, to show him he was loved. But the bitch of it was, he didn't really give a damn. She wasn't Nancy. And they both knew it.

Wendy got up silently and walked into the living room so he wouldn't see the tears bright in her eyes. In the kitchen she poured herself a fresh Bloody Mary and stood there for a moment with her eyes closed, trembling, wishing she could reach out to him and find him there. But she was beginning to think he would never be "there" for her. He wouldn't let himself be there for anyone.

She drained the drink with long steady gulps and set the empty glass down on the counter as she felt his hands float softly over her satiny bronzed skin. She spent every weekend in her garden, getting a suntan, alone. She said nothing as he stood there now, just behind her. She could feel the heat from his body, and she wanted him desperately, but she was tired of his knowing that, and of his being able to have her whenever he liked. Damn it, it was time she made it harder for him.

"I want you, Wendy." Her whole body ached for him at the words, but she wouldn't let herself. She kept her back to him, hating the gentleness of his hands as they traveled smoothly down her back and over her buttocks and then around and up toward her breasts.

"As you said earlier, 'So?' "

"You know I can't deal with that kind of pressure." His voice was as soft and smooth as her skin.

"It's not pressure, Michael. It's love. The sad thing is you don't know the difference. Is that what it was like with her, too?" She felt the hands stop and the arms grow stiff. But she couldn't stop herself. She wanted to hurt him, too. "Were you afraid to love her, too? Is it easier now that she's dead? Now you don't have to love anyone, and you can spend the rest of your life hiding behind the tragedy of how much you miss her. It certainly takes care of things, doesn't it?" She turned slowly to face him now, and there was hatred brewing in his eyes.

"How can you say a thing like that? How dare you?" For a moment he reminded her of his mother, almost as hard, almost as cold. But not quite. No one could equal Marion. "How dare you twist the things I've told you."

"I'm not twisting, I'm asking. If I'm wrong, I'm sorry. But I'm beginning to wonder if I am wrong." She leaned against the counter, staring at him, and then he grabbed her by the shoulders and pulled her toward him. "Michael . . ."

But he said not a word, he only crushed his mouth down hard on hers, and at the same time tore away the top of her bikini, and then pulled hard at the bottom and it came away instantly in his hand. The little gold clasps at the sides had broken. But by the time Wendy reached the kitchen floor in his arms, she hated herself more than she hated him because she knew in her heart that she wanted to be there. At least he was alive, at least he was making love to her, whatever it took. But it took too much, and she knew it. It was costing a piece of her soul.

As they lay there panting and damp, ten minutes later, Wendy could hear the kitchen clock ticking in the silence. Michael said nothing. He only stared out at the garden, looking strangely sad.

"Are you all right?" He should have been asking her, but she was asking him. The whole affair was crazy, and she knew it, but she couldn't seem to stop herself. Sometimes she wondered what would happen when it was over. Maybe he'd have Ben Avery fire her. She almost expected it. "Mike?"

"Hm? Yeah. I . . . I'm sorry, Wendy. Sometimes I'm really an incomparable ass." There were tears glistening in his eyes.

"Well, I'm not sure I can argue with you on that one." She looked up at him with a rueful smile and then kissed the tip of his chin. "But I seem to love you anyway."

"You could do a lot better, you know." For the first time in months he looked down at her and really seemed to see her. "Sometimes I hate myself for what I do to you. I just . . ." He couldn't go on, and she put her finger over his lips.

"I know."

He nodded silently and stood up as she lay looking up at him from the kitchen floor.

"Michael?"

"Yeah?" His face was softer now than it had been half an hour before. She had done something for him after all.

"Do you still miss her all the time?"

He waited for a long moment, and then nodded, with a look of pain in his eyes. And then, without saying anything more, he went into the bedroom to dress. Wendy got up slowly. She didn't bother with the broken bikini. It had seen a good summer's use anyway, and the little gold clips probably couldn't be fixed. She perched naked on one of the bar stools at the kitchen counter and thought about what she'd seen in his eyes. When he came back to the kitchen a few moments later, he found her still sitting there, lost in her own thoughts. She looked up in surprise, and then regret as she saw him wearing jeans and a white shirt open at the neck. He had his briefcase in one hand and a sweater in the other. The briefcase told her that he was going to the office after all, in spite of the fact that it was Sunday, and the sweater told her that he would be staying late. None of it was good news to Wendy.

"Will I see you later?" She hated herself for the question. She was asking . . . begging. Damn his hide. And worse yet, he was shaking his head.

"I'll probably work till two or three in the morning and then go back to my place. I have to dress there in the morning anyway." The brief gentleness of a few moments before was gone. He was Michael again, running away. She had already lost him in the ten or fifteen minutes since they'd made love. The situation was hopeless, yet she hated to give up. That kind of rejection just made her want to try harder and give more.

"I'll see you in the office tomorrow then." She tried not to sound miserable, even to smile as she walked him to the door, but she was glad when he left her quickly, with a vague peck on her forehead and without looking back, because when she closed the door she was already crying. Michael Hillyard was a lost cause.

Chapter 16

The countryside flew past them as he floored the accelerator of the black Porsche. It was a delicious feeling, almost like flying, and there was no one else on the road. They took a drive almost every Sunday now. Peter picked her up around eleven, and they drove south as far as they wanted. Eventually they would stop somewhere for lunch, and then walk for a while hand in hand, laugh at each other's stories of the past, and eventually drift back toward home. It was a ritual she had come to love. And in an odd way she was coming to love him. Peter was very special in her life now. He was giving her back all her dreams, along with some new ones.

Today they had stopped near Santa Cruz at a little country restaurant decorated like a French inn. They had had quiche and salade nicoise for lunch, with a very dry white wine. Nancy was getting used to meals like this. It was a long way from New England and county fairs and blue beads. Peter Gregson was a man of considerable sophistication. It was one of the things Nancy liked about him. He made her feel wonderfully worldly, even in her bandages and funny hats. But one could see more of her face now. The whole lower half of her face had been finished. Only the area around the eyes was still heavily taped, and the dark glasses covered most of it. Her forehead, too, was for the most part obscured. Yet from what one could see, he had not only wrought a miracle, he had done an exquisite job. Nancy herself was aware of it, and just knowing how she was beginning to look had given her an air of greater self-confidence. She wore her hats at a jauntier angle now and bought more striking clothes, of a more sophisticated cut, than she had worn before. She had lost another five pounds and looked long and sleek, like a beautiful jungle cat. She even played with her new voice now. She liked the new person she was becoming.

"You know, Peter, I've been thinking of changing my name." She said it with a sheepish little smile over the last of their wine. Somehow it had sounded less foolish when she'd discussed it with Faye. Now she was sorry she'd brought it up. But Peter instantly put her at ease.

"That doesn't surprise me. You're a whole new girl, Nancy. Why not a new name? Has anything special come to mind?" He looked at her fondly as he lit a Don Diego from Dunhill's. She had grown fond of their aroma, particularly after a good meal. Peter was introducing her to all the better things in life. It was a delightful way to grow up. "So, who's my new friend? What's her name?"

"I'm not sure yet, but I've been thinking of Marie Adamson. How does it sound to you?"

He thought for a moment and then nodded. "Not bad . . . in fact, I like it. I like it very much. How did you come to it?"

"My mother's maiden name, and my favorite nun."

"My, what an exotic combination." They both laughed and Nancy sat back with a small, satisfied smile. Marie Adamson. She liked it a lot. "When were you thinking of changing it?" He watched her through the thin veil of blue smoke.

"I don't know. I hadn't decided."

"Why not start using it right away? See how you like it. You know, you could use it on your work." He looked excited at the idea. He was always excited when he spoke of her work or his. And much to her astonishment and pleasure, he viewed her work and his in the same light, as though they were equally important. He had come to respect her talent a great deal. "Seriously, Nancy, why don't you?"

"What? Sign Marie Adamson on the prints I give you?" She was amused at how seriously he was taking her. He and Faye were the only ones who saw her work.

"You might broaden your horizons a little."

This was not a new subject between them, and she put up a hand and shook her head with a firm little smile. "Now don't start that again."

"I'm going to keep at it until you get sensible on the subject, Nancy. You can't hide your light under a bushel forever. You're an artist, whether you work in paints or on film. It's a crime to hide your work the way you've been doing. You have to have a show."

"No." She took another swallow of wine and looked out at the view. "I've had all the shows I want to have."

"Wonderful. I put you back together so you can hide in an apartment for the rest of your life, taking photographs for me."

"Is that such a terrible fate?"

"For me, no." He smiled gently at her and took her hand in his. "But for you, yes. You have so much talent, don't be stingy with it. Don't hide it. Don't do this to yourself. Why not have a show as Marie Adamson? There's anonymity in that. If you don't like the show or what it brings you, you scratch the name of Marie Adamson, and go back to taking pictures for me. But at least give it a try. Even Garbo was a success before she became a recluse. Give yourself a chance at least." There was a pleading note in his voice that pulled at her. And he had a good point about the anonymity of her new name. Maybe that would make a difference. But she felt as though they'd been over this ground a thousand times before. Something froze in her at the thought of being a professional artist again. It made her feel vulnerable. It made her . . . think of Michael.

"I'll think about it." It was the most positive response he'd ever gotten on the subject, and he was pleased.

"See that you do . . . Marie." He looked at her with a broad smile, and she giggled.

"It feels funny to have a new name."

"Why? You have a new face. Does that feel funny too?"

"Not really. Not anymore. Thanks to Faye, and to you, I've gotten used to it." Most women would have given their right arms to get used to that face, and she knew it.

"Should I start calling you Marie?" He was only teasing, until he saw a new light in her eyes. They were mischievous and wonderful and alive.

"As a matter of fact . . . yes. I think I'll try it on for size."

"Perfect. Marie. If I slip, step on my foot."

"No problem. I'll just hit you with my camera."

He signaled for the check and they exchanged a long, tender smile. After lunch they walked through the small beach town, peeking into shops, poking into narrow alleys, and wandering into galleries when something looked interesting. And everywhere they went Fred ran along behind them, equally accustomed to his Sunday ritual. He always waited in the car when they had lunch, and then shared their walks with them afterwards.

"Tired?" He looked at her carefully after they had meandered for an hour. Although she was gradually building up her endurance, Peter, more than anyone, was aware of how easily she tired. But in the seventeen months since the accident, she had had fourteen operations. It would be another year before she felt fully her old self, although anyone who didn't know her well would never suspect her occasional fatigue.

She always looked vivacious, but an hour's walk still required an effort. "Ready to go back?"

"Much as I hate to admit it, yes." She nodded ruefully, and he tucked her hand in his.

"A year from now, Marie, you'll outrun me in any race."

She laughed at both the idea and his easy use of her new name. "I'll accept that as a challenge."

"I'm afraid you'll win. You have one great advantage on your side."

"And what's that?"

"Youth."

"So do you." She said it earnestly, and he laughed with a shake of his handsome head.

"May you always see me through such kindly eyes, my dear." But as he looked away there was a sad shadow lurking in his eyes. She caught only a glimpse of it, but she knew. There was no denying the age difference between them. No matter how much they enjoyed each other, how close they became, one could not deny the twenty-three-year gap. But she found that she didn't mind it; she liked it. She had told him that before, and sometimes he even believed her; it depended on his mood. But he never admitted just how much it bothered him. She was the first girl who had made him want to be young again, to throw away a decade or perhaps two, decades he had cherished but now found a burden in the face of her youth. "Nancy—" The new name was suddenly forgotten as he looked at her with great seriousness, a question in his eyes.

"Yes?"

"Do you . . . do you still miss him?" There was such pain in Peter's eyes when he asked that she wanted to put her arms around him and tell him it was all right. But she couldn't lie to him either. She was surprised to find that the question brought tears to her eyes as she shrugged and then nodded.

"Sometimes. Not always." It was an honest answer.

"Do you still love him?"

She looked very hard into his eyes before answering. "I don't know. I remember him as he was, and us as we were, but none of that is real anymore. I'm not the same person, and he can't be either. The accident must have left a mark on him. Maybe if we saw each other again we'd both find that we had nothing left together. Like this, it's hard to say. You're left with only dreams of the past. Sometimes I wish I could see him just to get it over with. But I . . . I've come to understand that I never will . . . see him again." She said it with difficulty but finality. "So I just have to put the dreams away."

"That's not so easily done." There was pain in his own eyes as he spoke to her. And suddenly she began to wonder if he had been through something similar. Perhaps that was why he always understood what she felt.

"Peter, how come you've never married?" They walked slowly toward the beach, with Fred at their heels, all but forgotten now. "Or shouldn't I ask?"

"No, you can ask. A lot of sensible reasons, I suppose. I'm too selfish. I've been too busy. My work has swallowed up my life. All of that. Also, I move too fast, I'm not really the sort to settle down."

"Somehow I don't believe that." She looked at him closely, and he smiled.

"Neither do I. But there's some truth in all those reasons." He seemed to pause for a long time, and then he sighed. "There are other reasons too. I was in love with someone for twelve years. She was a patient when we met, and I was very taken with her, but I avoided getting involved. She never knew how I felt until . . . until much later. We seemed destined to be constantly thrown together. At every party, every dinner, every social or professional function. Her husband was a doctor, too. You see, she was married. I resisted 'temptation,' as it were, for a year. And then I couldn't anymore. We fell in love, and we had a beautiful time together.

"We talked about getting married, running off together, having a child. But we never did. We simply went on as we were—for twelve years. I can't understand how we did it for so long, but I suppose things happen that way. They just go on and on and on, and one day you wake up and ten years have gone by, or eleven, or twelve. We kept finding reasons not to get married, for her not to get divorced—because of her husband, my career, her family. There were always reasons. Perhaps we preferred it the way it was. I don't know." He had never admitted that before, and Nancy watched him as he spoke. He was looking out at the horizon, and he seemed a thousand miles away even as he talked to her.

"Why did you stop seeing each other? Or—" Maybe they hadn't. As the thought came to her, she blushed. Maybe she was prying. It was possible that there was a great deal about Peter's life that she didn't know, and had no right to know. She had never thought of that before. "I'm sorry. I shouldn't have asked."

"Don't be ridiculous." His eyes and his thoughts came back to her with their usual gentleness. "There's nothing you can't ask me. No, she died. Four years ago, of cancer. I was with her most of the time, except on the last day. I think . . . I think Richard knew at the end. It didn't matter anymore. We had both lost her, and I think he was grateful that she didn't leave him in the years before. We mourned her together. She was an incredible woman. She was . . . very much like you." There were tears in his eyes when he looked at her, and Nancy felt tears come to her own eyes. Without thinking, she reached up with a careful hand and wiped the tears softly from his cheeks, and then without taking her hand away from his cheek she moved gently toward him and kissed him, softly, on the lips. They stood there for a long, silent moment, very close, with their eyes closed, and then she felt Peter's arms go around her, and she felt more at peace than she had in over a year. She felt safe. He held her that way for what seemed like a very long time, and then he bent his face down to hers and kissed her with the pent-up passion of four years. He had had other women since Livia had died, but there had been no one he had loved. Not until Nancy. "Do you know that I love you?" He stepped back and looked down at her with a smile she had never seen before. It made her feel at once happy and sad, because she wasn't sure she was ready yet to give him all that he was giving her. She loved him, but not . . . not the way his eyes told her he loved her.

"I love you, too, Peter. In my own peculiar way."

"That'll do for now." Livia had told him that at first, too. It was frightening, sometimes, how much alike they were. "You know, Faye helped me a great deal when she died. That was why I thought she'd be good for you." She had also helped him in other ways, but that didn't matter, not now.

"You were right. She's been wonderful. You both have." She took his hand then, and they began to walk back up the beach. "Peter . . . I . . . I don't know how to say this, but . . . I don't want to hurt you. I do love you, but I'm still packing up my past. Piece by piece, bit by bit. It may still take me a little time."

"I'm in no hurry. I'm a man of great patience."

"Good. Because I want you to be there when I'm ready."

"I'll be there. Don't worry." And the way he said it made her feel happy and warm. She wondered if perhaps she did love him more than she knew. And then as they walked along, she had a sudden thought. It frightened her and excited her, but she knew that she wanted to do it. He caught the sparkle in her eye when she looked up at him as they got back to the car. "And just what exactly do you have up your sleeve?"

"Never mind."

"Oh, God. Now what?" Several weeks before she had phoned him one morning at dawn, to tell him he had to get up to watch the sensational sunrise. "Nancy . . . no, Marie. From now on, it's Marie, and only Marie. But tell me, is Marie as outrageous as Nancy?"

"More so. She has all kinds of new ideas."

"Oh, no, spare me." But he didn't look as though he wanted to be spared. Not for a moment. "A little hint maybe? Just a small one?" But she was shaking her head and laughing at him as Fred hopped onto her lap and Peter started the car. "Well, I have an idea for you myself. The work on your face will be done by the end of the year. How about starting the new year with a show of the photographic artwork of Marie Adamson? Will you agree to that?"

"I might." She was actually beginning to like the idea, and something had happened that afternoon to make her feel brave again. Maybe telling him how she felt about Michael, hearing about the woman he had loved . . . being in his arms, being kissed by a man again. "I'll think about the show."

"No. Promise me. In fact—" He took the key out of the ignition, slipped it under him on the seat, and turned to smile at her. "I won't take you home until you agree to a show, and I hope you're too much of a lady to wrestle me for the key."

"Okay. You win." She ruffled Fred's fur and laughed. "I give up. I'll have a show."

"As easy as that?" He was stunned.

"As easy as that. But just how do you propose I go about getting myself shown?"

"Leave that to me. Is that a deal?"

"Yes, sir, it is." She trusted him with her work as much as she had with her face and her life.

"Darling, you won't regret it." He gently took her face in his hands, kissed her, and started the car again. It had been a beautiful day.

They drove home slowly along the coast, and Peter regretfully stopped the car in front of her house at six o'clock. He hated to see the day end. But he wanted her to rest.

"Okay, young lady. Get a good night's sleep. I want to see you in the office bright and early tomorrow." He was removing more of the bandages the next day, and two more operations were scheduled for the next two months. But by December she would be through with surgery, and in January she would be 'unveiled.'

"Do you want to come up?" She wasn't really sure she wanted him to, and was slightly relieved when he said no.

"We'll have dinner sometime this week. I'll have some news by then about the show."

"I won't be disappointed if you don't."

He smiled as she and Fred got out of the car, and she waved as she walked into the building. But she was already thinking of something else. She had thought of it on the beach as they walked back to the car, and now she knew it was something she had to do. Something she wanted to do. She walked straight to the closet without taking off her coat, and reached behind her clothes until she found it. She pulled it out into the hallway and looked at it for a long time before opening it. It was dusty, and she was almost afraid to open it, but she had to. Slowly, she pulled at the zipper, and the large black artist's portfolio opened at her feet, revealing sketches, a few small paintings, and some unfinished work. But at the top of the pile was what she was looking for. She sank down onto the floor and looked at it thoughtfully. She had intended it to be Michael's wedding present, a year and a half ago. The landscape with the boy hidden in the tree. She sat there holding it, and slowly the tears slid down her face. It had taken eighteen months to face that again. But she had now, and she was going to finish it. For Peter.

Chapter 17

It was a brisk, chilly day as Marie pulled down the brim of her white fedora, raised the collar of her bright red wool coat, and walked the last few blocks to Faye Allison's office. Fred was at her side, as always, and his collar and leash were exactly the same red as her coat. Nancy smiled down at him as they turned the last corner. She was in high spirits, which even the fog couldn't dampen. She ran up the steps to Faye's office, and let herself in.

"Hello! I'm here!" Her voice sang out in the warm, cozy house, and a moment later there was a quick answer from upstairs. Marie slipped out of her coat. She was wearing a simple white wool dress with a gold pin Peter had given her a few months before. Almost absentmindedly, she glanced in the mirror and pulled her hat to a jauntier angle and then smiled at what she saw. The glasses were at last gone, and she could finally see eyes when she looked in the mirror. Only a few narrow bands of tape remained, high on her forehead. And in a few weeks they would be gone, too. Finished. The job was done.

"Pleased with what you see, Nancy?" She suddenly

noticed Faye standing behind her, an affectionate smile on her face, and she nodded.

"Yes, I guess I am. I'm even used to myself now. But you're not!" There was mischief in her eyes as she turned and grinned impishly at her friend.

"What do you mean?"

"You keep calling me 'Nancy.' It's Marie now, remember? It's official."

"I'm sorry." Faye shook her head and led the way into the cozy room where they always talked. "I keep slipping."

"You certainly do." But Marie didn't look upset as she slid into her favorite chair. "I guess old habits are hard to break." Her face grew somber as she said the words, and Faye waited for the rest of her thoughts. "I've been thinking of that a lot lately. But I think I'm finally over him." She said it quietly, looking into the fire.

"Michael?" Marie only nodded and then finally looked up with great seriousness in her face. "What makes you think you're over him?"

"I think I decided to be. I don't have much choice. The fact of it is, Faye, it's been almost two years since the accident. Nineteen months to be exact. He hasn't found me. He didn't tell his mother to go to hell, that he had to be with me no matter what. Instead he just let it go." Her eyes looked for Faye's and then held fast. "He let me go. Now I have to let him go."

"That's not easy. You've expected a lot of him for a long time."

"Too long. And he let me down."

"How does that make you feel about yourself?"

"Okay, I guess. I'm mad at him, not at me."

"You're not angry at yourself anymore for your deal with his mother?" Faye was pressing a tender area and she knew it, but the ground had to be covered.

"I had no choice." The voice was cool and hard.

"But you don't reproach yourself?"

"Why should I? Do you suppose Michael reproaches himself that he let me down? That he never bothered to come to me after the accident? Do you think it's given him sleepless nights?"

"Is it still giving you sleepless nights, Nancy? That's what interests me."

"Marie, damn it. And no, it's not. I decided to put the dreams away. I've lived with this nonsense for too long." She sounded convincing, but Faye was still not entirely sure how the girl felt.

"So now what?" What would take Michael's place? Or who? Peter?

"Now I work. First, I take a vacation in the Southwest, over the Christmas holiday. There are some beautiful areas I want to photograph. I've already made my plans. Arizona, New Mexico. I might fly into Mexico for a couple of days." She looked pleased as she said it, but there was still something hard in her face, masking something sad. She had had another loss. She had finally let herself lose Michael. It had taken a very long time. "I'll be gone for about three weeks. That ought to take care of the holidays pretty nicely."

"And then what?"

"Work, work, and more work. That's all I care about right now. Peter got the show all set up for me. It's going to be in January. And you'd better be there!"

Faye smiled. "You don't think I'd miss it, do you?"

"I hope not. I've picked out some work for the show that I really love. You haven't seen most of it, nor has Peter. I hope he likes it too."

"He will. He loves everything you do. Which brings up a question, Nan . . . sorry, Marie. What about Peter? How do you feel about all that?"

Marie sighed and then looked back into the fire. "I feel a lot of different things about Peter."

"Do you love him?"

"In a way."

"Could he ever replace Michael in your life?"

"Maybe. I keep trying to let him take Michael's place, but something stops me. I'm not ready. I don't know, Faye . . . I feel guilty not to be giving him more. He does so much for me. And . . . I know how much he cares."

"He's a very patient man."

"Maybe too patient. I'm afraid to hurt him." She looked into Faye's eyes again, and her own were troubled. "I care about him a great deal."

"Then you'll just have to see what happens. Maybe you'll feel freer now that you've decided to let Michael go out of your life." Faye saw the muscles tighten around Marie's mouth as she heard the words. "Marie? You're not giving up on people are you? Giving up on love?"

"No. Why should I?" But the answer was too quick and too glib.

"You shouldn't. Michael failed you. He's one man, not all men. Don't forget that. There's someone out there for you. Maybe Peter, maybe someone else. But there's someone. You're a beautiful girl, and you're twenty-three years old. You have a whole life ahead of you."

"That's what Peter says, too." But she didn't look as though she believed it. And then she looked up at Faye with a nervous little smile that masked both fear and sorrow. "I made another decision, too."

"And what's that?"

"About us. I think I've about done it, Faye. I've said all I want to for a while. I'm ready to go out there, work my ass off, and beat the world."

"Why not just enjoy it?" There was something about the girl that still worried her. She had given up on something. There was something she no longer believed in. She had been betrayed, and in a sense she was quitting. She was ready to fight for her work, but not for herself. "You've been given a wonderful gift, Marie. The gift of beauty. Don't just hide that behind a camera."

But Marie was looking at her with marble-hard eyes. "It wasn't a gift, Faye. I paid for it with everything I had."

They exchanged Merry Christmases as she left, but there was a tinselly echo to the words, an emptiness that still bothered Faye as Marie Adamson pulled at her white fedora and walked off with a jaunty wave back at her friend of two years. It was almost as though she were saying good-bye to those two years and walking into a new life, leaving behind everything she had once loved.

Chapter 18

When Marie left Faye's office she caught a cab and
headed straight to Union Square. She had already
made the reservation; all she had to do now was stop
off and pay for the ticket. It would be the first trip
she had taken in years, the first since the weekend she
and Michael had spent in Bermuda. It had been
Easter and . . . She forced the thought from her mind
as the cab headed down Post Street into the downtown traffic. Fred sat on her lap staring at the cars
passing by and occasionally turning to look at his
mistress. He sensed something different; there was an
electricity about her that even the little dog could
feel as she pulled a cigarette out of her handbag and
lit it.

"Right here, miss?" The driver had stopped on the
corner of Powell and Post, next to the Saint Francis
Hotel, and Marie quickly nodded.

"This will be fine." She paid the fare, opened the
door of the cab, and let Fred hop out onto the pavement. She quickly followed, stubbed out the cigarette, and looked around. The ticket office was only

a few steps away, and she was rapidly inside. For once, there wasn't even a line, but it was still early in the day. Her appointments with Faye were always at eight forty-five. Were . . . had been . . . She suddenly realized again that she was through now. Free. Finished. Done. She was no longer seeing a psychiatrist. The thought frightened her a little. She felt both liberated and lonely, like celebrating and crying all at once.

"May I help you?" The girl behind the counter looked at her with a smile, and Marie smiled back. "Are you picking up tickets?"

"Yes, I am. I made reservations last week. Adams . . . McAllister." It was strange using the old name again; she hadn't in two months. But even the trip was symbolic. Legally, her name would be changed on January first. When she returned she would no longer be Nancy McAllister, she would be Marie Adamson, for good. But when she left she would still be Nancy. It was almost like a wedding trip, all by herself. It was the final step in the endless process that had taken almost two years. Marie Adamson was finally, officially going to be born. And Nancy McAllister could be forgotten forever. Hell, Michael had forgotten her; now she could forget her too. There was no one left to remember. Peter had seen to that. No one who had ever known her before would recognize her now. The delicate, perfectly etched face was someone other women dreamed of being, but no one she had known for the past twenty-four years. She wasn't a stranger anymore, but neither was she

Nancy McAllister. And the voice was different, too, smoother, deeper, more controlled. It was a subtle voice with sexual overtones, and she liked the way people listened to her now, as though she had more to say now that she had a different way of saying it. Her hands were graceful and delicate, her movements smoother and more mature after the ballet classes Peter had finally let her take once his work was far enough along. Yoga had added to the whole. And all of it completed the picture of Marie Adamson.

"That'll be a hundred and ninety-six dollars." The girl glanced at the computer and then the customer standing before her. She couldn't take her eyes off her—the perfect features, dazzling smile, and a grace when she moved that held everyone's attention. Everything about her made you want to ask, "who is she?" Marie wrote out her check, received her ticket, and walked back out into the December sunlight of Union Square. She held Fred in her arms so he wouldn't get stepped on, and smiled to herself as she wandered across the square. It was a beautiful day and she had a beautiful life. She was going away over the holidays; she was through with all those endless operations; she was starting a new life, a new career; she had an apartment she loved, a man who loved her. She couldn't ask for much more. She strolled into I. Magnin with a smile on her face and a bounce in her step, and decided to buy herself something pretty. An early Christmas present for herself, or maybe for the trip. She wandered from floor to floor, trying on hats, bracelets, scarves, jackets, handbags, a pair of boots, and a funny pair of gold lamé shoes. She finally settled on a soft white cashmere sweater, which with her silken skin and rich, dark hair made her look almost like Snow White. The thought amused her. And Peter would like it. The sweater molded her figure in a pleasing sort of way. Even her shape had changed in the last year, with the ballet and yoga; her body seemed to have hardened and stretched until she looked long and lean and wonderfully lithe.

She made her way to the main floor again, looking at the displays, watching the people, and finally she stopped to buy a box of chocolates for Faye. They were a suitably festive gift for the last day of therapy. She wrote on the card only, "Thank you. Love, Marie." What more could she say? Thank you for helping me forget Michael? Thank you for helping me survive? Thank you . . . As she played with the thoughts, she suddenly stopped. She looked as though she had seen a ghost, and when the saleswoman handed her back her charge card, she only continued to stare. Ben Avery stood just a few feet away, looking over some very expensive women's luggage. Marie remained where she was for what seemed like an eternity, and then edged closer. She had to see him, touch him, hear what he was saying. For an insane moment, she wondered if he would recognize her; she prayed that he would, and then she knew that he wouldn't and forced herself to be glad. This way she could watch him, stand near him, for as long as she wanted. She wondered how long it had been since he'd seen Michael, if he'd taken the job with the firm. She sidled up next to him and began fingering the suede attaché cases next to the pieces he was examining. Her eyes never left his face, and then suddenly he turned to look at her and smiled his old easy smile in her direction. But there wasn't even a glimmer of recognition; instead he looked her over admiringly and then reached out a hand to Fred.

"Hi there, little fella." The voice was so familiar that it made her feel almost weak, but she only stood there, feeling the warmth of his hand near hers as he patted the dog. She never would have imagined that just seeing a friend of Michael's would do this to her. But this was the first link she'd had with him since . . . She blinked back the tears and looked at the bags Ben had been looking over. Without thinking her hand went to the chain around her neck that he had given her on her wedding night. She still wore it.

"Buying Christmas gifts?" She felt foolish making chitchat with him, but she wanted to talk to him, and once again wondered if he'd recognize her, this time by her voice. But even she knew how different she sounded now. And again he looked at her with the blank easy smile passed between two strangers.

"Yes, for a young lady, and I can't decide what to get."

"What's she like?"

"Terrific."

Marie laughed. It was so like Ben. She almost wanted to ask him if it was serious this time, but she couldn't.

"She's got sort of red hair, and she's . . . about your height." He was looking Marie over again, and his eyes roamed over her figure almost hungrily. She didn't know whether to laugh or be upset, it was all so typically Ben.

"Are you sure she wants luggage?" It seemed a dull gift to Marie. She was hoping for something more exciting from Peter. Like maybe a new lens.

"We're going to be taking a trip together, so I thought . . . And the trip is kind of a surprise. I want to hide the tickets in the luggage."

Five hundred dollars on imported luggage to hide some tickets? Benjamin Avery, such extravagance! The last two years must have been good to him. "She's a lucky girl."

"No, I'm the lucky guy."

"Is this a honeymoon?" Marie was embarrassed at her own nosiness, but it was wonderful getting all this news of him, and maybe . . . maybe he'd . . . She kept her smile cool, pleasant, and detached as he shook his head.

"No. Just a business trip. But she doesn't know about it yet. Well, what do you think? The brown suede, or the dark green?"

"The brown suede with the red stripe. I think it's gorgeous."

"So do I." He nodded happily at Marie's choice and signaled to the salesgirl. He was taking three pieces, and asked her to ship them airmail to New York. Then he did live there. She had wondered. "Thank you for your help, er . . . uh . . . Miss . . ."

"Adamson. I thoroughly enjoyed it, and I apologize if I asked too many questions. The holidays always have a strange effect on me."

"Me too. But it's such a nice time of year. Even in New York, and that's saying a lot."

"Is that where you live?"

"When I'm home. I travel a great deal for my job."

That still didn't tell her if he was working for Michael, but she knew she couldn't ask. And suddenly, it made her ache, just standing there, being so near him, wanting to know about someone who no longer existed for her anyway—or shouldn't have. And then he looked at her again, as though something about her had bothered him. For a moment she felt her heart stop, but his smile told her that he had no idea who she was. She pulled at her hat a little to assure that he couldn't see the last of the tape and held Fred a little closer in her arms as Ben continued to stare at her.

"I know this is a crazy thing to ask," he said, "but . . . could I invite you somewhere for a drink? I'm leaving on a plane in a few hours, but we could hop over to the St. Francis, if . . ."

She returned the smile, but she was already shaking her head. "I'm afraid I have a plane to catch too. But thank you for the offer, Mr. Avery."

And then his smile faded slowly. "How did you know my name?"

"I heard the salesgirl say it."

She was quick with the response, and he shrugged and then looked at her with regret. She was an incredibly beautiful girl. And no matter how much he had come to love Wendy in the three months since their affair began, he could still have a drink with a pretty girl. It was too bad she was leaving town, too. And then he had a thought. "Where's your plane to, Miss Adamson?"

"Santa Fe, New Mexico."

He looked as disappointed as a schoolboy, and she laughed at the look on his face. "Damn. I was hoping you were going to New York. We could at least have enjoyed the flight together."

"I'm sure the young lady with the luggage would have appreciated that." Her eyes scolded him, but only a little, and they both laughed this time.

"Touché. Well, maybe next time."

"Do you come to San Francisco often?" She was intrigued again.

"No, but I will." And then with a look at the luggage and a smile, he added, "We will. My firm is doing a big project here. I'll probably be spending more time here than in New York."

"Then perhaps we'll meet again." But her voice sounded almost sad. It was only Ben after all. It didn't matter how often she saw him, he still wasn't Michael. The salesgirl broke into her reverie, and she realized it was time to go. She only looked at him for a long moment as he wrote out the check for the amount the salesgirl had tallied up, and then silently she squeezed his arm. He looked up in surprise, and she barely whispered, "Merry Christmas," before disappearing from where they had stood chatting for almost half an hour. He looked around when he had finished the check and was disappointed to find her gone. She had left so abruptly. He looked around the store as best he could through the throngs of Christmas shoppers, but she was nowhere to be seen. She had left by the side entrance, and was just then hailing a cab. She felt tired and heavyhearted. It had been a long morning.

She gave the driver the vet's address, dropped Fred off there, and jumped back in the cab to go home. She was already packed. All she had to do was pick up her bags and head for the airport. She felt a little unkind leaving Fred behind, but she didn't really want him with her this time, she was making too many stops in the three weeks she'd be gone. It was a trip she had to make alone. Her last moments as Nancy McAllister, the end of an old life, the beginning of a new. She took a last look around her apartment before she left, as though she expected never again to see it in quite the same way; and as she closed the door softly behind her, she whispered one word. She said it to herself, and to Ben, and to Michael, and to all those she had once loved or known or been . . . good-bye. There were tears in her eyes as she walked swiftly down the stairs with her camera bag and her suitcase tightly held in one hand.

Chapter 19

She wouldn't let Peter come to the airport. Just as she had left alone, now she wanted to return alone. There had been something magical about the trip. It was a time of peace and hard work. She had spoken to almost no one as she traveled; she had merely observed, and gotten lost in her own thoughts. But as the days went by, her thoughts were lighter than they had been on the day she left San Francisco. Seeing Ben Avery again had been a blow. It had revived too many memories. But that was over now. She knew it. She could live with it. Her new life had begun.

Christmas day got lost among the others, as she took photographs in the snow around Taos. She was tempted to ski, but she didn't. She had promised Peter to avoid the risk of an accident, or too much sun. And she had kept her word. So had he. She had told him when she was getting in but asked him not to be there, and he wasn't. She looked around the airport with relief. She was alone in an army of strangers. It was comforting to be lost in the crowd. It made her feel invisible and safe. She had spent a lot of time learning to be invisible in the last year and a half. Heavily bandaged most of the time, she had felt it important not to be seen. Now she attracted more attention than she had swathed in bandages: the very way she moved, the clothes she wore, the black stetson she had bought on her trip to hide the last bandages on her forehead, the black Levis and sheepskin coat, all contributed to her visibility simply because it was difficult to hide the kind of looks she had. But she was not yet aware of just how striking she was.

She got a cab just outside the terminal, gave the driver her address, and settled back, with a sigh, against the seat. She was tired. It was almost eleven o'clock, and she had gotten up at five that morning to take pictures. She looked at her watch and promised herself to be in bed by twelve. She had to. Tomorrow was another big day. She had stayed away right up to the last moment. At nine the next morning, Peter would remove the last of the tape. No one else had been aware that she was still wearing tape. But she knew. And now even that would be gone. She was going to spend the morning alone after she left his office, and then they were meeting again for a celebration lunch. No more operations, no more stitches, no more tape. She was just like everyone else now. Her new name had even become legal. Marie Adamson had been born.

The driver let her out in front of her building, and she walked slowly up the stairs, as though expecting to find a different apartment than the one she had left. But it was the same, and she was surprised to feel a sense of anticlimax. Then she laughed at herself. What did she want? She had told Peter not to meet her. Did she expect a brass band hiding in her bedroom? Peter under the bed? Something. She wasn't sure what. She peeled off her clothes and stretched out on the bed thinking of what she had come home to. She had a lot on her mind. What would it mean now that Peter's work on her face would be finished? What if she never saw him again? But that was crazy and she knew it. He had arranged the exhibition of her work, which opened the day after the final "unveiling" of her face. He cared about her as a person, not just as a reconstruction job. She knew that. But she felt oddly insecure as she lay there in the dark, wanting someone to tell her that everything was all right, that she wasn't alone, that she'd make it as Marie Adamson.

"Oh damn. What does it matter if I'm alone?" She stood up briskly and stared at herself in the mirror as she said the words, and then in irritation she picked up her camera and almost caressed it. That was all she needed. She was just tired from the trip. It was stupid to worry about being lonely, about her future, about Peter. . . . With a sharp sigh, she climbed into bed. She had better things to think about, like her work.

She woke up shortly after six the next morning and was dressed and out of the house by seven thirty. When she arrived at Peter's office at nine, she had already been to the produce market and then the flower market to take pictures. She had added another shot to her series on Chinatown. And she had picked up Fred at the vet.

"My, don't you look chipper this morning—and beautiful. That's a marvelous coat." Peter looked admiringly at the full-length coyote she had bought at a bargain price on a reservation in New Mexico. She wore it over jeans with a black turtleneck sweater and boots. And she had worn the black stetson until she got to his office. Now she held it in her hand for a moment, smiled at him in a way he had never seen before, and then poised over the wastebasket for only a fraction of a second, before crushing the hat into the bottom.

"And that, Dr. Gregson, is the last time I will ever wear a hat."

He nodded. He understood just how important the gesture was. "You won't ever have to again."

"Thanks to you." She wanted to kiss him, but her eyes told him what he needed to know, and as she looked at him she realized that she had missed him on her trip. He was someone different to her now. He would no longer be her doctor after that morning. He would be her friend, and whatever else she let him become. They had not yet resolved that, no matter how often he told her he loved her. She had not yet taken the last step, and he had never pushed her. "I missed you, Peter." She touched his arm softly as she sat down in the all too familiar chair, closed her eyes, and waited.

He watched her for a moment as he stood there, and then he took his usual seat on the little swivel stool in front of her. "You're in a hurry this morning."

"After twenty months, wouldn't you be too?"

"I know, darling, I know." She heard the clink of the delicate instruments in the little metal pan, and she felt the tape being pulled slowly from her forehead and her hairline. With every millimeter of skin it freed, she felt that much freer, until at last she felt nothing more, and she heard the little stool whoosh softly away from her. "You can open your eyes now, Marie. And go look in the mirror." She had made that trip a thousand times. At first only to see a tiny glimpse, a hint, a promise, and then bigger pieces of the puzzle. But she had never seen Marie Adamson's face free of tape, or stitches, or some reminder of what was being done. She had not seen her face completely bare since it had been the face of Nancy McAllister nearly two years before. "Go on. Take a look."

It was crazy. She was almost afraid to. But silently, she stood up and walked slowly to the mirror, and then she stood there with a broad smile, and a narrow river of tears gleaming on her face. He stood behind her, at a good distance. He wanted to leave her alone. This was her moment.

"Oh God, Peter, it's beautiful."

He laughed softly. "Not 'it's' beautiful, silly girl. You're beautiful. It is you, you know."

She could only nod and then turn to look at him. It wasn't so much that her face had changed without the few strips of tape on her forehead, but that it was over. She was entirely Marie now. "Oh Peter . . ." Without saying more, she walked into his arms and held him tight. They stood there that way in his office for a long time, and then he pulled away and gently wiped her tears. "Look, I can even get wet and I don't melt."

"And you can take the sun, though not excessively. And you can do anything you want to for the rest of your life. What's first on the agenda?"

"Work." She chuckled and sat down on the little swivel stool he had abandoned, and with her legs tucked up under her chin she spun herself around.

"God, she's going to break a leg in my office. That's all I need."

"If I do, I'm walking out of here anyway, love. I have a life to celebrate this morning."

"I'm glad to hear it." And apparently Fred was, too. He jumped up, wagged his tail, and barked, as though he had understood what she had said. They both laughed and Peter stooped to pat his head. "Are we still having lunch?"

There was an anxious look in his eyes and she was touched. She understood what he was feeling, too. Abandonment. Anxiety. Would she still want him in her life when she didn't need him anymore? He looked very vulnerable to her as he stood there, and she held out a hand to him. "Of course we're having lunch, silly. Peter . . ." Her eyes held fast to his. "There will always be time in my life for you. Always. I hope you know that. You're the only reason I have a life."

"No. Someone else is responsible for that." Marion Hillyard. But he knew how much she hated to hear the older woman's name, so he didn't say it. He never

understood why Marie reacted that way, but he
humored her on that point. "I'm glad I was around
to help. I always will be, if you need me . . . for . . .
for other things."

"Good. Then see that you feed me at twelve thirty."
The conversation had been serious enough. She stood
up and shrugged her way into the new coyote coat.
"Where shall we meet?"

He suggested a new restaurant down at the docks,
where they could watch the tugboats and ferries and
tankers cruising by on the bay, and the hills of
Berkeley beyond. "Does that sound all right to you?"

"It sounds perfect. I may just hang around down
there all morning and do some shooting."

"I'd be disappointed if you did anything else." He
swept open the examining room door with a bow, and
she winked as she left, but she did not go straight to
the docks as she had said. Instead, she went downtown
to shop. Suddenly, she wanted to buy something
fabulous to wear to lunch with Peter. It was the
most special day of her life, and she wanted to enjoy
every bit of it. In the cab, she glanced at her check-
book and was grateful for the money she had made
before Christmas on some of her work. It would
allow her to be extravagant for herself, and to buy
Peter something as well.

She found a pale fawn cashmere dress which molded
her figure breathtakingly beneath the fur coat, and she
stopped at the hairdresser and let him do her hair. It
was the first time in years that she had worn it back,
revealing her whole face. She bought big wonderful

gold earrings at the costume jewelry bar, and a beige satin rope with a gold seashell on it. Beige suede shoes and a bag, and the perfume she had always loved best, and she definitely looked ready for lunch with Dr. Peter Gregson. Or just about anyone else. She was a woman who would have stopped any man's heart.

Her last stop was at Shreve's where, as though by prearranged plan, she found precisely what she had wanted but hadn't known she would ever find. It was a little gold face made up as a watch fob, and she knew that Peter had a pocket watch he was fond of and occasionally wore. She would have the date engraved in it for him later, but for the moment this would have to do. She had it gift wrapped, hailed a cab, and arrived at the restaurant just as he was sitting down. She thought she might explode with joy as she watched his face while she approached. There were a number of others in the restaurant who watched her appreciatively too, but none with the tenderness of Peter Gregson.

"Is it really you?"

"Cinderella at your service. Do you approve?"

"Approve? I'm overwhelmed. What did you do all morning? Run around shopping?"

"But of course. This is a special day."

She did things to his feelings that he had thought couldn't be done. He wanted to kiss her there, in the restaurant. Instead he held tightly to her hand, and smiled a long happy smile. "I'm so glad you're happy, darling."

"I am. But not just because of the face. There's the show tomorrow, and . . . and my work, and my life

... and ... you." She said the last word very softly.

The moment meant so much to him that he could only make light of it. "I come after all those things, eh? What about Fred?"

They both laughed and he ordered Bloody Marys for the two of them, and then he thought better of it and changed the order to champagne.

"Champagne? Good heavens!"

"Why not? And I closed the office for the afternoon. I'm as free as can be—unless, of course—" He hadn't even thought of it—"you have other plans."

"Doing what for God's sake?"

"Working?" He felt sheepish for even asking.

"Don't be ridiculous. Let's go do something fun to-day."

He laughed at her answer. "Like what? What would you like to do most?"

She tried to think and couldn't come up with anything, and then she looked at him with a broad smile. "Go to the beach."

"In January?"

"Sure. This is California after all, not Vermont. We could drive over to Stinson, and go for a walk."

"All right. You're certainly easy to please." But beach walks with him had become special to her and she wanted a special place to give him her gift. She wasn't sure if she could hold out till then. But she did. She waited until late that afternoon, when they were walking hand in hand along the windswept beach. The fur coat protected her from the stiff breeze that was coming in with the fog.

"I have something for you, Peter." He looked at her

in surprise as she stopped walking, as though he didn't quite understand, and then she pulled out the little gift-wrapped box. "I'll have it engraved, if you like it."

"Marie, that's outrageous. You shouldn't . . . I didn't want . . ." He was touched and embarrassed as he opened the little box, and delighted when he saw the beautiful fob. He put an arm tightly around her shoulders. "Why did you do a thing like that?" he scolded softly.

"Because you're such a creep and you never do anything for me." He laughed at the mischievous look in her eyes and this time took her in his arms for a long, tender kiss that told her all that he felt. And this time, she kissed him as she never had before, with her body as well as her heart. It made him hungry for her in a way he could barely control.

"You'd better watch that, young lady, or I'll rape you here on the beach."

She swept open the coat with a teasing smile and laughed. "So?"

He only laughed back and pulled her into his arms again. What an extraordinary girl she was, and how well worth the wait she had been. He could let his feelings soar now: she was no longer his patient. "Darling . . . Marie. . . ." She silenced him with a long hungry kiss, and he pulled away for a moment, wondering if he was reading into her response the feelings he wanted to be there. But a current of desire was running between them that he knew he wasn't imagining. "Shall we . . . maybe we'd better go back."

She nodded quietly and followed him back to the car, but her expression wasn't as somber as his, and when they reached her apartment, she turned and looked at him with a smile. "I have something else for you, Peter. I'd like you to come upstairs if you have time."

"Are you sure?"

"Absolutely."

She walked up the stairs ahead of him in silence, and when she opened the door of the apartment, she didn't turn on the lights. She walked straight across the living room, turned her easel away from the window, and then turned on the light. What he saw was her landscape with the boy sitting partially hidden in the foliage of a tree. She had finished it for him before she left on her vacation, but she had been saving it for this day, if not for this moment. He looked at her now as though he didn't understand.

"It's for you, Peter. I started it a long time ago. And I . . . I finished it for you."

"Oh darling—" He walked toward it with bright eyes and a gentle look on his face, as though he couldn't believe what she'd done for him. It had been a day filled with emotion and surprises. For both of them. "I can't take that. I already have so much of your work. You give it all to me, and then you have nothing left to exhibit."

"You have photographs, Peter. This is different. This is a sign of my rebirth. It's the first time I've painted again. And . . . this painting used to mean a great deal to me. I want you to have it. Please." There were tears in her eyes now, and he walked toward her and took her into his arms.

"It's exquisite. Thank you. I don't know what to say. You've been so good to me."

"You don't have to say anything." And then she kissed him in a way that said it all, and this time he was sure, too. He didn't need to ask. He simply walked into the bedroom with her and, trembling with desire, slowly slipped off her clothes. And in the soft light of twilight, with the music of the foghorns bleating softly in the distance, they made love.

Chapter 20

"Darling, can you zip me up?" She turned her graceful ivory back to him, and he kissed her shoulder.

"I would much rather zip you down than up."

"Now, now, Peter, we don't have time." Marie looked at him warningly and they both laughed. He was wearing a dinner jacket, and she had just put on a beautifully cut black dress with soft dolman sleeves and a narrow waist in a fabric that allowed one to see her silhouette but nothing more. It was a striking dress, and Peter was suitably dazzled.

"I hate to tell you this, my love, but no one is going to be looking at your work. They're all going to be looking at you."

"Oh yeah?"

He laughed at her obvious disbelief and straightened the tie he wore with a soft blue shirt and his dinner jacket. Together they made a very striking couple.

"Did they hang everything the way you wanted them to? I never got time to ask you." When he had awakened at eight that morning, she was already gone. But late that afternoon he had arrived at her apartment, and an hour in bed had shown them that they had only begun to feed their hunger for each other. Then they had shared a half hour in the bath, catching up on each other's day. It was almost as though they had lived this way for years.

She smiled at him as she watched him finish dressing. "Yes, they put everything up exactly the way I wanted. Thanks to you. I get the feeling you told them to do it my way 'or else.' You or Jacques." The gallery owner was one of Peter's oldest and closest friends. "I feel thoroughly spoiled. The complete '*artiste*.'"

"That's how you should feel. Your work is going to be very important, darling. You'll see."

And indeed she did. The reviews in the paper the next day were spectacular. They sat around in her apartment over morning coffee, and grinned at what they read.

"Didn't I tell you?" He looked even more pleased with himself than she did. "You're a star."

"You're crazy." She plunked herself on his lap with a grin and rumpled the paper.

"You wait. You'll have every photographer's agent in the country calling you by next week."

"Darling, you are out of your mind." But he wasn't too far off. She was getting calls from Los Angeles and Chicago by the following Monday. She couldn't get over it, but she was thoroughly enjoying the whole thing. And she was amused by every phone call she got. Until the call from Ben Avery. It came on a Thursday afternoon, when she was developing some film. She heard the phone ring and she wiped her hands and walked into the kitchen to answer it. She assumed it was Peter. He had said he would call to let her know what time he could see her that evening. He had some kind of meeting scheduled for late afternoon. But she had plenty of darkroom work to keep her busy; there was a veritable avalanche of orders coming in as a result of the show.

"Hello?"

"Miss Adamson?"

"Yes." She didn't recognize the voice, and the smile she had been wearing for Peter rapidly faded.

"I don't know whether we've met or not, but I met a Miss Adamson the last time I was here. At I. Magnin's. I was doing some Christmas shopping. . . . I bought some luggage, and . . ." He felt like a total ass, and for what seemed like an eternity she said nothing.

So it was Ben. Damn. How had he found her? And why had he bothered to?

"I . . . was that you?"

She was tempted to say no, but why lie? "I believe it might have been."

"Good. Well, at least we've met. I'm actually calling you because I've just seen your work at the Montpelier Gallery on Post Street. I'm enormously impressed, as is my associate, Miss Townsend."

Marie was suddenly curious. Was that the girl he had bought the luggage for? But she didn't feel she could ask. Instead she sighed and sat down. "I'm glad you liked it, Mr. Avery."

"You remember my name!"

Oh, Jesus. "I have a memory for those things."

"How fortunate for you. I have a memory like a sieve, and in my business that's no asset, believe me. In any case, I'd very much like to get together with you to discuss your work."

"In what sense?" What the hell was there to discuss?

"We're doing a medical center here in San Francisco, Miss Adamson. It's going to be an enormous project, and we'd like to use your work in every building as the central theme of the decor. We're not quite sure how, but we know we want your pictures. We'd like to work it out with you. This could be the assignment of your career." He said it with tremendous pride, and he was obviously waiting for a gasp at the other end of the line, a shriek of enthusiasm, anything but what he heard.

"I see. And what firm are you representing?" She waited, holding her breath, but she already knew the answer before he said the words.

"Cotter-Hillyard, in New York."

"Well, no thanks, Mr. Avery, it's just not my speed."

"Why not?" He sounded stunned. "I don't understand."

"I don't want to get into it with you, Mr. Avery, but I'm not interested."

"Can we get together and discuss this?"

"No."

"But I've already spoken to . . . I—"

"The answer is no. Thank you for your call." And

then, very quietly, she placed the receiver back into the cradle and walked back to the darkroom door. She wasn't going to do business with them. That was all she needed. She was through with Michael Hillyard. He didn't want her as his wife; she didn't want him as her employer. Or anything else.

The phone rang again before she had closed the darkroom door. She knew it would be Ben again, but she wanted to settle the matter once and for all. She strode back to the phone, picked it up, and almost shouted into it. "The answer is no. I already told you that." But the voice on the other end was not Ben's, it was Peter's.

"Good God, what have I done?" He was half laughing, half stunned, and Marie felt herself relax at the sound of his voice.

"Oh Christ. I'm sorry, darling. I just had someone call me with an annoying request."

"As a result of the show?"

"More or less."

"The gallery shouldn't be giving out your number to crackpots. Why don't they take the messages there?" He sounded upset.

"I think I'll suggest that to Jacques."

Peter was disturbed at the thought of some crazy calling her. "Are you all right?"

"I'm fine." But she sounded shaken, and he could hear it.

"Well, I'll be there in an hour. Don't answer the phone till I get there. I'll handle it if anyone calls after that."

"Thank you, my love."

They exchanged a few more words and then hung up, and she found herself feeling guilty for not telling him the truth about the call. Ben Avery was no crackpot, he just worked for Michael Hillyard. But she didn't want to tell Peter that that was what had unnerved her. He didn't need to know how shaky she still was on the subject of Michael. But she was getting better every day. And fortunately Ben didn't call again that night. He waited until the next morning. And then surprised her again as she got ready to go to work.

"Hi, Miss Adamson. Ben Avery again."

"Look. I thought we got this thing settled last night. I'm not interested."

"But you don't even know what you're not interested in. Why not have lunch with my associate and me, and we'll talk? It can't hurt, can it?"

Oh yes it can, Ben, oh yes it can. "I'm sorry, I'm busy." She wasn't giving an inch, and sitting in his hotel room, Ben rolled his eyes at Wendy. It was hopeless. And he couldn't understand why. What the hell did she have against Cotter-Hillyard? It didn't make sense.

"How about tomorrow?"

"Look, Ben . . . Mr. Avery . . . I won't do it. I'm not interested. And I don't want to discuss it with you, your associate, or anyone else. Is that quite clear?"

"Unfortunately, yes. But I think you're making a huge professional mistake. If you had an agent, he'd tell you just that."

"Well, I don't. So I don't have to listen to anyone but myself."

"That's your mistake, Miss Adamson. But we'll keep in touch."

"It's nice of you to be interested, but really, don't bother."

"All right, all right. But I'll drop you a card. If you change your mind, call me. Here or in New York. I'll be at the Saint Francis till the end of the month, and then back at my office in New York. There's still plenty of time to discuss this."

Maybe for you, but not for me. It's two years too late. "I'm afraid I don't agree." And once again, she hung up. This time she left the phone off the hook when she went back to the darkroom.

Chapter 21

It was a freezing February day as Ben Avery huddled turtlelike in his coat, and ran all the way from the subway exit to his office on Park Avenue. There would be snow by the end of the day—he could feel it in the air—and it seemed as though daylight had barely emerged. It was not quite eight o'clock in the morning. But he had an enormous amount of work to do. This would be his first day back from the coast, and the big meeting with Marion was scheduled for ten thirty that morning. He had mostly good news for her.

There were already a number of people in the lobby of the building and the elevator was almost full as he rode upstairs. Even at that hour, the business world was bustling. After the slower pace of San Francisco, and even Los Angeles, it was a shock to be back in the mainstream again. In Mecca, people started early. But at least there seemed to be no one else at work on his floor when he walked down the long, beige-carpeted, wood-paneled hall to the office Marion had given him when he'd joined the firm. It was smaller and far less handsome than Mike's office, but it was well put together. Marion spared no expense on the offices of Cotter-Hillyard.

Ben looked at his watch as he shrugged out of his coat and rubbed his hands together for a moment to get warm. There was no getting used to the freezing winds and damp cold of New York. Some winters he wondered if he'd ever get warm, and why he put up with it when there were cities like San Francisco, where people lived in a temperate dream world all year long. Even his office felt icy cold. But he had no time to waste. He emptied the contents of his briefcase on his desk, and began to sort through the papers and reports. Everything had gone splendidly. With one minor exception. And maybe something could still be done about that. He looked at his watch again after a few moments, grew pensive, and then decided to give it a try. It would be a major coup if he could come into the meeting with that one last piece of good news.

Ben had brought home a few samples of Marie Adamson's work; he had had to buy them at the gallery. But he had been sure they were worth the investment; once Marion and Michael got a look at her style, and saw just how good she was, Marion herself would probably get into the act, and talk the girl into signing. He smiled at the thought that would have sent shivers up Marie's spine.

He dialed her number and waited. It was an insane thing to do. In San Francisco, it was five fifteen in the morning, but maybe if he could get her half asleep . . .

"Hello?" She sounded groggy when she answered the phone.

"Uh . . . Miss . . . Miss Adamson, I'm terribly sorry to do this to you, but this is Ben Avery in New York. I'm going into a meeting this morning with the head of our firm, and I want more than anything to tell her that you'll work with us on the medical center. I just thought that—" But he already knew he had done the wrong thing. He could sense it in the silence that overwhelmed him from the other end, and then suddenly she came alive.

"At five o'clock in the morning? You called to tell me about your meeting with . . . for Chrissake, what kind of crazy business is this? I told you no, didn't I? What the hell do I have to do? Get an unlisted phone number?" As he listened to her, he closed his eyes, partially in embarrassment, and partially because of something else. The voice. It was strange. He didn't know why, but it sounded familiar. And it didn't sound like Marie Adamson. It was higher, younger, and different enough to strike a chord of memory that bothered him. Whom did she sound like? But he couldn't remember. "Haven't you gotten the message yet, for Chrissake?"

Her angry words brought him back to the present and the reality that he was indeed speaking to Marie Adamson, and she was far from pleased with his phone call. "I'm really sorry. I know this was an insane thing to do. I just hoped that—"

"I told you. No. I will not listen to, discuss, consider, ponder, or further speak to you about your lousy medical center. Now leave me alone." And with that she hung up on him again, and he sat there with the dead phone in his hand, smiling sheepishly.

"Okay, guys. I blew it." He said the words to himself, or thought he did. He hadn't seen Mike leaning easily in the doorway.

"Welcome home. What did you blow?" Mike didn't look particularly concerned. He looked very pleased to see his friend as he sauntered into the room and sat down in one of the large, comfortable leather chairs. "It's good to see you back, you know."

"Nice to be back. But it's damn cold in this town. Jesus, after San Francisco, I may never readjust."

"We'll be sure to keep you on the Southern route from now on, O delicate one." He grinned at his friend. "And what was that phone call about?"

"The one and only hair in my soup on this trip." He ran a hand through his hair in irritation and sat back in his chair. "Absolutely everything went the way we wanted. Your mother is going to be in ecstasy over the reports. With one exception. Granted it's a minor problem, but I wanted everything to be perfect."

"Should I start worrying?"

"No. I'm just pissed. I found an artist. A girl. A marvelous photographer. I mean really a huge talent, Mike, not just some kid with a Brownie. She is brilliant. I saw her current show in San Francisco, and I wanted to sign her for the lobby decor in all the main buildings. You know, the photographic motif we all okayed at the last meeting before I left."

"And?"

"And she told me to drop dead. She won't even discuss it." He looked beaten as he said it.

"Why? Too commercial for her?" Mike looked unimpressed.

"I don't even know why. She went into a tailspin from the first time I called her. It just doesn't make any sense."

But Mike was smiling at him with an expression of cynical amusement. "Of course it makes sense, my naïve friend. She's just holding out for big money. She knows who we are, so she figures she'll play hard to get and hit us up for a fat contract. Is she really that good?"

"The best. I brought you some samples of her work. You'll love them."

"Then maybe she'll get what she wants. Show me later. First, there's something I want to ask you." Mike looked momentarily serious. This was a subject he'd been meaning to bring up for weeks.

"Anything wrong?" Ben was quick to pick up on his mood.

"No, in fact I feel like a horse's ass even asking you. It shows how out of touch I've been. But . . . well . . . is there something between you and Wendy?"

Ben searched his face for a moment before answering. Mike looked curious, but not hurt. Of course, Ben had known about Wendy's affair with Mike. But it was no secret that Mike had never cared about her. Still, Ben found it a little odd picking up his old friend's castoff. This had been the first time it had happened, and he had never been quite sure how

Mike would take it when he found out. And the truth was, he and Wendy were in love. They had spent an incredible month together on the business trip to the coast. Wendy had teasingly called it their honeymoon.

"Well, Avery, what's up? You haven't answered my question." But now there was a small smile playing around Mike's mouth. He already knew.

"I feel like a jerk for not telling you sooner. But the answer is yes. Does it bother you, Mike?"

"Why should it? I'm embarrassed to admit that I . . . well, I haven't exactly kept up with things. I'm sure Wendy told you how wonderfully attentive I was." He sounded bitter at the last words, but Ben's tone was gentle in reply.

"She never said anything, except that she thought you weren't a very happy man. That doesn't exactly come as a shock to either of us, pal, does it?" Mike nodded silently. "I didn't move in on your scene with her, Mike. I want you to know that. You two had stopped going out for a while. And to tell you the truth, I always did have kind of a soft spot for her."

"I suspected that when you hired her. She's a hell of a nice girl. Better than I deserved." And then he smiled again. "And probably better than you deserve too. Hey, wait a minute." There was pure mischief in his eyes now. "Is this serious by any chance?"

Ben grinned at his friend and then nodded. "I think so."

"Jesus. You mean it? You're thinking of getting married?" He was stunned. Where had he been? Why hadn't he noticed? Of course, Ben had been away for a month, but still . . . he hadn't paid attention to things like that in two years. "I'll be goddamned. Married, Avery. Jesus. Are you sure?"

"I didn't say that. But we're thinking about it. I'd say the odds are all for it. Do you have any objections?" But they both knew he was only teasing. The awkward moment was already past.

"No objections whatsoever." He sat there shaking his head, with a grin on his face. "I feel like I missed a page here and there. Or have you been particularly discreet?"

"No, not at all. You've just been particularly busy. All work and no play. It will make you rich and celebrated in your field, but totally out of touch with office gossip." Ben was only half teasing, and Mike knew it.

"You could have told me, you jerk."

"You're right and I'm sorry, and when there's big news to report, I will. Speaking of which, will you be my—" And then he could have bitten off his tongue for what he had started to ask. He had been acting as Mike's best man the night of the accident, and now he had almost asked Mike to be his. "Never mind. There's plenty of time." Mike stood up, nodded, and went to shake hands with his friend, but there was something dark and hidden in his eyes again. He knew only too well what Ben had been about to say.

"Congratulations, old man." The smile was genuine, but so was the pain. "And don't worry about the photographer in San Francisco. If she's really as good as you say we'll hit her with a fat contract and a good deal, and she'll give in. She's just playing games."

"I hope you're right."

"Trust me. I am." Mike saluted smartly and then disappeared as Ben mused over what they had said. He felt better now that Mike knew. He was only sorry for his own stupid tactlessness. Even after all this time, any reference to Nancy caused explosions of agony in his friend's eyes. He hated himself for bringing it up, but it had seemed a natural question to ask and he hadn't thought first. He shook his head with regret and then went back to the work on his desk. He had barely an hour before the big meeting with Marion. And it seemed like only moments later when Wendy knocked on the open door and beckoned him with a smile.

"Come on, Ben. We have to be in Marion's office in five minutes."

"Already?" He looked up nervously from his desk, and then smiled as he looked at her. She was just exactly what he had always wanted. "By the way, I told Mike this morning." He looked pleased with himself.

"Told him what?" Her mind was on the medical center in San Francisco and the meeting with Marion. Meetings with the great white goddess of architecture always scared the hell out of her.

"I told him about us, silly. I think he was actually pleased."

"I'm glad." She didn't really care, but she knew it meant something to Ben. She really didn't give a damn about Mike anymore, one way or the other. He had been unkind and unfeeling, absent from every moment they had ever spent together. It was almost as though nothing had ever happened between them. "Ready for the meeting?"

"More or less. I tried the Adamson girl again this morning. She told me to go to hell."

"That's a shame." They talked about it quietly as they walked down the hall to the private elevator that led to Marion's ivory tower in the penthouse. Everything on that floor was the color of sand, even the elevator, which was entirely carpeted, floor, ceiling, and walls. It was like traveling upward in a soundless, plush, creamy-beige womb, until suddenly you reached the floor which housed Marion's office with its spectacular view. Wendy could feel her palms grow moist on the file she was carrying. Marion Hillyard always made her feel like that, no matter how pleasant she was: Wendy had seen what lay beneath the poise and the charm.

"Nervous?" Ben whispered it softly as they walked around a bend to the chrome and glass door to Marion's conference room.

"You bet." They laughed with each other and then quietly took their seats in the long, plant-filled room. There was a Mary Cassatt on one wall, an early Picasso on another, and ahead of them lay all of New York, a magnificent view that always made Wendy feel almost dizzy as she sat there on the sixty-fifth floor. It was like taking off in a plane, except for the silence. Marion always seemed to move surrounded by a hush.

There were twenty-two people seated at the long smoked-glass conference table when Marion finally walked into the room flanked by George, Michael, and her secretary Ruth. Ruth carried an armful of files and George and Michael were engaged in an earnest conversation. Little by little George had been turning over the reins over to Michael, and was surprised to find it a relief. Only Marion seemed interested in the group, and she looked around at the faces, making sure everyone was there. She looked the same sandy color as her decor today, but Wendy assumed it was simply New York pallor. She had grown so accustomed to seeing tanned faces on the West Coast that it was a bit of a shock to come back to New York and realize how pale everyone still was in the dead of the Eastern winter.

But Marion looked as chic as ever in a dress that appeared to be Givenchy or Dior, of simple, heavy black wool, relieved by four rows of very large, perfectly matched pearls. Her nail polish was dark, and she seemed to be wearing very little makeup. Even Michael thought she looked unusually pale and was probably working too hard on this project, and ten other projects as well. His mother had her finger in every pie baked by the firm. That was just the way she was. And Michael was following in her footsteps. She admired the total dedication of his work for the past two years. That was how successful empires were kept healthy, infused by the life's blood of those who nurtured them. Sacred guardians. Keepers of the holy grail.

Marion was the first to speak. She reached over for

the first folder in front of Ruth and began questioning the group, department by department, discussing the various problems that had come up in the last meeting, and checking up on their solutions. All went well until she got to Ben, and even there she was immensely pleased with what he and Wendy had to say. They explained their progress in San Francisco, the results of their meetings, all the new developments, and she checked off a list in front of her and looked over at Michael with pleasure. The San Francisco job was taking shape splendidly.

"We only had one problem." Ben said it a little too softly and her eyes were instantly on him again.

"Oh? And what was that?"

"A young photographer. We saw her work and liked it very much. We wanted to discuss the possibility of signing her for the lobby art in all the major buildings. But she wouldn't talk to us."

"What does that mean?" Marion did not look pleased.

"Just that. When she found out why I called her, she almost hung up on me." Marion raised an eyebrow in query.

"Did she know whom you represent?" As though that would change everything. Michael concealed a smile, as did Ben. Marion had such overwhelming pride in the firm, she expected everyone to want to do business with them.

"Yes. I'm afraid that didn't sway her. If anything, it seemed to anger her more."

"Anger her?" For the first time all morning there

was color in Marion's face, but her expression was grim. Who did she think she was, this young woman who turned up her nose at Cotter-Hillyard?

"Well, maybe anger is the wrong word. Maybe scared her off would be more appropriate." It wouldn't, but it suited the need of the moment. To pacify Marion. The two bright red spots in her cheeks began to fade, to everyone's relief, especially Ben's.

"Is she worth pursuing?"

"I think so. And we brought back some samples of her work to show you. I hope you'll agree."

"How did you get samples of her work if she wouldn't agree to discuss the job with you?"

"We bought them from her gallery. It was an extravagance, but if there's any problem with it, I'd be happy to buy them from the firm myself. She does beautiful work." And with that, Wendy quietly went to a table near the back wall and came back with a good-sized portfolio from which she took three very handsome color photographs Marie had shot in San Francisco. One was a park scene, its composition simple; it showed an old man seated on a bench, watching some small children at play. The picture could have been sentimental, but wasn't: it was compassionate. The second was a wharf scene, the vitality of its crowds not detracting from the grinning shrimp vendor who dominated the foreground. And finally, a shimmering view of San Francisco at dusk—the city as tourists and residents alike loved to see it. Ben said nothing. He merely propped up the photographs and stood back. They were enlarged so that everyone could see clearly how fine the work was. Even Marion sat in silence for a long time, before finally nodding.

"You're right. She is worth pursuing."

"I'm glad you agree."

"Mike?" She turned to her son, but he seemed lost in thought as he looked at the work. There was something haunting and familiar about the quality of the art, the nature of the subjects. He wasn't sure what it was, but it instantly put him in a pensive mood that he fought to shake off. He wasn't sure why the photographs bothered him as they did, but even he had to agree that they were remarkably good work and would enhance any building with the Cotter-Hillyard name on it.

"Do you like them as much as I do?" Marion persisted. He looked at his mother with a silent, sober nod.

"Ben, how do we get her?" Marion wasted no time.

"I wish I knew."

"Money, obviously. What sort of girl is she? Did you meet her at all?"

"Oddly enough, I met her the last time I was in San Francisco. She's a strikingly beautiful girl. In an almost unreal way. She's almost too perfect. All you can do is stare at her. She's poised, pleasant—when she wants to be—and obviously gifted. Used to be an artist, before she took up photography. She looked expensively dressed so I don't suppose she's starving. In fact, the gallery owner said that she has some sort of sponsor. An older man. A doctor I think he said, a famous plastic surgeon. At any rate, she doesn't need the money. And that's really all I know."

"Then maybe money isn't the answer." But suddenly Marion looked as pensive as her son. She had had a mad, unreasonable thought. It would be an outrageous coincidence, but what if . . . "How old is this girl?"

"Hard to say. She was wearing kind of a big hat the first time I met her; it sort of hid her face. But I'd say she's . . . I don't know, twenty-four, twenty-five maybe. At the most twenty-six. Why?" He didn't understand that question at all.

"I was just curious. I'll tell you what, Ben. I'm sure you and Wendy did your best, and it's quite possible that there's no getting to this girl at all, but I'd like to give it a try. Leave me the information, and I'll get in touch with her myself. I have to be in San Francisco anyway, sometime in the next few weeks. Maybe she'll feel more awkward turning down an old woman than a young man."

Ben smiled at the reference to an "old woman." Marion Hillyard looked anything but the part. A tough middle-aged dynamo perhaps, but a withered grandmama she would never be. But his smile grew serious as he watched her face. She was growing paler by the moment, and he suddenly wondered if she were ill. But she never gave him or anyone else time to inquire. She stood up, expressed her satisfaction with the meeting, got the information she needed from Ben, and thanked everyone for coming upstairs. When she left the room the meeting was over. The brass-bordered door to her office closed softly behind Ruth a moment later, and the rest of them flowed slowly toward the elevator, commenting on the progress of the job. Everyone seemed pleased, and relieved that Marion had been too. Usually someone set her off, but today she had been almost uncharacteristically mellow, and once again Ben found himself wondering if she were ill. He was among the last to leave the conference room, and Wendy had already gone downstairs when Ruth came rushing out of the inner sanctum and signaled for Michael. She looked terribly frightened.

"Mr. Hillyard! Your mother . . . she's . . ."

But it was George who reacted first, literally running to her office, with a thunderstruck Michael and Ben at his heels. And once there, it was again George who knew what to do. Where to find the pills, which he rapidly gave her with a small glass of water, supporting her, with her son's help, from her desk chair to the couch. She was a pale grayish-green, and she seemed to be having a great deal of difficulty breathing. For a terrified moment, Mike found himself wondering if she was dying, and he felt tears spring to his eyes. He rushed to the phone to call Dr. Wickfield, but she waved weakly from the couch, and then spoke in a barely audible whisper.

"No, Michael . . . don't call . . . Wick. Happens . . . all . . . the time." Michael looked instantly at George. This was news to him, but it couldn't be to George, or he wouldn't have known where to find the pills, what to do. Jesus. How much of the world around him had he grown totally oblivious to in recent months? As he looked at his mother, pale and trembling on the couch, he began to wonder just how sick she was. He knew that she saw rather a lot of Dr. Wickfield, but he had always assumed that was to make sure she was fit, not because she had any major problems. And this certainly appeared to be major. And a glance at the little bottle of pills George had left on the desk confirmed Michael's fears. They were nitroglycerin, standard treatment for heart trouble.

"Mother—" Michael sat down in a chair next to her, and took her hand. "Does this happen often?" He was almost as pale as she, but she opened her eyes and smiled at him, then at George. George knew.

"Don't worry about it." The voice was still soft, but stronger now. "I'm fine."

"You're not fine. And I want to know more about this." Michael spoke, and Ben found himself wondering if he were intruding, but he didn't want to leave, either. He was too stunned by what he had seen. The great Marion Hillyard was human after all. And she looked terribly vulnerable and frail as she lay there in the expensive black dress which only made her look paler. She was the color of very fine parchment as she talked to her son, but her eyes were more alive than they had been a moment before.

"Mother . . ." Michael was going to press until she told him.

"All right, darling, all right." She took a little breath and slowly sat up on the couch, swinging her feet back to the floor and looking straight into the eyes of her only child. "It's my heart. You know I've had the problem for years."

"But it was never serious."

"Well, now it is." She was matter of fact. "I may

live to be a very nasty old woman, or then again I may not. Only time will tell. In the meantime, the little pills keep me going, and I manage. That's all there is to say."

"How long has this been going on?"

"A while. Wicky started worrying about it two years ago, but it's gotten quite a lot worse this year."

"Then I want you to retire." He looked like a stubborn child as he sat staring worriedly at his mother. "Immediately."

She only laughed and smiled up at George. But this time her ally's face told her he was worried, too. "Not a chance, darling. I'll be here till I drop. There's too much to do. Besides, I'd go crazy at home. What would I do all day? Watch soap operas and read movie magazines?"

"It sounds perfect for you." They all laughed. "Or—" He looked at his mother and then at George. "You could both retire, get married, and go enjoy yourselves for a change." It was the first time Michael had openly acknowledged George's attentions of the past twenty years, and George blushed crimson. But he did not look displeased.

"Michael!" His mother almost sounded like herself again. "You're embarrassing George." But oddly enough, she too looked neither shocked nor appalled at the idea. "In any case, my retirement is out. I'm too young, sick or not. You're stuck with me, I'm afraid, for the duration."

Michael already knew he had lost the battle. But he was going to give up by inches. "Then at least be sensible for God's sake, and stop traveling. You don't have to go to San Francisco. I can do all that myself. Don't be such a busybody. Stay home and take care of yourself."

She only laughed at him and got up and walked to her desk. She looked rattled and tired and pale as she sank into her desk chair while they all watched her with terrible concern in their faces.

"I do wish you'd go away and stop looking so maudlin. *All* of you. I have work to do. Even if you apparently don't."

"Mother, I'm taking you home. Today at least." Michael looked belligerent as he watched her, but she only shook her head.

"I'm not going. Now go away, Michael, or I'll have George throw you out." George only looked amused at the idea. "I may leave early, but I'm not leaving now. So thank you for your concern and ta ta. Ruth." She pointed to the door, which her secretary obediently opened, and one by one they helplessly filed out. She was stronger than all of them, and she knew it.

"Marion?" George stopped in the doorway with a worried look in his eyes.

"Yes?" Her face softened as she looked at him, and he smiled.

"Won't you go home now?"

"In a little while."

He nodded. "I'll be back in half an hour."

She smiled, but she could hardly wait for the door to close behind him. There was no doubt in her mind about what had caused the attack. She couldn't afford to get excited about anything anymore. It was really becoming a terrible nuisance. She looked at her watch as she dialed the number Ben had given her and listened to the phone ring three or four times. She didn't know why she was so certain, but she was. Had been from the moment Ben started to describe Marie Adamson. She would try to see the girl when she went to San Francisco; maybe then she'd know for sure. Or maybe not. Maybe the changes would be too great. She wondered if she'd really know. And then, as she wondered, the girl answered the phone. Marion took a breath, closed her eyes, and spoke smoothly into the receiver. No one would have known she'd had an attack half an hour before. Marion Hillyard was, as ever, totally in control.

"Miss Adamson? This is Marion Hillyard, in New York."

The conversation was brief, cold, and awkward, and Marion knew nothing more when she hung up than she had when she dialed. But she would know. In exactly three weeks. They had an appointment at four o'clock on a Tuesday afternoon in three weeks. Marion marked it on her calendar, and then sat back and closed her eyes. The meeting might tell her nothing, and yet . . . there were some things she had to say. She only hoped she lived another three weeks.

Chapter 22

The clock seemed to tick interminably as she sat in
the living room of her suite at the Fairmont. It offered
an impressive view of the bay and Marin County beyond, but Marion Hillyard was not interested in the
view. She was thinking about the girl. What had become of her? What did she look like? Had Gregson
really wrought the wonders he had promised two
years before? Ben Avery had seen a stranger when he
met Marie Adamson. But what about Michael—
would he still recognize her? And was she in love
with someone else now, or, like Michael, had she
become bitter and withdrawn? It made Marion think
of her son again as she waited for this stranger who
might indeed turn out to be the girl Michael had once
loved. But what if she wasn't? She could be just anyone, a local photographer who had caught Ben Avery's
eye. Maybe her theory was all wrong. Maybe . . .

She crossed and uncrossed her legs, and then
reached into her handbag again for her cigarette case.
It was a new one. George had given it to her for
Christmas, with her initials set in lovely sapphires

along the side of the handsome gold case. She lit her cigarette with the matching lighter, took a long quiet drag, and sat back in her chair for a moment with her eyes closed. She was exhausted. It had been a long flight that morning, and she should have given herself a day to rest before seeing the girl. But she was too anxious to put the meeting off for another day. She had to know.

She looked up at the mantel clock again. It was four fifteen. Seven fifteen in New York. Michael would still be at his desk. Avery would already be off gallivanting with that girl from the design department. Her mouth pursed as she thought of them. He wasn't a serious boy, like Michael. But then again . . . She sighed. He wasn't unhappy like Michael, either. Had she done the wrong thing? Had she been totally mad two years before? Had she asked too much of the girl? No. Probably not. She had been the wrong girl for Michael. And in time, perhaps, he'd find someone. There was no reason why he shouldn't. He certainly had everything it took: looks, money, position. He was going to be president of one of the leading companies in America. He was a man with power and talent, gentleness and charm.

Her face softened again as she thought of him. How good and strong he was . . . and how lonely. She sensed that, too. He even maintained a certain distance from her. It was as though some part of him had never bounced back. At least the drinking and brooding had stopped, but only to be replaced by a bleak, jagged determination that showed in his eyes.

Like a man who has struggled through the desert for too long, determined to make it, but no longer quite sure why. And yet he had so much to be happy about, such a good life to enjoy. But he never took time to enjoy anything. She wasn't even entirely sure he enjoyed his work, not the way she did. Not the way his father and grandfather had. She thought of her own husband with tenderness again, and then slowly her thoughts drifted to George. How good he had been to her in these recent years. It would have been impossible to continue her work without him. He took the burdens from her shoulders as often as possible, and left her only the interesting decisions, the creative work, and the glory. She knew how often he did that for her. He was a man of great strength, and at the same time great humility. She wondered why she hadn't paid closer attention to all his virtues a dozen or so years before. But there had never been time. For him, or anyone. Not since Michael's father. Maybe the boy wasn't so unlike her after all.

She was smiling to herself when the buzzer at the door of the suite suddenly interrupted her thoughts. She started, as though for a moment she had forgotten where she was. It was four twenty-five. The girl was twenty-five minutes late. But secretly, she was glad for the time alone.

She set her face in a dignified mask and walked sedately to the door. Her navy blue silk dress and four rows of pearls suited her perfectly, as did the smooth coif, the perfect manicure, the artful makeup that made her look more like forty-five than her nearly sixty years. She would still be a beautiful woman in twenty years, if she lived that long. Nothing defeated Marion Hillyard, not even time. She congratulated herself on that as she opened the door to the elegant young woman with the artist's portfolio in her hand.

"Miss Adamson?"

"Yes." Marie nodded with a small taut smile. "Mrs. Hillyard?" But she knew. She had not seen Marion that May night because her eyes had been bandaged, but she had seen enough photographs around Michael's apartment. She would have recognized his mother in a back alley in Tokyo. This was the woman who had haunted her dreams for two years. This was the woman she had once wanted as her mother and friend, but no more.

"How do you do?" Marion extended a cool, firm hand, and they shook hands ceremoniously just inside the door, before Marion made a gesture toward the suite. "Won't you come in?"

"Thank you."

The two women eyed each other with interest and caution, and Marion seated herself easily in a chair near the table. She had had room service set up a tea service there and some soft drinks for her guest. It seemed a great deal of trouble to go to for a girl who had already cost her almost half a million dollars. *If* this was the girl. She eyed her carefully, but she could see nothing. There was no resemblance to any of the photographs she had seen over the years. This was not the same girl. At least she didn't seem to be. But Marion sat back to watch her, and listen. She

would always remember that torn, broken voice as
they had made the agreement.

"What may I offer you to drink? Tea? Soda? We
can order a drink if you like."

"No, thank you, Mrs. Hillyard. I'd really just prefer
to . . ." But her voice trailed off as they watched
each other, the pretext of their meeting almost forgotten as the older woman appraised the younger,
watched her move, studied the shape and texture of her
hair, and then glanced quickly at the overall picture
again. She was a terribly pretty girl, in very expensive
clothes. Marion found herself wondering if she were
spending her living allowance on outfits like that one.
Her wool dress bore the distinct mark of Paris, her
suede handbag and shoes were Gucci, and her unas-
suming beige trench coat was lined in a dark fur that
looked to Marion like possum.

"That's a very attractive coat, by the way. Must be
a marvelous weight for this city. I envy you the easy
climate. I left New York in two feet of snow. Or
rather," she smiled winningly at the girl, "two inches
of snow, and twenty-two inches of slush. Do you
know New York?"

It was a loaded question and Marie knew it, but
she could answer it honestly. She had lived in New
England, but spent little time in New York. Had she
married Michael, she would have lived there. But
she hadn't. Her face set and something hardened in
her voice. "No, I don't know it very well. I'm not really
a big-city person." She was pure Marie now, there
wasn't a trace of Nancy.

"I find that hard to believe. You look extremely 'big-city' to me." Marion smiled at her again, but it was the smile of a barracuda eying a small and tender minnow.

"Thank you." And then without further ado, Marie reached toward her portfolio, put it on her lap as Marion watched her, and unzipped the case. She smilingly handed Marion a thick black book with copies of her work. The book was large and unwieldy, and the older woman seemed to falter as she took it. It was then that Marie noticed the violent trembling of her hands, and how weak she was when she tried to hold the book. Time had not been kind to Marion Hillyard after all. Was it possible that some of her own ugly prayers had been answered? She watched the woman intently, but Marion seemed to regain her composure as she silently turned the pages.

"I can see why Ben Avery was so anxious to sign you for our center. You do extraordinarily fine work. You must have been at this for years." For once it was an innocent question, and Marie shook her head.

"No, photography is new to me. I was a painter before."

"Ah yes, Ben mentioned that." Yet Marion seemed surprised. She had actually forgotten this might be Nancy McAllister she was talking to, she was so engrossed in the beautiful work. "Are you as good as this at painting?"

"I thought I was." Marie smiled at the woman. An almost eerie exchange was going on. She felt as though she were watching Marion Hillyard through a trick mirror: she could see Marion plainly, yet the person Marion saw was actually someone else. Marie thought that she alone knew the secret. "I like photography just as much now."

"Why did you change?" Marion looked up, intrigued.

"Because everything in my life changed very suddenly, so much so that I became a new person. The painting was part of that old life, that old me. It hurt too much to bring it with me." Marion almost winced at the words.

"I see. Well, the world hasn't suffered a loss, from what I can see anyway. You're a marvelous photographer. Who got you started? Undoubtedly one of the local greats. There are so many out here."

But Marie only shook her head, with a small smile. It was strange. She had come here to hate this woman, and now she found that she couldn't. Not quite. She didn't like her. But she couldn't hate her, either. She looked so tired and frail beneath the bravado and the pearls. She wore a death mask carefully concealed with good makeup, but beneath the veneer lurked the sorrows of autumn, with winter already clutching at her heels. Marie forced herself back to the woman's question, trying to remember what that question was. . . . Oh, yes.

"No, actually, it was a friend who got me started. My doctor, in fact. He's been responsible for getting me launched as a photographer. He knows everyone in town."

"Peter Gregson." The words were soft and dreamy

on Marion Hillyard's lips, as though she hadn't meant to speak them, and then they were both shocked into silence.

"Do you know him?" Why had the woman said that? Did she know? But she couldn't. Had Peter . . . No, he'd never do that.

"I . . . yes . . ." Marion hesitated for a long moment and then looked at her squarely. "Yes, Nancy, I do. He did a beautiful job on you." It was a long shot. A wild guess. But she had to say it, even if she made a fool of herself. She had to know.

"There must be some misunderstanding. My name is Marie—" and then, like a rag doll, she crumpled. There were tears in her eyes as she stood up and walked away to stand at the window with her back to the room. "How did you know?" The voice was shattered and angry. The voice of two years before. Marion sat back in her chair, tired but relieved. Somehow it comforted her to know she had been right. She had not made this difficult trip for nothing. "Did someone tell you?" Marie demanded.

"No. I guessed. I don't even know why. But I had a feeling the first time Ben mentioned you to us. The details fit."

"Did—" Goddamn. She wanted to ask her about him. She wanted to . . . Would this never leave her life? Would they never go away? "Why did you come here? To reconfirm our little deal?" Marie wheeled on her heels at the window, to stare at the woman who tormented her. "To make sure I'd stick with my promise?"

"You've already proven that." Marion's voice was tired and gentle, and uncharacteristically old. "No, I'm not even sure I understand it myself, but I came to see you. To talk to you. To find out how you are, if indeed it was you."

"Why now? Why should I be so interesting after two years?" Suddenly there was venom in Marie's voice, and hatred in her eyes. The hatred she had dreamed of spewing for months. "Why now, Mrs. Hillyard, or were you just curious to take a look at Gregson's work? Was that it? Well, how do you like your four hundred-thousand-dollar baby? Was it worth it?"

"Why don't you answer that? Was it? Are you pleased?" She hoped so. She suddenly, desperately hoped so. They had all paid such a high price for that new face. It had been wrong. Suddenly she was sure of it. But it was too late. They were not the same people anymore. She could see that in the girl as much as she could in Michael. It was far, far too late, for either of them. They would have to find their dreams somewhere else. "You're a very beautiful girl now, Marie."

"Thank you. Yes, I know Peter did a good job. But it was like making a deal with the devil. A face for a life." With a ragged sigh Marie sank into a chair.

"And I'm the devil." Marion's voice trembled as she looked at the girl. "I suppose it's an obscene thing to say to you now, but at the time I thought I was doing the right thing."

"And now?" Marie looked at her squarely. "Is

Michael happy? Was it worth getting rid of me, Mrs. Hillyard? Was the mission a success?" Christ, she wanted to hit her. Just haul off and demolish her, in her ladylike dress and her pearls.

"No, Marie, Michael isn't happy, anymore than you are. I always thought he'd pick up his life again. I assumed you'd do the same. Something tells me, though, that you haven't. Not that I have any right to ask."

"No, you don't. And Michael? He's not married?" She hated herself for it, but she prayed for a no.

"Yes, he is." Marie almost felt herself gasp and then catch her breath again. "To his work. He lives, eats, sleeps, and breathes it. As though he hopes to get lost in it forever. I hardly ever see him."

Good, you bitch. Good! "Then would you say you'd been wrong? I loved him, you know. More than anything in life." Except my face . . . oh, God . . . except . . .

"I know. But I thought it would pass."

"Has it?"

"Perhaps. He never mentions you."

"Did he ever try to find me?"

Marion slowly shook her head. "No." But she did not tell her the reason why. She did not tell Marie that Michael thought she was dead. The lie weighed on her even as she said the word, and she saw the girl's face set in a fresh mask of hatred.

"All right then, why am I here? Just to satisfy your curiosity? To show you my work? Why?"

"I'm not sure, Nancy. I'm sorry . . . Marie. I simply had to see you. To know how it had gone with you.

I . . . I suppose it's maudlin to say it, but I'm dying, you know." She looked faintly sorry for herself as she faced the girl, and then she was annoyed for having told her. But Marie did not appear moved. She stared at the woman for a very long time and then in a soft, broken voice she spoke to her again.

"I'm sorry to hear it, Mrs. Hillyard. But I died two years ago. And it sounds to me as though your son did, too. That's two of us. On your hands, Mrs. Hillyard. To be honest with you, it's hard for me to feel a great deal of sympathy for you. I suppose I should be grateful to you. I suppose I should thank you from the bottom of my heart that men turn and stare at me every day, instead of running from me in horror. I suppose I should feel a lot of things, but I don't. I don't feel anything for you now, except sorry for you, because you've ruined Michael's life, and you know it. Not to mention what you did to mine."

Marion nodded silently, feeling the full weight of the girl's reproach. She knew it all herself. Secretly, she had known it for two years. About Michael anyway. She hadn't known about the girl. Maybe that was why she had to come. "I don't know what to say."

"Good-bye will be fine." Marie picked up her coat and her portfolio and walked to the door of the suite. She stopped for a moment at the door, her hand on the knob, her head bowed, and tears beginning to creep down her face. She turned slowly then, and saw tears running down Marion's face as well. The older woman was speechless with her private agony, but the young girl managed to catch her breath and speak again. "Good-bye, Mrs. Hillyard. Give . . . give Michael . . . my love." She closed the door softly behind her, but Marion Hillyard didn't move. She felt her heart rip through her lungs with long searing pains. Gasping for air, she stumbled toward the buzzer that would summon a maid. She managed to press it once before passing out.

Chapter 23

His heels rapped hollowly in the hospital corridor as he almost ran to her room. Why had she insisted on coming out alone? Why did she always have to be so damned independent, still, after all these years? He knocked softly on the door, and a nurse opened it with a pointed look of inquisition.

"Is this Mrs. Hillyard's room? I'm George Calloway." He looked nervous and tired and old, and he felt that way, too. He had really had enough of this nonsense. And he was going to tell her so as soon as he saw her. He had said as much to Michael before leaving New York.

The nurse smiled at the sound of his name. "Yes, Mr. Calloway, we've been expecting you." Marion had only been in the hospital since six o'clock that evening. George had managed to arrive in San Francisco by eleven o'clock local time. It was now just after midnight. That was about as fast as anyone could make the trip. Marion's smile acknowledged that when the nurse opened the door to let George step inside, and slipped quietly past him into the hall.

"Hello, George."

"Hello, Marion. How do you feel?"

"Tired, but I'll live. At least that's what they tell me. It was only a small seizure."

"This time. But what about next time?" He looked leonine as he paced the room, glaring at her. He hadn't even stopped to kiss her, as he usually did. He had too much to say.

"We'll worry about next time when it gets here. Now sit down and relax, you're making me nervous. Do you want something to eat? I had the nurse save you a sandwich."

"I couldn't eat."

"Now stop that. I've never seen you like this, George. It wasn't serious, for heaven's sake. Don't be like that."

"Don't tell me how to be, Marion Hillyard. I've been watching you destroy yourself for far too long, and I'm not going to tolerate it anymore."

"You're quitting?" She grinned at him from the bed. "Why don't you just retire?" She was suddenly amused at the whole scene, but she was less amused in a moment when he returned to face her with something immovable in his face.

"That's exactly what I'm going to do, Marion. Retire."

She could see that he was serious. This was all she needed. "Don't be ridiculous." But she wasn't so sure she could jolly him out of this one. She sat up in bed with a nervous smile.

"I'm not. It's the first intelligent decision I've made

in twenty years. And do you know who else is retiring, Marion? You are. We're both retiring. With no notice at all. I discussed it with Michael on the way to the airport. He was good enough to drive me out, and he said to tell you that he's sorry he couldn't come but he's just too tied up at the moment. He thinks our retiring is a fine idea. And so do I. In fact, no one is interested in what you think of it, Marion. The decision is made."

"Are you crazy?" She sat up in bed and glared at him in the dim room. "And just exactly what do you think I'll do with myself if I retire? Knit?"

"I think that's a fine idea. But the first thing you'll do is marry me. After that, you may do anything you like. *Except*"—his voice rose menacingly on the word —"work. Is that clear, Mrs. Hillyard?"

"Aren't you at least going to ask me to marry you? Or are you just telling me? Or is this an order from Michael, too?" But she wasn't angry. She was touched. And relieved. She'd had enough. She'd done enough, in the best and worst senses of the word. And she knew it, too. The meeting with Marie had driven the point home that afternoon.

"We have Michael's blessing, if that makes any difference." And then his voice softened as he approached her bed and reached for her hand, which he held gently in his. "Will you marry me, Marion?" He was almost afraid to ask after all this time, but he had finally spoken to Michael about it in the anxious moments before his flight, and Michael had said something strange to him about "celebrating their love." George had not really understood, but he had been grateful for the encouragement. "Will you?" He held her hand a little tighter as he waited.

She nodded slowly, with a warm, tired smile, and a look of near regret. "We should have thought of this years ago, George." But she wanted to say something else too . . . that she wasn't sure if she had the right . . . not after. . . .

"I thought of it years ago, but I never thought you'd accept."

"I probably wouldn't have. Fool that I am. Oh George," she sighed and fell back against the pillows, "I've done such stupid things in my life." Her face suddenly showed the agony of the afternoon, and he watched her, puzzled by the torment he saw mixed with the fatigue.

"What a silly thing to say. I can't think of a single foolish thing you've done in all the years I've known you." He kept a gentle hold on her hand and stroked it lovingly. He had wanted to do that for years, in just that way. "Don't torment yourself with nonsense from the past."

But Marion was sitting up very straight, and she looked at him from the bed, her hand cold and taut in his.

"What if the 'nonsense,' as you call it, destroyed people's lives? Do I have a right to forget that, George?"

"Why, Marion, what could you have done to destroy someone's life?" He suddenly wondered if the doctor had given her some powerful drug. Or perhaps this last attack had affected her mentally. She wasn't making sense.

But she settled back among her pillows and closed her eyes. "You don't understand."

"Should I?" His voice was gentle in the dimly lit room.

"Perhaps. Maybe, if you knew, you wouldn't be so anxious to marry me."

"Don't be absurd. But if that's how you feel, then I think I have a right to know what's bothering you. What is it?" He never let go of her hand, and at last she opened her eyes. She stared at him for a long time before she spoke.

"I don't know if I can tell you."

"Why not? I can't think of anything that would shock me. And I can't imagine anything about you that I don't know." They had had no secrets from each other for years. "I'm beginning to think the seizure this afternoon just rocked you a bit."

"The truth I had to face did that." Her tone was one he had never heard from her, and when he looked at her again there were tears in her eyes. He wanted to put his arms around her and make it all better, but he understood now that she really did have something very important to tell him. Could she have been having an affair with someone for all these years? The idea suddenly shocked him. But he could even have accepted that. He loved her. He had always loved her. He had waited too long for this moment to let anything spoil it.

"Did something special happen this afternoon?" He

watched her very closely, waiting for the answer, but her eyes only closed as the tears poured silently down her cheeks, and at last she nodded and whispered "Yes."

"I see. Well, relax now. Let's not get all excited about it." She was beginning to worry him. He didn't want her to have another seizure.

"I saw the girl."

"What girl?" What in God's name was she talking about?

"The girl Michael was in love with." The tears stopped for a moment, and she sat up very straight and looked at him. "Do you remember the night of Michael's accident, when he came down to the city to see me? You came in, and he stalked out. He was furious. He had come down to tell me that he was going to marry that girl. And I showed him that . . . that report I'd had done on her . . ."

Her voice drifted off for a moment as she remembered, and George's brow furrowed deeper. She must be confused by some drug. That was the only explanation. That girl had died in the accident.

"Marion dear, you couldn't have seen the girl. As I recall, she . . . she uh . . . passed on in the—"

But Marion shook her head, her eyes never leaving his. "No, George. She didn't. I said she did, and Wicky kept his mouth shut, but the girl lived. Her face was destroyed, though. Everything but her eyes." George watched her silently but he was listening. This was a distraught Marion, an agonized Marion, but it wasn't a crazy Marion. He knew she was telling the truth. "I went into her room that night and offered her a deal." He waited, silently. She closed her eyes as though in pain, and he squeezed her hand tighter.

"Are you all right?"

She nodded quietly and opened her eyes again. "Yes. Maybe I'll feel better once I tell you. I offered her a deal. Her face in exchange for Michael. There are a lot of prettier ways to say it, but that's what it boils down to. Wicky said he knew of one man in the country who could restore her face. It would cost a fortune, but he could do it. I told her about it, offered to pay for it and anything else she needed until all the operations were over. I offered her a whole new life, a life she'd never had, as long as she agreed not to seek out Michael again."

"And she agreed?"

"Yes." It was a small, rocklike word.

"Then she couldn't have loved him very much anyway. And you did a damn nice thing offering to pay for the surgery. Hell, if they'd loved each other so much, neither one of them would have accepted that."

"You don't understand, George." Her tone was icy now. But her anger was against herself, not George. "I wasn't honest with either of them. I told Michael she was dead, for God's sake, and I knew damn well that she never expected Michael to honor the agreement. That's probably why she agreed to it. That and the fact that she had no choice. She had nothing left. Except me—offering her a deal with the devil, as she herself put it today. George, you know Michael never would have accepted that agreement either, if he'd known the truth. He'd have gone back to her in a moment."

"He hasn't suffered in the interim. He's recovered. Maybe they wouldn't even like each other now." He was desperately looking for balm for her wounds, but he had to admit that it was a pretty nasty wound, and it must have been damned hard to live with. He knew Marion had thought she was acting in Michael's best interests, but she had played a very serious game with his life. "That's true, you know, they've probably grown to be quite different. They might not even want each other now."

"I realize that." She leaned back, with a sigh. "Michael is obsessed with his work. He has no love, no gentleness, no time, nothing. There's nothing left, and I know it better than anyone. And she. . . ." She thought back painfully to that afternoon. "She's exquisite. Elegant. Beautiful. And bitter, angry, filled with hate. They'd make a charming couple."

"And you think you did all that?"

"Knowing what you know now, don't you agree?" In spite of herself, her eyes filled with tears again. "I was wrong to come between them, George, I know that now."

"Maybe the damage can be repaired. And in the meantime, you've given the girl her life back. A better life, in some ways."

"And she hates me for it."

"Then she's a fool."

Marion shook her head. "No. She's right. I had no right to do what I did. And if I had any courage at all, I'd tell Michael." But in spite of himself, George hoped she would not do that. Michael's anger would destroy her. Her son would never feel the same about her again.

"Don't tell him, darling. There's no point now." Marion saw the fear in his eyes, and she smiled.

"Don't worry. I'm not that brave. But he'll find out. In time. I'll see to that. He has a right to know. But I hope he'll hear it from her, if she takes him back. Maybe then he'll forgive me."

"Do you think there's a chance of that? That she'll take him back, I mean?"

"Not really. But I must do what I can."

"Oh God—"

"I started this. Now I owe it to both of them to do something. Maybe nothing will come of it, but I can try."

"And you've kept in touch with her during all this time?"

"No. I saw her again for the first time today."

"Now I understand. And how did that happen?"

"I arranged a meeting. I wasn't even sure it was she, but I suspected. And I was right." She sounded pleased with herself, and he smiled for the first time in half an hour.

"It must have been quite a meeting." Now he understood the fresh seizure. It was a wonder it hadn't killed her.

"It could have been worse." Her voice grew gentle, and her eyes filled with tears again. "It could have been much worse. All it really did was show me how wrong I'd been, that I'd destroyed her life as well as his."

"Stop that. You didn't destroy either one of them. You've given Michael a career any man would give his life for, and you've given her something no one else could have."

"What? Heartbreak? Disillusionment? Despair?"

"If that's how she feels she's an ingrate. What about a new face? A new life? A new world?"

"I suspect it's a very empty world, except for her work. In that sense, she's very much like Michael."

"Then maybe they'll build something together again. But in the meantime, what's done is done. You can't punish yourself forever over this. You did what you must have thought right at the time. And they're young, darling. They have full lives ahead of them. If they waste them, it's their own doing. What we mustn't do is waste ours." He wanted to say "we have so little time left," but he didn't. He leaned closer to her as she lay on the bed, and she raised her arms to him. He held her very tight and felt the warmth of her body in his arms. "I love you, darling. I'm sorry you went through all that alone, without telling me. You should have told me two years ago."

"You'd have hated me for it." Her voice was muffled by his shoulder and her sobs.

"Never. Not then and not now. I could never do anything but love you. And I respect you for telling me about this now. You didn't have to. You could have hidden it. I would never have known."

"No, but I would. And I had to know what you thought."

"I think the whole thing has been an agony for everyone. Now, do what you can about it, and then let it go. Drop it from your thoughts, your heart, your conscience. It's over. And we have a new life to begin. We have a right to that life. You've paid dearly for everything you've had. You don't have to punish yourself for anything. We're going to get married, and go away, and live our life. Let them work out their own."

"Do I really have a right to that?" She looked younger again when he looked into her face.

"Yes, my love, you do." And then he kissed her, gently at first, and then hungrily. To hell with Michael and the girl and all of it. He wanted Marion, with her good and her bad, her genius and her outrageousness, all of it. "And now, you are going to forget about all this, and go to sleep, and tomorrow we are going to sit down and plan the wedding. Start thinking about sensible things like what kind of dress to order and who's to do the flowers. Is that clear?"

She looked up at him and laughed.

"George Calloway, I love you."

"It's a good thing, because if you didn't, I'd marry you anyway. Nothing would stop me now. Is that clear?"

"Yes, sir." They were beaming at each other when the nurse finally stuck her head into the room. It was one in the morning. And special instructions from the doctor or no, he had to leave. George nodded that he understood, and with a gentle kiss, a touch on the hand, and a smile that nothing could have dimmed, he reluctantly left the room. And in her bed, Marion

felt enormously relieved. He loved her anyway. And
George had restored a little of her own faith in herself. And then with a look at the clock, she decided
to give Michael a call. Maybe she could do something
about all that right now. To hell with the time difference. She didn't have a moment to waste. None of
them did. She turned to the phone in the darkened
room and dialed his apartment in New York. It took
him four rings to find the phone and answer groggily
with a muffled 'llo?

"Darling, it's me."

"Mother? Are you all right?" He quickly switched
on the light and tried to force himself awake.

"I'm fine. I have something to tell you."

"I know. I know. George told me." He yawned and
smiled at the phone and then blinked at the clock.
Jesus. It was five o'clock in the morning in New York.
Two in San Francisco. What the hell was she doing
up, and where was her nurse? "Did you accept?"

"Of course. Both his proposals. I'm even going to retire. More or less." Michael laughed at her last words.
That sounded like her. George was going to have his
hands full, but he was pleased for the two of them.
"But I'm calling about something else." She sounded
very businesslike and firm, and he groaned. He knew
the tone.

"Not business at this hour. Please!"

"Nonsense. There is no hour for business. I wanted
to tell you that I saw that girl."

"What girl?" His mind was a blank. It had been an
incredible day. Three meetings, five appointments, and

the news that his mother had had another seizure, alone in San Francisco.

"The photographer, Michael. Wake up."

"Oh. Her. So?"

"We want her."

"We do?"

"Absolutely. I can't pursue it now. George would have my head. But you can."

"You must be kidding. I have too much to do. Let Ben handle it."

"She already turned him down. And she's a young woman with style, intelligence, and character. She is not going to deal with underlings."

"She sounds like a pain in the ass to me."

"That's how you sound to me. Now listen to me. I don't care what you have to do to sign her, but do it. Woo her, win her, fly out to see her, take her to dinner. Be your best charming self. She's worth it. And I want her work in the center. Do it for me." She was actually wheedling. She smiled to herself. This was new.

"You're crazy, and I don't have time." He was lying in bed, grinning to himself. His mother was going nuts. "You do it."

"I won't. And if you don't, I'll come back to the office full time and drive you round the bend." She sounded as though she meant it, and he had to laugh.

"I'll do it, I'll do it."

"I'll hold you to that."

"Jesus. All right. Are you satisfied? Can I go back to sleep now?"

"Yes. But I want you to follow this up right away."

"What's her name again?"

"Adamson. Marie Adamson."

"Fine. I'll take care of it tomorrow."

"Good, darling. And . . . thank you."

"Good night, you crazy old bat. And by the way, congratulations. Can I give away the bride?"

"Of course. I wouldn't dream of having anyone else. Good night, darling."

They each hung up, and at her end Marion Hillyard was finally at peace. Maybe it wouldn't work. Maybe it was too late. The two years had taken a hard toll on both of them. But it was all she could do. No, that wasn't true. She could have told him the truth. But with a small sigh, as she drifted off to sleep, she admitted to herself that she wasn't quite that ready for sainthood yet. She'd help them along a little. But she wouldn't do more than that. She wouldn't tell Michael what she had done. He would probably find out eventually, but perhaps, by then, there would be enough happiness to cushion the blow.

Chapter 24

George kissed her tenderly on the mouth and the soft music began again. Marion had hired three musicians to play at the wedding in her apartment. There were roughly seventy guests, and the dining room had been cleared as a ballroom. The buffet had been set up in the library. And it was a perfect day. The very last day in February and a clear, cold, magnificent New York day. Marion was completely recovered from her little mishap in San Francisco, and George looked jubilant. Michael kissed her on both cheeks, and she posed between her husband and her son for the photographer from the *Times*. She was wearing champagne lace to the floor and both George and Michael were formally dressed in striped trousers and cutaways. George wore a white carnation as his boutonniere, Michael a red one, and the bride carried delicate beige orchids, specially flown in from California along with the lavish show of flowers around the apartment. Her decorator had seen to it himself.

"Mrs. Calloway?" It was Michael offering her his arm to the buffet as she laughed girlishly at the new name and then smiled at George. "Celebrate it," as Nancy had said, and that was what they had done. Michael was pleased for them both. They deserved it. And they were spending two months in Europe to relax. He couldn't get over how sensible she had been about stepping out of the business. Maybe she had been ready to retire after all, or maybe her heart was finally frightening her after all this time, but she and George had been wonderful to work with as they transferred the power from their hands to his. He was the president of Cotter-Hillyard now, and he had to admit that he didn't mind the way it felt. President ... at twenty-seven. He had made the cover of *Time*. And that had felt good, too. He supposed his mother and George would make *People* with the wedding.

"You look very elegant, darling." His mother beamed at him as they swept into the library. It was filled with flower trees and tables laden with food. And the walls seemed to be lined with additional servants.

"You look pretty snazzy yourself. And the house doesn't look bad either."

"It's pretty, isn't it?" She seemed amazingly young as she flitted away from him to talk to some of the guests and give last-minute instructions to the servants. She was totally in her element, and as excited as a girl. His mother, the bride. He smiled to himself again at the thought.

"You're looking very pleased with yourself, Mr. Hillyard." The voice was soft and familiar, and when he turned to find Wendy right at his elbow, he was no longer embarrassed to see her. She was wearing the diamond solitaire Ben had given her for Valentine's Day when they got engaged. They were getting married the following summer. And he was to be best man.

"She looks lovely, doesn't she?"

Wendy nodded and smiled at him again. For once he looked happy, too. She had never really figured him out, but at least it didn't bother her anymore, now that she had Ben. Ben made her happier than any other man ever had.

"But I'm sure you'll look lovely next summer too. I have a weakness for brides." It seemed very unlike him and Wendy smiled again. She liked him much better, now that she shared his friendship with Ben.

"Trying to chase after my fiancée, old man?" It was Ben at their elbow, juggling three glasses of champagne. "Here, these are for you two. And by the way, Mike, I'm in love with your mother."

"Too late. I gave her away this morning." Ben snapped his fingers as though at a loss and all three laughed as the music began in the dining room. "Oops, I think that means me. The son gets the first dance, and then George cuts in on me. Emily Post says . . ." Ben laughed at him and gave him a shove as he disappeared toward the door to do his duties.

"He looks happy today," Wendy said softly after Mike had left.

"I think he is, for once." Pensively, he sipped his champagne, and a moment later smiled at Wendy again. "You look happy today, too."

"I'm always happy, thanks to you. By the way, did you follow up on that girl in San Francisco, the photographer? I keep meaning to ask you, and I never have time."

But Ben was shaking his head. "No, Mike said he'd take care of it."

"Does *he* have time?" Wendy looked surprised.

"No. But he'll probably manage anyway. You know Mike. He's going out there next week, for that and four thousand other reasons."

No, Wendy thought to herself, I don't know Mike. No one does. Except maybe Ben. But sometimes she even wondered if Ben knew him as well as he liked to think he did. Used to maybe. But did he still?

"Care to dance, lady?" He set down his glass and put an arm around her to guide her to the next room.

"Love to."

But they'd only been dancing for a moment, it seemed, when Michael cut in on them. "My turn."

"The hell it is. We just got started. I thought you were dancing with your mother."

"She ditched me for George."

"Sensible of her." The three of them had been shuffling around together on the dance floor and Wendy was starting to laugh. Seeing the two of them together this way was like getting a glimpse of the Ben and Michael of years gone by. This was the kind of occasion they had once thrived on. A good healthy dose of champagne, an occasion worth celebrating, and they were off.

"Listen, Avery, are you going to get lost, or aren't you? I want to dance with your fiancée."

"And what if I don't want you to?"

"Then I dance with both of you, and my mother

throws us out?" Wendy was grinning again. They were like two kids, dying to raise hell at a birthday party. They were just breaking into a song about "a girl in Rhode Island" that was beginning to worry her.

"Listen you two, this is supposed to be twice as much fun. Instead, I'm getting both my feet walked on at once. Why don't we all go have some wedding cake?"

"Shall we?" Ben and Michael eyed each other, nodded in unison, and each obligingly took one of Wendy's arms and led her off the floor, as Michael looked over her head and winked at Ben.

"Cute, but I think she's crocked. Did you notice the way she danced? My shoes are practically ruined."

"You should see mine." Ben spoke in a stage whisper, over her left shoulder, and Wendy sharply elbowed them both.

"Listen, you creeps, has anyone seen *my* shoes? Not to mention my poor aching feet, dancing with you two drunken louts."

"Louts?" Ben looked at her, horrified, and Michael started to laugh as he accepted three plates of wedding cake from a uniformed maid, and then proceeded to juggle the plates, almost dropping two.

"Never mind her. The cake looks terrific. Here." Michael handed a plate to each of the other two, and the three leaned against a convenient column and watched the action as they ate, eyeing dowagers in gray lace, young girls in pink chiffon, cascades of pearls, and a river of assorted gems.

"Jesus, just think what we could make if we held

them up." Michael looked enchanted with his idea.

"I never thought of that. We should have done it years ago. Up at school, when we were broke." They nodded sagely at each other, as Wendy looked at them with a suspicious grin.

"I'm not sure I should trust you two alone while I go to powder my nose."

"Not to worry. I'll keep an eye on him, Wendy." Michael winked broadly and polished off another glass of champagne. Wendy had never seen him like this, but he amused her. Ben had been right. He was human after all. Seeing him that way, giddy and silly, was like meeting him five years before, or even two.

"I don't think either of you could uncross your eyes long enough to keep an eye on anything, let alone each other."

"Bull . . . I mean . . . oh, go to the can, Wendy, we're in great shape." He accepted two more glasses of champagne, handed one to Michael, and waved his fiancée off in the direction of the ladies' room. "She's a hell of a girl, Mike. I'm glad you didn't get mad when I told you about . . . about us."

"How could I get mad? She's just right for you. Besides, I'm too busy for that stuff."

"One of these days you won't be."

"Maybe so. In the meantime, the rest of you can run off and get married. Me, I have a business to run." But for once he didn't look grim when he said it. He looked over his glass of champagne with a grin, and toasted his friend. "To us."

Chapter 25

The plane set down gently in San Francisco as Michael snapped shut his briefcase. He had a thousand things to do in the week to come. Doctors to see, meetings to attend, building sites to visit, architects to organize, and people, and plans and demands and conferences, and . . . damn . . . that photographer, too. He wondered how he'd find time for it all. But he would. He always did. He'd give up sleeping or eating or something. He took his raincoat out of the overhead rack where he had folded it, put it over his arm, and followed the other passengers out of first class. He felt the stewardesses' eyes on him. He always did. He ignored them. They didn't interest him. Besides, he didn't have time. He looked at his watch. He knew there would be a car waiting for him at the terminal. It was two twenty in the afternoon. He had done a full day's work in half a day at the office in New York, and now he had time for at least four or five hours of meetings here. Tomorrow morning he had a breakfast conference scheduled for seven. That was the way he ran his life. That was the way he liked it.

All he cared about was his work. That and a handful of people. Two of whom were happily off in Majorca by now, at the house of friends, and the other of whom was in Wendy's good hands in New York. They were all taken care of. And so was he. He had the medical center to pull together. And it was coming along beautifully. He smiled to himself as he walked into the terminal. This baby was his.

"Mr. Hillyard?" The driver recognized him immediately, and he nodded. "The car is over here."

Michael settled back in the car while the driver retrieved his luggage from the chaos inside. It was certainly pleasant to be in San Francisco again. It had been a freezing cold March day when he left New York, and it was sixty-five in San Francisco that afternoon. All around him, the world was already green and lovely and lush. In New York, the trees were still barren and brittle and gray, and green would be a forgotten color for another month. It was hard waiting for spring in New York. It always seemed as though it would never come. And just when you gave up, and decided that nothing would ever be green again, the first buds would appear, bringing back hope. Michael had forgotten how pleasant spring was. He never noticed. He didn't have time.

The driver took him straight to his hotel, where some minor employee of the company had already checked him in and seen to it that his suite was in order for the first meeting. He had reserved two suites, one in which he could stay, the other for meetings. And if necessary there could be conferences held simultaneously in both. It was nine o'clock that night

before he was through with his work, and tiredly he
called room service and asked for a steak. It was midnight
in New York, and he was beat. But it had been
a fruitful few hours, and he was pleased. He settled
back on the couch, pulled off his tie, threw his feet
up on the coffee table, and closed his eyes. And then
it was as though he heard his mother's voice in the
room. "Did you call that girl?" Oh, Christ. The words
sounded loud in the suddenly quiet room, which still
reeked of cigarette smoke, and the round of Scotches
they'd ordered at the end. But the girl . . . well, why
not? He had the time, while he waited for his steak.
It might keep him from falling asleep. He reached
for his briefcase, found the number in a file, and
dialed from where he sat. The phone rang three or
four times before she answered.

"Hello?"

"Good evening, Miss Adamson, this is Michael Hillyard."

She felt herself almost gasp and had to sharply
control her breathing. "I see. Are you in San Francisco,
Mr. Hillyard?" Her voice was clipped and
brusque; she sounded almost angry. Maybe he had
gotten her at a bad time, or maybe she didn't like
to be called at home. He didn't really care.

"Yes, I am, Miss Adamson. And I was wondering if
we might get together. We have a few things to discuss."

"No. We have absolutely nothing to discuss. I
thought I made that very clear to your mother." She
was trembling all over and clutching the phone.

"Then perhaps she forgot to relay the message." He

was beginning to sound as uptight as she. "She had a mild heart attack just after her meeting with you. I'm sure it had nothing to do with the meeting, but she didn't tell me a great deal about what either of you said. Understandably, given the circumstances."

"Yes." Marie seemed to pause. "I'm sorry to hear it. Is she all right now?"

"Very much so." Michael smiled. "She got married last week. Right now she's in Majorca."

How sweet. The bitch. She ruins my life and goes on a honeymoon. Marie wanted to grit her teeth, or slam down the phone.

"But that's neither here nor there. When can we meet?"

"I've already told you. We can't." She almost spat the words through the phone, and he closed his eyes again. He was really too tired to be bothered.

"All right. I concede. For now. I'm at the Fairmont. If you change your mind, call."

"I won't."

"Fine."

"Good night, Mr. Hillyard."

"Good night, Miss Adamson."

She was surprised at how quickly he ended the conversation. And he hadn't really sounded like Michael. He sounded worn out, as though he didn't really give a damn. Just what had happened to him in the last two years? She sat wondering for a long time after she hung up the phone.

Chapter 26

"Darling, you're so solemn-looking. Is anything wrong?" Peter looked at her across the lunch table, and she shook her head, toying with her glass of wine.

"No. I'm just thinking of some new work. I want to start a new project tomorrow. That always keeps me preoccupied." But she was lying and they both knew it. Ever since Michael had called the night before, she had been catapulted back into the past. All she could think of was that last day. The bicycling, the fair, the gaudy blue beads, burying them at the beach, and then dressing in the white eyelet dress and blue satin cap to run off and marry Michael . . . and then his mother's voice as she lay bandaged and unseeing in her hospital bed. It was like having a movie shown constantly before her eyes. She couldn't get away from it.

"Darling, are you all right?"

"Fine. Really. I'm sorry I'm such bad company today. Maybe I'm just tired." But he had seen the haunted look, and there was a troubled little frown between her eyes.

"Have you seen Faye lately?"

"No, I keep meaning to call her for lunch, and I never have time. Ever since the show," she smiled gratefully at him, "I've spent half my time in the darkroom and the other half racing around town with my camera."

"I didn't mean socially. Have you seen her professionally?"

"Of course not. I told you, we finished before Christmas."

"You never told me if that was her decision or yours, to finish the sessions."

"Mine, but she didn't disagree." Marie was hurt that he seemed to think she needed more work with the psychiatrist. "I'm just tired, Peter. That's all."

"I'm not so sure. Sometimes I think you're still haunted by . . . well, by events of two years ago." He said it carefully, watching her face. And he was dismayed when he saw her almost visibly cringe.

"Don't be ridiculous."

"It's perfectly normal, Marie. People have been tormented by things like that for ten and twenty years. That's a very traumatic thing to live through, and even if you were unconscious after the accident, some part of you way down deep will always remember what happened. If you can put it to rest, you'll be free of it."

"I have and I am."

"Only you can judge that. But I want you to be sure. Otherwise, subtly, it'll affect you for the rest of your life. It will limit your abilities, cripple your life.

... Anyway, there's no need to go on. Just think about it carefully. You may want to see Faye for a while longer. It wouldn't do any harm." He looked worried.

"I don't need to." Her mouth was set in a firm line, and he patted her hand. But he didn't apologize for bringing it up. He didn't like the way she looked.

"All right. Shall we go then?" He smiled at her more gently and she tried to return the smile, but he was right, of course. She was obsessed with having talked to Michael.

Peter paid the check and helped her into the navy blue velvet blazer she had worn with the white Cacharel skirt, and delicate silk blouse. She was always impeccably dressed, and Peter loved being seen with her. "Shall I take you home?"

"No. I thought I'd stop at the gallery. I want to discuss some things with Jacques. I want to change around some of the pieces. Some of my earlier work is getting more play now than the recent work. I want to switch that around."

"That makes sense." He put an arm around her shoulders as they walked out into the spring sunshine. The morning fog had burned off and it was a beautiful warm day. The attendant brought around the black Porsche in a few moments, and Peter held open the door as Marie slipped inside. She smoothed down her skirt and smiled at him as he took his place behind the wheel. She knew now just how much she mattered to him. Sometimes she wondered, though, if he loved her because he had created her, or perhaps because she remained somewhat unattainable. Often it made her feel guilty that she wasn't freer with him. But despite the affection she felt for him, there was always a shadow of reserve between them. It was her fault, she knew it. And maybe he was right. Maybe she would always be haunted and crippled by the accident. Maybe she should go back and see Faye.

"You're not very talkative today, my love. Still thinking of the new project?"

She nodded with an embarrassed smile and then ran a delicate hand over the back of his neck. "Sometimes I wonder why you put up with me."

"Because I'm lucky to have you. You're very special to me, Marie. I hope you truly know that."

But why? Sometimes she wondered. Was she like the other woman he had loved? Had he made her that way? It was an eerie thought.

She settled back in her seat for a moment and closed her eyes, trying to relax, but they flew open again as she felt Peter swerve in the bulletlike little car. As she opened her eyes, all she could see was a sleek red Jaguar hurtling toward her side of the car, head on, as its driver swooped around a double-parked truck. For some reason the driver of the Jaguar had overshot his mark, and was well into the opposite lane, until he was almost nose to nose with Marie. She stared wide-eyed in horror, too terrified to make a sound. But in an instant, the incident was over. Peter had avoided the car, and the delinquent Jaguar had sped off in the opposite direction, running a red light. But Marie sat frozen and terrified in her seat, clutching the dashboard, her eyes staring straight ahead, her jaw

trembling, her eyes filled with unshed tears, her mind
rooted to something it had seen twenty-two months
before. Peter realized instantly what was happening,
stopped the car, and reached out to take her in his
arms, but she was too stiff to move, and as he
touched her, the car was suddenly filled with her
screams. She howled from the very bottom of her
soul, and he had to shake her and pull her into his
arms to subdue her.

"Shhh . . . it's all right, darling. It's all right. Ssshhhh.
It's all over now. Nothing like that will ever happen
again. It's all over." She subsided into terrified sobs,
the tears streaming down her face, her whole body
trembling as she let herself fall against him while he
held her. It was almost half an hour before she stopped,
and lay back exhausted in her seat. He watched her
silently for a time, stroking her face and her hair,
holding her hand and letting her feel that she was
indeed safe. But he was deeply troubled by what he
had seen. It proved what he had thought all along.
When at last she had stopped shaking and she rested,
quiet, next to him, he spoke to her softly but firmly
and she closed her eyes. "You have to go back to
Faye. It isn't over for you yet. And it won't be until
you face it and heal it."

But how much more could she face? And what was
there to heal? Her love for Michael? How could she
heal that? How could she tell Peter that she had
spoken to him on the phone; and that it had made
her want to hold him and kiss him and feel his hands
on her again? How could she tell Peter that? Instead

she looked at him with tired eyes and silently nodded.

"I'll give it some thought."

"Good. Shall I take you home?" His voice was very soft, and she nodded. She didn't have the strength to go to the gallery now. And they didn't speak again until they reached her house. "Do you want me to take you up?" But she only shook her head and kissed him on the cheek.

The only words she said to him as she got out of the car were, "Thank you." And she didn't look back when she got out. She slowly climbed up the stairs, the burden of twenty-two lonely months heavy on her shoulders. If only Michael had never called. It had brought back all the pain. And for what? What was the point? He probably didn't give a damn anyway. He just wanted her photographs. Well, let him buy someone else's work, the bastard. Why the hell couldn't he leave her alone?

She let herself into her apartment and went straight to the bed. Fred was leaping and jumping at her feet, and instantly joined her on the bed, but she wasn't in the mood. She pushed him to the floor, and lay there for a long time, staring at the ceiling, wondering if she should call Faye, or if there was any point in that either. She was just beginning to doze in fitful exhaustion when the phone rang and she jumped up with a start. She didn't really want to answer it, but it was probably Peter wanting to know if she was all right, and she didn't have the right to worry him anymore than she already had that afternoon. Slowly, she reached for the phone.

"Hello." It was a soft broken word from her lips.

"Miss Adamson?" Oh Jesus, it wasn't Peter, it was . . .

She closed her eyes to fight back the tears as an endless sigh shook her entire body. "For God's sake, Michael, leave me alone." She hung up the phone, and at the other end Michael stared at the receiver in total confusion. What the hell was this all about? And why had she called him Michael?

Chapter 27

Marie looked tired and drawn the next morning when she walked into the gallery with Fred. She was wearing a black pants suit with a brilliant green sweater that set off her coloring to perfection. But she looked unusually pale after a long, sleepless night, in which, at least ten thousand times, she had relived her last day with Michael and the accident that followed. She felt as though she would never get away from it if she lived to be a thousand years old. And she felt at least a hundred that morning.

"You look as though you've been working too hard, my love." Jacques smiled at her from behind the desk in his office. He was wearing his standard uniform. Impeccably tailored French blue jeans grafted to his body, black turtleneck sweater, and suede St. Laurent jacket. On him the combination looked perfect. "Or are you staying up too late with our favorite doctor?" He was an old friend of Peter's, and he had already grown fond of Marie.

She smiled in answer and sipped the coffee he had poured. It was strong and dark, a café filtre, the only kind he ever served. He brought it over from France, along with countless other precious items without which he could not survive. She loved to tease him about his chauvinism and his expensive tastes. She had bought him toilet paper imprinted with the Gucci logo for his birthday. That and a briefcase from Hermès, which was slightly more his style. But he had liked the joke, too.

"No, I haven't been partying. Maybe too much time in the darkroom."

"Crazy girl. A woman like you should be out dancing."

"Later. After I do some more work." She started describing her new idea for a series on San Francisco street life, and he nodded in satisfaction.

"Ça me plaît, Marie. I like it. Okay. Do it as soon as you can." He was about to go into the details with her when there was a knock on his office door. It was his secretary, making hushing gestures. "Aha! Probably one of your girls." Marie loved to tease him, and he grinned and shrugged "helplessly" as he walked around the desk to confer with the secretary just beyond the door. He listened to her whispered words, and then nodded, looking exceedingly pleased. He gave one final affirmative sign, and then walked back in and sat down, looking at Marie as though he were about to bestow a wonderful gift.

"I have a surprise for you, Marie." And with that, she heard another knock on the door. "Someone very important is interested in your work." The door swung open before she had time to fully understand the meaning of his words, or their implication, and suddenly she found herself turning around to face Michael. She almost gasped, and felt the cup of steaming dark coffee tremble in her hand. He was very handsome in a dark blue suit, white shirt, and dark tie, and he looked every bit the magnate he was.

Marie set down the coffee cup to take his outstretched hand, and he was impressed with how poised she looked in Jacques's office. It hardly seemed possible that this was the girl who had answered the phone the night before, with agony in her voice, begging him to leave her alone. Maybe she had other problems, with men perhaps. Maybe she'd been drunk. You never knew with artists. But none of his thoughts showed on his face, nor did her discomfort show on hers.

"I'm awfully glad to meet you at last. You've led me a merry chase, Miss Adamson. But then, as talented as you are, I suppose you have that right." He gave her a benevolent smile, and she looked at Jacques, who was standing behind his desk extending a hand toward Michael. He was extremely impressed by Cotter-Hillyard's interest in Marie's work. Michael had made it quite clear to the secretary that his interest was professional, not for his own collection or even for his office. He wanted her work for one of the largest projects the company had ever done, and Jacques was overwhelmed. He could hardly wait until Marie heard. Even her cool reserve would be shattered over this. But she looked as unruffled as ever, at least for the moment. She sat very still in her chair, avoiding Michael's gaze, and with an icy little smile on her lips. "May I get right to the point and explain to you both what I have in mind?"

"But of course." Jacques waved at the secretary to pour Michael some coffee, and sat back to listen as Michael went on to explain in full detail what he wanted to do with Marie's work. It was a project any artist would have fought for, but at the end of the discussion Marie seemed unmoved. She nodded very quietly and then turned to look at Michael.

"I'm afraid my answer is still the same, Mr. Hillyard."

"You've discussed this before?" Jacques looked confused, and Michael was quick to explain.

"One of my associates, my mother, and I myself have all contacted Miss Adamson at her home. We've mentioned this project to her, though only briefly, and her answer has been a firm no. I was hoping to change her mind."

Jacques looked at her in stupefaction. Marie was shaking her head.

"I'm sorry, but I can't do it."

"But why not?" The words were Jacques's. He was almost frantic.

"Because I don't want to."

"May we at least know your reasons?" Michael's voice was very smooth, and it held something new, the knowledge of his own power. Marie was irritated to find she liked this side of him. But it did nothing to change her mind.

"Call me a temperamental artist if you like. Whatever. The answer is still no. And it will stay no." She put down her cup, looked at the two men, and stood up. She held out a hand to Michael and somberly shook his hand. "Thank you, though, for your interest. I'm sure you'll find the right person for your project. Maybe Jacques can recommend someone. There are several wonderful artists and photographers associated with this gallery."

"But I'm afraid we only want you." He sounded stubborn now, and Jacques looked apoplectic, but Marie was not going to lose this battle. She had already lost too much.

"That's unreasonable of you, Mr. Hillyard. And childish. You're going to have to find someone else. I won't work with you. It's as simple as that."

"Will you work with someone else in the firm?"

She shook her head again and walked to the doorway.

"Will you at least give it some thought?"

Her back was to Michael as she paused for an instant in the doorway, but once again she only shook her head, and then they heard the word no as she disappeared with her little dog. Michael did not waste a moment with the stunned gallery owner, who remained seated at his desk. He ran out into the street after her, shouting "Wait!" He wasn't even sure why he was doing it, but he felt he had to. He got to her side as she began to walk hurriedly away. "May I walk with you for a moment?"

"If you'd like, but there isn't much point." She

was looking straight ahead, avoiding his eyes as he strode doggedly beside her.

"Why are you doing this? It just doesn't make any sense. It is personal? Something you know about our firm? A bad experience you've had? Something about me?"

"It doesn't make any difference."

"Yes it does, damn it. It does." He stopped her and held fast to her arm. "I have a right to know."

"Do you?" They both seemed to stand there for an eternity, and finally she softened. "All right. It's personal."

"At least I know you're not crazy."

She laughed and looked at him with amusement. "How do you know? Maybe I am."

"Unfortunately, I don't think so. I just think you hate Cotter-Hillyard. Or me." It was ridiculous though. Neither he nor the firm had had any bad press. They weren't involved in controversial projects, or with dubious governments. There was no reason for her to act like this. Maybe she'd had an affair with someone in the local office and had a grudge against him. It had to be something like that. Nothing else made sense.

"I don't hate you, Mr. Hillyard." She had waited a long time to say it as they walked along.

"You sure do a good act." He smiled, and for the first time he looked like a boy again. Like the kid who used to tease her with Ben in her apartment. That glimpse of the past tore at her heart and she looked away. "Can I invite you out somewhere for a cup of coffee?" She was going to refuse, but maybe it would be better to get it over with once and for all. Maybe then he'd leave her alone.

"All right." She suggested a place across the street, and they walked there with Fred at their heels. They both ordered espressos, and without thinking she handed him the sugar. She knew he took two, but he only thanked her, helped himself, and set the bowl down. It didn't seem unusual to him that she had known.

"You know, I can't explain it, but there's something odd about your work. It haunts me. As though I've seen it before, as though I already know it, as though I understand what you meant and what you saw when you took the pictures. Does that make any sense?"

Yes. A great deal of sense. He had always had a wonderful understanding of her paintings. She sighed and nodded. "Yes, I guess it does. They're supposed to do something like that to you."

"But they do something more. I can't explain it. It's as though I already know . . . well, your work. I don't know. It sounds crazy when I say it."

But don't you know me? Don't you know these eyes? She found herself wanting to ask him those questions as they quietly drank their coffee and discussed her work.

"I get the terrible feeling you're not going to give in. You won't, will you?" Sadly, she shook her head. "Is it money?"

"Of course not."

"I didn't think so." He didn't even mention the

enormous contract he had in his pocket. He knew it would do him no good, and perhaps make things worse. "I wish I knew what it was."

"Just my eccentricities. My way of lashing out at the past." She was shocked at her own honesty but he didn't seem to be.

"I thought it was something like that." They were both at peace now as they sat in the little Italian restaurant. There was a sadness to the meeting too, a bittersweet quality Michael couldn't understand. "My mother was very taken with your work. And she's not easy to please." Marie smiled at his choice of words.

"No, she isn't. Or so I've heard. She drives a very hard bargain."

"Yes, but she made the business what it is today. It's a pleasure to take over from her. Like a perfectly run ship."

"How fortunate for you." She sounded bitter again, and once more Michael didn't understand. In a little nervous gesture he ran his hand across a tiny scar on his temple, and abruptly Marie set down her coffee cup and watched him. "What's that?"

"What?"

"That scar." She couldn't take her eyes from it. She knew exactly what it was. It had to be from . . .

"It's nothing. I've had it for a while."

"It doesn't look very old."

"A couple of years." He looked embarrassed. "Really. It was nothing. A minor accident with some friends."

He tried to brush it off, and Marie wanted to throw her coffee in his face. Son of a bitch. A minor accident. Thanks, baby. Now I know everything I need to know. She picked up her handbag, looked down at him icily for a moment, and held out her hand.

"Thanks for a lovely time, Mr. Hillyard. I hope you enjoy your stay."

"You're leaving? Did I say something wrong?" Jesus. She was impossible. What the hell was wrong with her now? What had he said? And then he found himself shocked at the look in her eyes.

"As a matter of fact, you did." She in turn was shocked at her own words. "I read about that accident of yours, and I don't think it was what anyone would call minor. Those two friends of yours were pretty well banged up, from what I understand. Don't you give a damn about anything, Michael? Don't you care anymore about anything but your bloody business?"

"What the hell is wrong with you? And what business is it of yours?"

"I'm a human being, and you're not. That's what I hate about you."

"You are crazy."

"No, mister. Not anymore." And with that, she turned on her heel and walked out, leaving Michael to stare at her. And then, as though pushed by an invisible force, he found himself on his feet and running after her. He had dropped a five-dollar bill on the little marble table and fled in her wake. He had to tell her. He had to . . . No, it hadn't been a minor accident. The woman he loved had been killed. But what right did she have to know that? He didn't get a chance to tell her, though, because when he reached the street, she had just slipped into a cab.

Chapter 28

She had just gotten to the beach and was setting up her tripod when she suddenly saw the figure approach. His determined step puzzled her until she realized who it was. Michael, damn it. He walked down the beach and over the small dune, until he stood in front of her, blocking her view.

"I have something to say to you."

"I don't want to hear it."

"That's tough. Because I'm going to tell you anyway. You have no right to pry into my private life and tell me what kind of human being I am. You don't even know me." Her words had tormented him all through the night. And he had found out from her answering service where she was. He wasn't even sure why he had come here, but he had known he had to. "What right do you have to make judgments about me, damn you?"

"None at all. But I don't like what I see." She was cool and removed as she changed lenses.

"And just exactly what do you see?"

"An empty shell. A man who cares about nothing

but his work. A man who cares about no one, loves nothing, gives nothing, is nothing."

"You bitch, what the hell do you know about what I am and do and feel? What makes you think you're so almighty together?" She stepped around him and focused on the next dune. "Damn you, listen to me!" He reached for her camera and she dodged him, turning on him in fury.

"Why don't you get the hell out of my life?" Like you have for the last two years, you bastard . . .

"I'm not in your life. I'm trying to buy some work from you. That's all I want. I don't want your pronouncements about my personality, or my life, or anything else. I just want to buy some stinking photographs." He was almost trembling, he was so angry, and all she did was walk past him to the portfolio that lay on a blanket on the beach. She unzipped it, looked into a file, and pulled out a photograph. Then she stood up and handed it to him.

"Here. It's yours. Do whatever the hell you want with it. Then leave me alone."

Without saying a word he turned on his heel and walked back to the car he'd left parked in the road.

She never turned to look at him, but went back to work until the light began to dim and she could work no longer. Then she drove back to her apartment, scrambled some eggs, heated some coffee, and headed for the dark room. She went to bed at two in the morning, and when the phone rang, she didn't answer it. Even if it was Peter, she didn't care. She didn't want to speak to anyone. And she was going back to the beach at nine the next morning. She set her alarm for eight and fell asleep the moment she hit the bed. She had freed herself of something back there on the beach. And she had to be honest with herself: even if she hated him, at least she had seen him. In an odd way, it was a relief.

She showered and dressed in less than half an hour the next morning. She was wearing well-worn work clothes, and she sipped her coffee as she read the paper. She left the apartment on schedule, a few minutes before nine, and she was already thinking of her work as she hurried down the steps with Fred. It was only when she reached the foot of the steps that she looked up and gasped. Across the street was an enormous billboard mounted on a truck, driven by Michael Hillyard. He was smiling as he watched her, and she sat down on the last step and started to laugh. He was really crazy. He had taken the photograph she had given him, had it blown up and mounted, and then driven it to her door. He was grinning as he left the truck and walked toward her. And she was still laughing when he sat down next to her on the step.

"How do you like it?"

"I think you're a scream."

"Yeah, but doesn't it look good? Just think how your other stuff would look blown up and mounted in the medical center buildings. Wouldn't that be a thrill?" He was a thrill, but she couldn't tell him that. "Come on, let's go have breakfast and talk." This morning he wasn't taking no for an answer. He had cleared his morning schedule just for her. And she found his determination touching as well as amusing. She just wasn't in the mood for another fight.

"I should say no, but I won't."

"That's better. Can I give you a ride?"

"In that?" She pointed to the truck and started laughing again.

"Sure. Why not?"

So they hopped into the cab of the truck and headed down to Fisherman's Wharf for breakfast. Trucks were a familiar sight there, and no one was going to walk off with a photograph that size.

Surprisingly, it was a very pleasant breakfast. They both put aside the war, at least until the coffee.

"Well, have I convinced you?" He looked very sure of himself as he smiled at her over his cup.

"No. But I've had a very nice time."

"I suppose I should be grateful for small favors, but that's not my style."

"What is your style? In your own words."

"You mean you're giving me a chance to explain myself, instead of your telling me what I am?" He was teasing, but there was an edge to his voice. She had come too close to home with some of her comments the day before. "All right, I'll tell you. In some ways you're right. I live for my work."

"Why? Don't you have anything else in your life?"

"Not really. Most successful people probably don't. There just isn't room."

"That's stupid. You don't have to exchange your life for success. Some people have both."

"Do you?"

"Not entirely. But maybe one day I will. I know it's possible anyway."

"Maybe it is. Maybe my incentive isn't what it used to be." Her eyes grew soft at the words. "My life has changed a great deal in the last few years. I didn't wind up doing any of the things I once planned to. But ... I've had some damn nice compensations." Like becoming president of Cotter-Hillyard, but he was embarrassed to say it.

"I see. I take it you're not married."

"Nope. No time. No interest." How lovely. Then it was probably just as well they hadn't married after all.

"You make it sound very cut-and-dried."

"For the moment it is. And you?"

"I'm not married either."

"You know, for all your condemnation of my way of life, I can't see that yours is all that different from mine. You're just as obsessed with your work as I am with mine, just as lonely, just as locked away in your own little world. So why are you so hard on me? It's not very fair." His voice was soft but reproachful.

"I'm sorry. Maybe you're right." It was hard to argue the point. And then, as she thought over what he had said, she felt his hand on hers, and it was like a knife in her heart. She pulled it away with a stricken look in her eyes. And he looked unhappy again.

"You're a very difficult woman to understand."

"I suppose I am. There's a lot that would be impossible to explain."

"You ought to try me sometime. I'm not the monster you seem to think I am."

"I'm sure you aren't." As she looked at him, all she wanted to do was cry. This was like saying good-bye to him. It was knowing, all over again, what she could never have. But maybe she would understand it better now. Maybe she would finally be able to let go. With a small sigh she looked at her watch. "I really should get to work."

"Have I gotten any closer to a yes in answer to our proposal?"

"I'm afraid not."

He hated to admit it, but he would have to give up. He knew now that she would never change her mind. All his efforts had been for nothing. She was one very tough woman. But he liked her. He was surprised just how much, when she let down her guard. There was a softness and a kindness that drew him to her in a way that he hadn't been drawn to anyone in years. "Do you suppose that I could talk you into having dinner with me, Marie? Sort of a consolation prize, since I don't get my deal?" She laughed softly at the look on his face and patted his hand.

"I'd like that sometime. But not just now. I'm afraid I'll be going out of town." Damn. He had really lost this one, round after round.

"Where are you going?"

"Back east. To take care of some personal business." She had made the decision in the last half hour. But now she knew what she had to do. It was not a question of burying the past, but unburying it. In a way, Peter had been right. And now she was sure. She had to "heal it" as he had said.

"I'll call the next time I'm in San Francisco. I hope I'll have better luck."

Maybe. And maybe by then I'll be Mrs. Peter Gregson. Maybe by then I'll be healed. And it won't matter anymore. Not at all.

They walked quietly back to the truck, and he dropped her off at her apartment. She said very little when she left him. She thanked him for breakfast, shook his hand, and walked back up the steps. He had lost. And as he watched her go he felt an overwhelming sadness. It was as though he had lost something very special. He wasn't quite sure what. A business deal, a woman, a friend? Something. For the first time in a long time, he felt unbearably alone. He shoved the truck into gear, and drove grimly through Pacific Heights and up the hill back to his hotel.

Marie was already on the phone to Peter Gregson.

"Tonight? Darling, I have a meeting." He sounded flustered, and he was in a hurry between patients.

"Then come after the meeting. It's important. I'm leaving tomorrow."

"For where? For how long?" He sounded worried.

"I'll tell you when I see you. Tonight?"

"All right, all right. Around eleven. But that's really foolish, Marie. Can't this thing wait?"

"No." It had waited two years, and she had been crazy to let it sit for that long.

"All right. I'll see you tonight." He had hung up in a hurry, and she called the airline to make a reservation, and the vet to make arrangements for Fred.

Chapter 29

Marie had been lucky. There had been a cancellation that afternoon, so now she found herself sitting in the familiar, comfortable room she had not visited in months. She sat back against the couch and stretched her legs toward the unlit fireplace, as though by habit, staring absently at her feet in delicate sandals. Her thoughts were so far away that she didn't hear Faye come in.

"Are you meditating or just falling asleep?"

Marie looked up with a smile as Faye sat down in the seat across from her. "Just thinking. It's good to see you." Actually, she was surprised how good it felt to be back. There was a feeling of homecoming in just being there, an ease about fitting back into an old and happy groove. She had had some good moments in that room, as well as some difficult ones.

"Should I tell you that you look marvelous, or are you already tired of hearing it?" Faye beamed at the girl, and Marie laughed.

"I never get tired of hearing it." Only with Faye would she dare to be that honest. "I guess you want

268

to know why I'm here." Her face sobered as she looked into the other woman's eyes.

"The question certainly crossed my mind." They exchanged another rapid smile, and then Marie seemed to get lost in her own thoughts again.

"I've seen Michael."

"He found you?" Faye sounded stunned, and more than a little impressed.

"Yes, and no. He found Marie Adamson. That's all he knows. One of his underlings has been hounding me about my work. Cotter-Hillyard is doing a medical center out here, and they seem to want my photographs blown up to enormous proportions as part of the decor."

"That's very flattering, Marie."

"Who gives a damn, Faye? What do I care what he thinks of my work?" But that wasn't entirely true either. She had always basked in the warmth of his praise, and even now there was a certain satisfaction in knowing that she had caught his attention again, with her work. "Anyway, his mother was out here a while back, and I told her the same thing I'd been telling them. No. I'm not interested. I won't sell to them. I won't work with them. Period."

"And they've pursued it?"

"Ardently."

"That must feel good. Do any of them realize who you are?"

"Ben didn't. But Michael's mother did. I think that's why she set up the meeting." Nancy fell silent and stared at her feet. She was a long way away, back in that hotel room, the day she had seen Marion.

"What did it feel like when you saw her?"

"Terrible. It reminded me of everything she'd done to me. I hate her." But there was more in her voice, and Faye heard it.

"And?"

"All right." Marie looked up with a sigh. "It made everything hurt all over again. It reminded me of how much I had once wanted her to like me, to love me even, to accept me as Michael's wife."

"And she still rejected you?"

"I'm not sure. I guess so. She's sick now. She seems different. She seemed almost sorry about what she'd done. I gather Michael hasn't been particularly happy in the last two years."

"And how did you feel about that?"

"Relieved." She said it with a soft, tired sigh. "And then I realized that it doesn't make any difference how he's been. It's all over for us, Faye. All of that was years ago. We're different people now. And the fact is that he never came back to me. He probably wouldn't even be running after me for my work now, if he knew who I really was—who I used to be. But I'm not Nancy McAllister anymore, Faye. And he's not the Michael I knew."

"How do you know?"

"I saw him. He's callous, hard, driven, cold. Oh I don't know, maybe there's something there. But there's a lot of new stuff too."

"How about pain? Loss? Disappointment? Grief?"

"No, Faye, how about betrayal, abandonment, desertion, cowardice? Those are the real issues, aren't they?"

"I don't know. Are they? Is that how you still feel when you see him?"

"Yes." Her voice was hard again now. "I hate him."

"Then you must still care for him a great deal." Marie started to deny it, but then she shook her head as tears sprang to her eyes. She looked at Faye for a long time without speaking. "Nancy, do you still love him?" She had purposely used the old name.

The girl sighed deeply and let her head fall back against the couch before answering, and when she did, she looked at the ceiling and spoke in a monotone. "Maybe Nancy still loves him, what little bit of her is left. But Marie doesn't. I have a new life now. I can't afford to love him anymore." She looked up at Faye with sorrow.

"Why not?"

"Because he doesn't love me. Because that's not real. I have to let it go now. Totally, completely. I know that. That isn't why I came here today, to cry on your shoulder about still being in love with Michael. But I needed to tell someone how I feel. I can't really talk to Peter about it; it would upset him too much, and I needed to get some of this off my chest."

"I'm glad you did come, Marie. But I'm not sure you can just decide to let something go as simply as that, and have it fall away from you from one moment to another."

"In truth, it fell away from me two years ago, I just didn't let go until now. I told myself I had, but I hadn't. So . . ." She sat up straight again and looked squarely at Faye. "I'm leaving for Boston tomorrow to attend to some business."

"What kind of business?"

"Letting-go business." She smiled for the first time in an hour. "There are some things I left unfinished back there, some things that Michael and I shared. I've let them stand as a monument to us, because I always thought he'd be back. Now I have to go back there and take care of it."

"Do you really think you're ready to handle that?"

"Yes." She sounded sure of herself, even to Faye.

"Is that what you really want to do?"

"Yes."

"You don't want to tell Michael who you are, or rather who you were, and see what happens?"

Marie almost shuddered. "Never. That's over. Forever. And besides," she sighed again, and looked down at her hands, "that wouldn't be fair to Peter."

"You have to think about being fair to Marie."

"That's why I'm going to Boston tomorrow. But I keep thinking, too, that maybe after this I'll be free to make some kind of real commitment to Peter. He's such a nice man, Faye. He's done so much for me."

"But you don't love him."

It was frightening to hear someone else say the words, and Marie instantly shook her head. "No, no, I do!"

"Then why the problem making a commitment?"

"Michael always stood between us."

"That's too easy, Marie. That's a cop out."

"I don't know." She paused for a long time. "Something always stopped me. Something isn't . . . there. I guess I haven't really let myself be there. In some ways I was waiting for Michael, and in some ways it just hasn't felt . . . I don't know, it just doesn't feel right, Faye. Maybe it's me."

"Why do you think it doesn't feel right?"

"Well, I'm not sure, but sometimes I get the feeling that he doesn't know me. He knows me, Marie Adamson, because that's the person he helped create. He doesn't know the person I was or the things I cared about before the accident."

"Could you teach him about that, Marie?"

"Maybe. But I'm not sure he wants to know. He makes me feel loved, but not for myself."

"Well, there are a lot of other fish out there, you know."

"Yes, but he's a good man, and there's no reason why it shouldn't work."

"No. Unless you don't love him."

"But I *do* love him." She was getting agitated as they spoke.

"Then relax, and let that problem take care of itself. You can come back here and discuss it with me, if you like. First, let's deal with your feelings about Michael."

"I just want to get this trip east over with. Then I'll be free."

"All right, then do that, but come and see me when you get back. Sound okay to you?"

"Very okay." In a way, she was glad to be back. It was a relief.

With that, Faye looked at her watch regretfully and stood up. It had already been an hour and a half, and she had to teach at the university in an hour. "Will you call for an appointment when you get back?"

"The minute I do."

"All right then, and be good to yourself when you go back there. Don't torment yourself about the past. And if you have any problems, call me."

It was comforting to know that she could do that, and as she left, her mood felt lighter than it had all afternoon. Their conversation was going to make it easier for her to explain her decision to Peter.

Chapter 30

"Boston? But why, Marie? I don't understand." Peter looked tired and irritable, which was rare. But it had been a long day and a tiresome meeting. All this nonsense about the new medical center. And he had to meet with the architects in the morning. Why did he have to be on the committee? He had better things to do with his time. "I think you're crazy to make the trip."

"No, I'm not. I have to. And I'm ready. The past is over for me. Completely."

"So completely over that when we almost had an accident in the car the other day you had hysterics for an hour. It's not over."

"Darling, you have to trust me. I'm going to do the only thing I've left unfinished, and then I'll be free. I'll be back the day after tomorrow."

"It's insane."

"No. It's not." Her voice was so quiet and firm that it stopped him, and he sat back on the couch with a tired sigh. Maybe she knew what she was doing after all.

"All right. I don't understand. But I have to hope that you know what you're doing. Will you be okay back there?"

"I'll be fine. Trust me."

"I do, darling. It's not that I don't trust you. It's that . . . oh, I don't know. I don't want you to get hurt. May I ask you a totally crazy question?"

Oh Jesus. She hoped it wasn't that one. Not yet. But that wasn't what he had on his mind as he watched her carefully from the couch. "Go ahead." She waited, as though for surgery.

"Do you know that Michael Hillyard is in town?"

"I do." She was strangely calm.

"Have you seen him?"

"Yes. He came to the gallery. He wants me to do some work for a new project of his out here. I turned him down."

"Did he know who you were?"

"No."

"Why didn't you tell him?"

Now was the time for her to tell him about the deal with Michael's mother, but it was too late. It didn't matter anymore. "It didn't make any difference. The past is over."

"Are you sure?"

"Yes. That's why I'm going to Boston."

"Then I'm glad." And then he looked momentarily worried. "Does the trip have anything to do with Hillyard?" But he knew it couldn't. He was seeing Michael Hillyard in the morning.

Marie firmly shook her head. "No. Not the way

you mean. It has to do with my past, Peter. And it has to do with only me. I don't want to say any more about it than that."

"Then I'll respect that."

"Thank you."

He wanted to make love to her that night, but he didn't. Instead, he left quietly, with a gentle kiss. He sensed that she needed to be alone.

It was a peaceful night, and she still felt that way when she dropped off Fred at the vet the next morning. She knew exactly what she was doing, and why, and she knew it was right.

She caught the plane with plenty of time to spare, and she arrived in Boston at nine P.M. local time. She thought about driving out that night, but that was asking too much of lady luck. So she put it off until the following morning. She had already rented the car. All she had to do was drive there, and then drive back. She was taking the last plane home.

She felt like a woman with a sacred mission as she went to bed in the motel that night. She had no desire to see the city, to call anyone, or go anywhere. She wasn't really there. It was all like a dream, a two-year-old dream, and she would relive it only one last time.

Chapter 31

"Dr. Gregson?"

"Yes?" He was still distracted when his secretary came into the room. He had just spoken to Marie at the airport. He still had a queasy feeling about the trip, but he had to respect her feelings about something as personal as this. Still, he would feel better when she got back the next day. He looked up and tried to pay attention to his nurse. "Yes?"

"A Mr. Hillyard here to see you. He says you're expecting him. And there are three of his associates with him."

"Fine. Send him in." Christ. That was all he needed now. But why not? At least he'd get a look at the boy. He was actually young enough to be his son. What a miserable thought. He wondered if Marie ever thought of that.

The four men came in and shook hands with the doctor, and the meeting got under way. They wanted to enlist his support to make their new medical center a success. They already had fifteen of the more illustrious doctors on their "team," and there was no doubt that the buildings would be ideally located and magnificently appointed. It was an easy choice to make. Gregson agreed to take new offices there, and was willing to talk to some of his colleagues. But even though his responses were mechanical, he watched Michael with fascination throughout the meeting. So this was Michael Hillyard. He didn't look like a formidable opponent. But he looked young, and handsome, and very sure of himself. And in an unsettling way, Peter began to realize how much like Marie he was. There was a similarity of energy, of determination, and even of humor. The realization made Peter feel shut out, and suddenly, too, he understood. He sat very quietly for a long time, watching Michael and saying nothing at all. He wasn't even listening to the meeting anymore; he was adjusting to the reality he had avoided for so long. It made him wonder, too, exactly why Marie had gone east that morning. Was it really to destroy the last shreds of the past, or to honor them?

For the first time, Peter wondered if he had a right to interfere. Just watching Michael, he felt as though he were seeing another side of Marie, a side he had no knowledge of. This man represented a part of her life that he didn't even understand, a part he had never wanted to know. He had wanted her to be Marie Adamson. She had never been Nancy to him. She had been someone new, someone who had been born in his hands. But now he recognized there was someone else. All the pieces of the puzzle began to fit, and he felt a sense of resignation as well as loss. He had been fighting an unfightable war, and he had been trying to recapture his own past. Marie was indeed someone new, but there were glimpses in her of the woman he had once loved, the woman who had died. . . . He had cherished those glimpses of Livia as well as the reality of the girl he had brought to life. Maybe he had no right to do that. He had never before had such free rein with a patient, because Marie had had no one to rely on but him. It allowed him to be everything to her . . . everything except what he wanted to be now. Watching Michael, he realized that his own role in Marie's life had been very like a father's. She didn't realize it yet, but one day she would.

The meeting was over when they stood up to shake hands, and Michael's three associates were already out of the office, waiting for him in the anteroom beyond. Gregson and Michael were exchanging pleasantries, when suddenly everything stopped, and Michael stared fixedly at something over the older man's shoulder. It was the painting she had been doing two years before . . . it was to have been his wedding present . . . it had been stolen from her apartment by those nurses after she died. And now it was in this man's office, and it was finished. Mesmerized, Michael walked toward it before Gregson could stop him. But nothing would have stopped him. He stood there, staring, looking for the signature, as though he already knew what he would see. There, in tiny letters in the corner, were the words. Marie Adamson.

"Oh, my God . . . oh, my God . . ." It was all he

could say as Gregson watched him. "But how? It isn't
. . . oh, Jesus . . . God . . . why didn't someone tell
me? What in . . ." But he understood now. They had
lied to him. She was alive. Different. But alive. No
wonder she had hated him. He hadn't even suspected.
But he had been haunted by something in her, and in
her photographs, all that time. There were tears in his
eyes as he turned to look at Gregson.

Peter looked at him sorrowfully, afraid of what
would come. "Leave her alone, Hillyard. It's all over
for her now. She's been through enough." But even
as he said it, the words lacked conviction. Just looking
at Michael that morning, he wasn't sure that Michael
should stay away from her at all. And something deep
inside him wanted to tell him where she was.

But Michael was still staring at him with a look of
astonishment. "They lied to me, Gregson. Did you
know that? They lied to me. They told me she was
dead." His eyes were brimming with tears. "I've spent
two years like a dead man, working like a robot, wishing I had died instead of her, and all this time—" For a
moment he couldn't go on, and Gregson looked away.
"And when I saw her this week, I never knew. I . . . it
must have killed her . . . no wonder she hates me. She
does, doesn't she?" Michael sank into a chair, staring
at the painting.

"No. She doesn't hate you. She just wants to put it
behind her. She has a right to do that." *And I have a
right to her.* He wanted to say the words, but he
couldn't bring himself to. But suddenly it was as
though Michael had heard his thoughts. Michael

had just remembered what he'd heard about Marie having a sponsor, a plastic surgeon. The words suddenly rang in his ears, and just as suddenly the anger and pain of two years was upon him. He jumped to his feet and grabbed Gregson's lapels.

"Wait a minute, damn it. What right do you have to tell me that she wants to 'put it behind her'? How the hell do you know? How can you even begin to understand what we had together? How can you know what any of that meant to her, or to me? If I get out of her life without saying a word, then you have it all your way, is that it, Gregson? Is that what you want? Well, to hell with you! This is my life you're playing with, mister, and it seems to me that enough people have played with it already. The only person who can tell me she wants this thing finished is Nancy."

"She already told you to leave her alone." His voice was quiet, as he looked into Michael's eyes.

Michael backed away from him now, but there was hope mixed in with the anger and confusion in his face. For the first time in two years there was something alive there. "No, Gregson. Marie Adamson told me to leave her alone. Nancy McAllister hasn't said a word to me in two years. And she's going to have a lot of explaining to do. Why didn't she call me? Why didn't she write? Why didn't she let me know she was alive? And why did they tell me she was dead? Was that her doing, or ... or someone else's? And as a matter of fact"—he hated to ask the question because he already knew what he would hear—"who paid for her surgery?" His eyes never left Gregson's face.

"I don't know the answers to some of your questions, Mr. Hillyard."

"And the ones you do have the answers to?"

"I'm not at liberty to—"

"Don't give me that—" Michael advanced on him again, and Peter put up a hand.

"Your mother has paid for all of Marie's surgery, and for her living expenses since the accident. It was a very handsome gift." It was what Michael had feared, but it didn't really come as a shock. It fitted the rest of the picture he saw now, and maybe in some insane, misguided way his mother had thought she was doing it for him. At least she had led him back to Nancy now. He looked at Gregson again, and nodded.

"And what about you? Just exactly what is your relationship with Nancy?" Now he wanted to know it all.

"I don't know that that concerns you."

"Look, damn it . . ." His hands were at the other man's coat again, and Peter held up a hand in defeat.

"Why don't we stop this now? The answers are all in Marie's hands. What she wants, who she wants. She may not want either one of us, you know. For whatever reasons, you haven't contacted her in two years, nor has she contacted you. And as for me, I'm almost twice her age, and for all I know, suffering from a Pygmalion complex." He sat down heavily in his desk chair and smiled ruefully. "I almost think she could do better than either one of us."

"Maybe, but this time I want to hear it from her myself." He looked at his watch. "I'm going over to her place right now."

"It won't do you much good." Peter watched him and stroked his beard. He almost wished the boy luck. Almost. "She called me from the airport just before you got here this morning."

Once again Michael looked shocked. "Now what? Where was she going?"

For a long moment Peter Gregson hesitated. He didn't have to tell him anything. He didn't have to . . . "She was going to Boston."

Michael looked at him for one moment, and a shadow of a smile flitted through his eyes as he dashed for the door. He stopped, glanced back, and saluted Peter with a full-blown smile. "Thank you."

Chapter 32

She was up at dawn. Awake, alive. She felt better than she had in years. She was almost free now. In a few hours she would be. As though that childish promise had held her for all this time. And only because she had let it. Its only power had been the power she had given it.

She didn't even bother with breakfast. She only drank two cups of coffee, and got into the rented car. She could be there in two hours, by ten o'clock. Back at the hotel at noon. She could catch a plane back to San Francisco and be home by late afternoon. She might even be able to pick up Peter at the office and surprise him. Poor man, he had been so patient about the trip.

She found herself thinking about him as she drove along, wishing she had given him more, wishing she had been able to. Maybe after today that would change too. Or was it that . . . she didn't even let herself finish the question. Of course, she loved him. That wasn't the point.

She drove through the New England countryside, barely noticing anything she passed. The landscape was still gray and dark; the new leaves had not yet emerged. It was as though the countryside too had lain buried for two years. It was nine thirty when she passed Revere Beach, where the fair had been, and she felt a little jolt in her heart when she recognized the place. She followed an old road which wandered along the coast, and then she came to a stop, and got out of the car. She was stiff, but not tired. She was exhilarated, and nervous. She had to do this . . . had to . . . she could already see the tree from where she stood. She stood staring at it for a long time, as though it held all the secrets, knew her story too well, as though it had waited for her return. She walked slowly toward it, as though going to meet an old friend. But it was no longer a friend. Like everything and everyone she had once loved, it was a stranger. It was just another marker on Nancy McAllister's grave.

She stopped when she reached it, and then walked the last steps across the sand to the rock. It was still there. It hadn't moved. Nothing had. Only she and Michael had moved, in opposite directions and to different worlds. She stood there for a very long time, as though trying to summon the strength and the courage to do it. And at last she bent down and began to push. The rock moved after a few moments, and quickly, with a stick, she dug under it for what she sought. But there was nothing there. She dropped the rock, breathless, and then with fresh strength, she pushed it again, until this time she could see that they were gone. Someone had already taken the beads. She let the rock slip back into place just as she heard his voice.

"You can't have them. They belong to someone else.

To someone I loved. To someone I never forgot."
There were tears in Michael's eyes as he spoke to her.
He had waited half the night for her to come. It had
taken a chartered jet to get him there before she
arrived. But he would have flown on his own wings if
he had had to. He held out a hand now, and she saw
the beads, still caked with the sand from under the
rock. Her own eyes filled with tears when she saw
them. "I promised never to say good-bye. I never did."
His eyes never left hers as he stood there.

"You never tried to find me."

"They told me you were dead."

"I promised never to see you again if . . . if they
gave me a new face. I promised because I knew you'd
find me. And then . . . you didn't."

"I would have, if I'd known. Do you remember your
promise to me?"

She closed her eyes and spoke solemnly, like a
child, and for the first time in a long time, it was the
voice of Nancy McAllister, the voice he had loved,
not the smooth new one she had learned. "I promise
never to forget what lies buried here. Or what it
stands for."

"Did you forget?" The tears were sliding slowly
from his eyes now. He was thinking of Gregson, and
of the two years that had passed.

But she shook her head. "No. But I tried very hard
to."

"Are you willing to remember now? Nancy, will
you—" But then he couldn't speak. He only walked
toward her and took her very tightly into his arms. "Oh
God, Nancy, I love you. I always have. I thought I

would die when you did ... when I thought you had.
I died the moment they told me."

But she was crying too hard to speak, remembering
the endless days and months and years of waiting
for him, and then giving up hope. She held tightly
to him, like a child to a doll, as though she would
never let go. And at last she caught her breath and
smiled. "Darling, I love you, too. I always thought
you'd find me."

"Nancy ... Marie ... whatever the hell your name
is—" They both laughed like children through their
tears. "Will you please do me the honor of becoming
my wife? This time like civilized people, at a wedding,
with everyone there, and music and ..." He was thinking of his mother's wedding only a few weeks before. It
was odd how totally free of anger he was. He should
have hated his mother for what she had done. Instead,
he wanted to forgive. He had Nancy back now. That
was all he cared about. He smiled down at her in his
arms, thinking of their wedding. But she was shaking
her head, and he thought his heart would stop.

"Do we really have to wait that long? Do all that
stuff about music and people and—"

"Are you suggesting—" He didn't even dare say it,
but she nodded in his arms.

"Yes. Why not? Now. I don't want to wait again. I
couldn't bear it. Every moment I'd be afraid that
something would happen again. Maybe this time to
you."

He nodded silently, and held her tight as the surf
roared in softly and the pale eastern sun peeked
through the clouds. He understood.